LUNCH . . . WITH A SIDE OF MURDER

They were digging more deeply into their Thai food when Caprice's cell phone played.

"I'd better check this," she said to Roz. "Juan is at the house we're going to be staging and he might have run into a problem."

But when she glanced at the screen, she saw Ace's face. Uh oh, just what was she going to say to him? She swiped the screen and put the phone to her ear. "Hi, Ace. What's up?"

"Caprice . . ." Ace's voice sounded strained and very strange. "I'm at Alanna's house," he continued as if there was something wrong with that.

"Does Alanna need something?"

"No, she—" There was silence . . . absolute silence.

"Ace? What's going on?"

"Alanna's here, Caprice, but the thing is—she's not breathing. Her eyes are wide open. She has no pulse. I think she was strangled!"

Books by Karen Rose Smith

STAGED TO DEATH

DEADLY DÉCOR

GILT BY ASSOCIATION

DRAPE EXPECTATIONS

Published by Kensington Publishing Corporation

Drape Expectations

Karen Rose Smith

KENSINGTON PUBLISHING CORP.
http://www.kensingtonbooks.com

KENSINGTON BOOKS are published by

Kensington Publishing Corp.
119 West 40th Street
New York, NY 10018

All Kensington Titles, Imprints, and Distributed Lines are
available at special quantity discounts for bulk purchases
for sales promotions, premiums, fund-raising, and ed-
ucational or institutional use. Special book excerpts or
customized printings can also be created to fit specific
needs. For details, write or phone the office of the
Kensington special sales manager: Kensington Publishing Corp., 119 West 40th Street, New York, NY 10018,
attn: Special Sales Department, Phone: 1-800-221-2647.

Kensington and the K logo Reg. U.S. Pat & TM Off.

ISBN-13: 978-1-61773-770-1
ISBN-10: 1-61773-770-4
First Kensington Mass Market Edition: August 2015

eISBN-13: 978-1-61773-771-8
eISBN-10: 1-61773-771-2
First Kensington Electronic Edition: August 2015

10 9 8 7 6 5 4 3 2 1

Printed in the United States of America

I dedicate this mystery to my aunt,
Rose Cacciola,
who taught me the basics
of home decorating.

Acknowledgments

I would like to thank Officer Greg Berry, my law enforcement consultant, who so patiently answers all my questions.

Chapter One

Caprice De Luca's cocker spaniel bounded up the wide staircase, keeping close beside her.

"Why do you think Ace wants to see us?" she asked Lady, her golden-colored, seven-month-old pup.

Lady gave a bark and Caprice stopped mid-staircase to smile and ear-ruffle her dog. Lady was a lower-pack, stay-close dog who responded easily to praise, attention, and conversation. Caprice was about to engage in more conversation, when suddenly she heard Ace Richland's baritone call to her from his mansion's second-floor hall. "We're in the secure room."

Ace was a rock star legend making a comeback. He'd bought this estate in Kismet, Pennsylvania, after Caprice had staged it to sell with a Wild Kingdom theme. He'd wanted a place to relax away from the glitz, glamour, and glare in order to reconnect with his twelve-year-old daughter. Her mother enjoyed sole custody, so Trista spent the odd weekend with him.

Caprice wondered who was with Ace. He'd said, "*We're* in the secure room." Was his daughter here this weekend? When Ace had phoned her, he hadn't told her why he wanted to meet with her. Maybe he had another room he wanted her to redecorate.

But certainly not the secure room, with its climate control and digitally coded locking mechanism.

Ace had told her she could bring Lady, but she didn't know if he wanted her dog in *that* room. The previous owner had stored expensive artwork in there. Upon Caprice's suggestion, Ace used the room for his vast collection of guitars.

When she reached the room with Lady, Caprice said, "Stay," giving her dog a hand motion for the command. At seven months old, Lady still had a lot of pup in her.

Lady whined for a moment. She liked Ace and had probably already caught his scent.

Caprice pulled a treat from the little pouch belt she wore and rewarded Lady with it. Though praise usually did the trick, Caprice still liked to give the pup something extra every now and then.

"She can come in," Ace called. "All the guitars are hanging on racks, and she certainly can't hurt this rubber floor."

Caprice walked into the room, letting Lady wait a moment so she didn't receive confusing signals. Ace *wasn't* alone; a blond woman stood there. Her shoulder-length, perfectly coifed, waved hair and her jeweled necklace and earrings screamed, *Lots of money here!* Her perfectly matched cranberry-colored sweater and slacks, evidently bought from a designer rack, shouted, *Sophistication!* Manolo Blahnik shoes accentuated her long legs.

Although Caprice knew fashion, she indulged in her own fashion sense, mostly wearing vintage and retro styles. On this March day, with the wind blowing, she'd opted for her red bell-bottoms, one of her favorite

Beatle T-shirts in red and black, a crocheted yellow vest, and her platform boots. After all, this wasn't a professional visit, she didn't think. Ace was sort of a friend.

Now he gave her one of his wicked grins. "Let Lady come inside and I'll introduce you."

Caprice turned toward Lady, patting her hip, and said, "Come, girl."

Lady bounded toward her, wiggled at her feet for a few minutes, and then ran right over to Ace.

Immediately he crouched and petted the dog's head. "You're such a good girl. Just like Brindle."

Ace's daughter had adopted another one of the pups in the litter that Caprice had delivered and named her Brindle.

The blonde cleared her throat and Ace got to his feet. Caprice watched Lady for her opinion of Ace's guest.

Her dog stayed close to Ace, with wary eyes on the blonde.

Lady was a good judge of character, but Caprice should at least have a conversation with the woman before she sized her up too quickly.

"Caprice, meet Alanna Goodwin. Alanna, Caprice De Luca, home stager extraordinaire. If it weren't for her staging, I never would have bought this place."

So *this* was Alanna Goodwin. Caprice had heard gossip about Ace and the Southern born-and-bred Alanna. Supposedly he'd met the widow at a black-tie function in Harrisburg before Christmas and had been dating her ever since. Now that Caprice had a good look at her, she remembered this woman attending an at-home concert Ace had given for the drop of his new single last month.

Caprice extended her hand to shake Alanna's. Alanna gave her outfit a look, somewhat like the look

Caprice's sister Bella often gave her when she criticized her fashion sense.

But then the Southern beauty smiled winningly. "Hello, Caprice, it's so good to meet you. Ace speaks highly of you."

"Well, good," Caprice said with a smile. "I speak highly of him."

Ace gave a chuckle. "As I told you, Caprice says her mind. But she's usually right on the mark with staging and decorating."

Caprice wondered what Ace was up to. Drumming up business for her? She was booked up at the moment. When the economy had taken a downturn and her home-decorating business had hit a snag, she'd transformed her business into a unique staging service with high-end customers, and the endeavor had been successful. However, she never turned business away.

"Do you need my professional services with something?" she asked Alanna.

"Ace insists you're the best." Alanna looked toward Ace adoringly. "Do you want to ask her, or should I?"

Ace's boyish look and a twinkle in his eye told Caprice he wanted a favor.

As he moved closer to Alanna, Lady came to stand with Caprice.

He said, "Alanna's going to sell her Kismet house and move in with me. I'd like you to stage it to sell. You can fit her in, can't you?"

He gave Caprice a little wink, and she knew what that meant. He was playing the friend favor card. After all, he'd done a couple of favors for her, which included leading a teenager onto the right track in life. Ace was a good guy under the razzmatazz rock legend exterior, and she would help if she could.

She mentally reviewed her professional commitments.

She hadn't intended to schedule a new client for another two months.

"Ace said you do your best work under pressure, although I don't know how he knows that," Alanna commented with a probing glance.

If she was honest with herself, and she usually was, Caprice had already sized up Alanna just as Lady had. She sensed there was an edge of steel in the Southern beauty, and she wondered if they'd clash or mesh on the best staging course to take if she accepted her as a client.

Alanna sweetly but cuttingly asked, "Have you been in Ace's guitar room before?"

Maybe Alanna just wanted to know if she was a threat. There had never been anything romantic between Caprice and Ace.

Caprice explained, "I've been in here before when I was staging the house. I'm the one who suggested that he use it for his guitars."

"Caprice has been in my home more than most people," Ace added. "She redecorated Trista's room before she came to stay for the first weekend, and then redecorated it again when I got it all wrong."

"All wrong?" Alanna asked with a perfectly formed eyebrow quirking up.

"I wanted it in pink and ruffles, trying to keep Trista a little girl. She hated it. But she and Caprice put their heads together and came up with exactly what Trista liked. Caprice will do a good job for you, Alanna. I know she will."

The best course to take was to see Alanna's house as soon as possible. So much for having a free Sunday afternoon.

She asked Alanna, "How does tomorrow afternoon

suit? I can take a look at your house and you can decide if you'd like me to stage it."

After Alanna gave Caprice a once-over again, including Lady in the assessment, Alanna nodded. "I'll pencil you in. But just so you know, I have a cat. You'll probably want to leave your dog at home."

A stiff March breeze whisked past Caprice's restored yellow Camaro on Sunday afternoon as she drove toward Alanna Goodwin's estate, a few miles outside of Kismet. Winter had been long and harsh this year. That sometimes happened in Pennsylvania. She'd spent many nights curled up on her sofa in front of a blazing fire—Lady on the floor beside her and her cat, Sophia, on the afghan on the back of the sofa—as she worked on home-staging designs. But today, the promise of spring was faintly in the air.

As she turned down one rural road after another, she appreciated the bucolic setting with its rolling hills, groves of maples, sweet gum, and sycamores. She considered the older neighborhood where she lived, residing in a 1950s Cape Cod that was just perfect for her and her animals. She was five minutes away from everything in Kismet, yet close enough to Harrisburg, York, D.C., and Baltimore to draw clients from there.

Her Camaro made a *vroom* as she took the last turn leading to Alanna's house. She drove her work van more than she used to, so when she had Lady along, her dog could be housed in her crate in the back. It was safer for her pup that way. Today she appreciated the responsiveness of her Camaro, and the exhilaration she felt when she drove it.

Lady was home alone this afternoon on another trial run. The pup's training was going well. Instead of penning her in the kitchen, Caprice had been giving her the run of the downstairs when she wasn't going to be away more than an hour or so. For more than an hour, she used pet gates at the kitchen doorways. Lady and Sophia were buddies now, so no worries there. Toys that released food crunchies when batted about also kept Lady busy and out of trouble.

Alanna Goodwin's house, White Pillars, was easy to spot. Caprice had Googled Alanna after meeting her. The widow's deceased husband, Barton Goodwin, a self-made multimillionaire, had built the edifice for them twelve years ago when he'd moved them from Mississippi to Kismet. He'd died about a year ago. Apparently, Alanna wasn't still in mourning and was ready to move on with her life.

Caprice tried not to be judgmental. She didn't like anybody judging *her*. Still . . . Alanna and Ace? They just didn't seem to fit together quite right.

Alanna's home resembled a plantation mansion. Tall white pillars, which had given the estate its name, surrounded two sides of the house. Along the east side of the mansion stretched a screened-in veranda, which Caprice imagined might also extend along the back. As she parked in the driveway, pulled her patent leather purse with her electronic tablet from the seat beside her, and climbed out of her car, she stared up at the mansion. The entrance somehow managed to be both formidable and southerly inviting. She felt as if she was traveling through the Old South and had come upon a historical showplace.

Caprice pressed the bell. Alanna herself opened the huge white door, smiled easily, and after a "hello" invited Caprice inside.

Today, Caprice had dressed in loose-legged khaki slacks, with a military-cut jacket reminiscent of one that the Beatles had worn at their landmark Shea Stadium concert. Her low navy patent pumps coordinated with her purse. As she stepped into the house, her straight, long, dark brown hair swished over her shoulder. She was ready for this meeting. She just hoped Alanna Goodwin was, too.

"What do you want to do first?" Alanna asked.

"Let me have a look around. A theme is already presenting itself, but I want to make sure. I'll run it by you after I take a look at everything."

Right away, Caprice could see Alanna's furnishings were all Southern hospitality blended with traditional appeal. In the foyer, a crystal chandelier with large prisms dangling from it, hung directly above a round pedestal table with a three-foot-tall flower arrangement. Lilies projected a sweet scent that probably permeated the adjoining rooms. If Alanna had a cat, she shouldn't have lilies anywhere in the house. They were toxic to felines.

As Caprice moved forward, she could see early- to mid-nineteenth-century-style paintings of landscapes decorated the walls in the living room. She was pretty sure the mid-nineteenth-century antiques were *not* reproductions, especially the pine safe with its punched tin panels depicting antebellum mansions. High-backed, floral-upholstery-trimmed chairs in dark wood complemented two velvet settees. But those settees gave the room an overly heavy, unwelcoming mood.

As Caprice stepped into the dining room, admiring the dark wood table and its solid wood chairs made unique by ornamental backs and arms, a beautiful white Persian cat suddenly appeared. It blinked at Caprice and meowed.

"Well, hello there! Just who are you?"

The cat gave another meow, then walked slowly

toward Caprice, ending up beside her and rubbing against her leg. Without hesitation, Caprice automatically dropped down and held out her hand.

The animal sniffed it and butted her head against Caprice's palm. Caprice laughed, touching the soft-as-cotton long hair. "You're a beauty."

"And she knows it," Alanna said. "That's Mirabelle. She's declawed. You don't have to worry about her scratching you."

Declawed—so she wouldn't mar any of Alanna's furniture, carpet, or heavy drapes. Caprice tried not to look too aghast. When trained correctly, a cat didn't have to damage anything. Apparently, Alanna hadn't wanted to put the effort into teaching Mirabelle to use a scratching post.

Mirabelle kept by Caprice's side as she rounded the long dining-room table, with its green eyelet runner and ornate stand in the center, which held a display of fruit and nuts. In the kitchen, pie safes, glass-fronted cabinets and hutches provided additional storage to display decorative plates and large tureens. Too many furniture pieces made the room look cluttered.

As Caprice toured the rest of the house, Mirabelle followed her the whole way. Every once in a while, Caprice stooped and petted her, and the cat responded affectionately as if she was starved for the attention. That really wasn't fair. Caprice didn't know what kind of a pet owner Alanna was.

At one point, Alanna said, "I can tuck her away so she doesn't bother you."

Caprice wasn't exactly sure what Alanna meant by that. But she already liked the cat, who just seemed to want company. "She's fine with me."

However, pets aside, by the time she returned downstairs, she wasn't sure how Alanna and Ace were going

to combine their very different styles. She didn't think
Ace would particularly like heavy armoires and four-
poster beds, pie safes, and ornate sculptures. Yet, maybe
it was Alanna's Southern charm that had attracted Ace
to her. Who knew?

In the living room, Caprice sat on an uncomfortable settee, and Alanna on a chair beside it.

Mirabelle stood at Caprice's feet and looked up at
her lap.

But Alanna shook her finger at the cat. "Oh no. You
go over there and sit on your bed."

Caprice took one look at the ornate, shiny brass cat
bed low to the floor, not placed in any direct sunlight,
and wondered why any cat would like to sleep on it.
She knew cats preferred high places, windows, and
sunshine in as many forms as they could get it. But
Mirabelle must have been used to listening to her
owner because she went to the bed, folded her paws
under her, and didn't look particularly happy.

Caprice told herself if she wanted Alanna as a client,
even only as a favor to Ace, she really should bite her
tongue and be pleasant.

So she tried to be. "I think it's easy to see what the
theme for your staging should be—Antebellum Ecstasy.
We'll play up all the best parts of Southern hospitality
and emphasize the charm of living in a Southern mansion. You really should be able to keep most of your
furnishings here, but one of the first rules of staging is
to de-clutter."

"De-clutter? I don't understand."

"Even though I plan staging themes, I have to make
sure a prospective home buyer can imagine moving in
their possessions. Besides that, too many pieces of
furniture take away from the beauty of each one. Many
of my clients rent a storage shed or begin selling the

furniture they don't intend to take with them when they move."

"I'm not exactly sure what I'd be moving into Ace's," Alanna said with a pensive look. "We haven't discussed that."

"You should make a list," Caprice advised her. "There are also advantages to incorporating a few more inviting pieces and colors rather than the deep wines and dark browns in most of these rooms."

"I'm not changing my color schemes."

Aha. The resistance she'd expected from this woman. "I'm not suggesting you change them. I'm suggesting you incorporate lighter colors with them."

She motioned to the draperies in the living room, the heavy tiebacks with the fringe. "For instance, just think about removing those draperies, hanging sheers, letting in more daylight. That will make the room more inviting."

"I am *not* taking down my draperies. They go with the house. They're part of its character."

Caprice swallowed a retort and reminded herself Alanna could be the love of Ace's life. "Mrs. Goodwin, would you like to sell the house quickly?"

Alanna looked trapped. "Yes, I want to sell the house quickly. That's the whole point of hiring you. I'm ready to make a home for me and Ace."

Caprice nodded, seeing that in her statement Alanna seemed sincere. "Why don't I make a list of suggestions of pieces of furniture you can remove. Instead of removing the draperies entirely, maybe we could take away the tiebacks and the dark semi-sheers and use something more see-through. I'll compromise with you, Mrs. Goodwin. But you have to remember, whatever I suggest will aid in selling the house. For example, I would never remove your Oriental carpet. But I might add a shawl over the back of one of the dark chairs to complement the lighter blue in the rug. I might take away the dark velvet throw pillows and use a pale green that might match the sheers. I could move in a taupe love seat and remove the two ornate settees. Do you see the changes I'm talking about?"

Today, Alanna was dressed in a pale gray cashmere sweater and deeper gray slacks. The pearls and earrings she wore were classically beautiful. This woman should be able to understand easily what Caprice wanted to do.

Alanna cast a glance around the first floor of her home. She sighed. "I understand." After a moment, she added, "It will be hard to leave this. But I'm ready."

Knowing Ace wasn't alone in this new romantic adventure and his daughter, Trista, would be along for the ride, Caprice couldn't help but ask, "Have you and Trista spent time together?"

At that question, Alanna's face took on a look almost the same as when she talked about her cat. "I'm not concerned about Trista. We've met, but she doesn't live with Ace. She's simply a now-and-then weekend daughter. That's a shame, of course, but that's just how it's going to be."

That seemed to be a line drawn in the sand for Alanna. However, as she finished with her conclusion, a shadow passed over her face. Alanna was about five years older than Caprice, maybe in her late thirties. It was hard to tell. From her background research, Caprice had learned Alanna had begun her professional life as a journalist in Mississippi. She'd met Barton Goodwin when she'd interviewed him for a story and they'd married a few months later. Apparently, Barton had invented a new kind of scaffolding for construction sites, and his company had established enterprises worldwide. He'd moved them to Kismet to be closer to

Washington, D.C., Baltimore, and New York. With his sudden heart attack, Alanna had inherited a fortune.

From her research, Caprice had surmised Alanna didn't seem to have much to do with the day-to-day running of Goodwin Enterprises, but she did sit on the board of directors. Maybe she wished she and Barton had had children. Often when women reached their late thirties, they thought about that more. However, Caprice was just guessing. She didn't know Alanna and doubted she'd get to know her. The widow seemed to be the type of woman who usually kept her guard up—a mint julep with more bite than sweetness.

Caprice took her electronic tablet from her purse. "If you don't mind, I'm going to return upstairs and make that list for you of the pieces you can remove—that is, if you're interested in hiring me."

"Ace would be disappointed if I didn't."

"I can e-mail you a proposal tonight."

After considering Caprice's services once more, Alanna nodded and gave Caprice a fake smile. "Make your list. I promise I'll consider each suggestion seriously."

Caprice doubted that she would. But if they could compromise, they could make this house staging a real success.

When Caprice returned to the living room twenty minutes later, she found Alanna seated at a rolltop desk in the side parlor adjacent to the larger room. Mirabelle was no longer in sight and she wondered if Alanna had "tucked" her away.

This room possibly served as Alanna's office. She didn't mean to sneak up on Alanna, but the woman seemed focused on something at her desk. As Caprice looked over Alanna's shoulder, she spied a photo of a little girl who looked to be about six.

Caprice's charm bracelet, which she wore almost every day now, must have jingled as she shifted her tablet in her hand because Alanna started, then quickly slipped the photo back into the desk drawer. Caprice wondered who the child was.

That was none of her business.

She asked Alanna, "Do you have an e-mail address where I can send the proposal and my list of notes?"

Alanna rattled off her address. As she did, the porcelain-and-gold decorative phone on her desk jangled. Alanna said, "Could you excuse me a minute? I'm expecting a call."

"I can see myself out."

Alanna shook her head. "There is something else I'd like to ask you."

As Caprice wondered what that could be, she moved away from the parlor into the living room to give Alanna privacy.

Still, she could hear the conversation, although Alanna kept her voice low.

"It worked. That's what matters," Alanna said. After she listened a few moments, Alanna murmured, "It's not sabotage when it's for his own good. Keep me up to date."

Without even a good-bye, she set the handset on the receiver. Glancing at Caprice, Alanna manufactured a smile and joined her in the living room.

Wanting to get back home to her animals, thinking about taking Lady to the dog park before she put together Alanna's proposal, Caprice said, "You wanted to ask me something?"

Alanna studied her. "Are you and Ace good friends?"

Caprice picked up her purse from the settee, where she'd left it, and made eye contact with Alanna. "I don't know if we're *good* friends. We've talked to each other about some things that matter. I like his daughter a lot. Last summer, I found a stray dog who was pregnant. When she had her litter, Ace and his ex-wife said Trista could have one of her pups. Trista and I've talked a lot about the dogs and training them, and Ace has been around for that, too."

"I care about him deeply," Alanna said firmly, as if that was in doubt.

Caprice wasn't exactly sure what to say to that. If Ace was in love and had found a soul mate, she was all for it. But had Ace dated Alanna long enough to really know her?

"I wish you two all the best," Caprice responded sincerely.

But after Caprice left, after she climbed into her Camaro and headed for home, she wasn't sure what that "best" would be.

Chapter Two

Caprice pulled inside her garage and parked beside her van. But she didn't press the remote to put the garage door down. After she climbed out of the car, she ignored the door, which led to her back porch and the yard, where Lady liked to run and play. Instead, she studied the van with its psychedelic colors on the side, the flowers, and the name of her business in turquoise letters—CAPRICE DE LUCA–REDESIGN AND HOME STAGING.

She knew she should go into the house and write up Alanna's proposal. But she was antsy. She could easily call her sister Nikki, who catered her open houses. They'd have to put their heads together for Alanna's. Or she could round up Lady and go visit her sister Bella and her husband and three kids. Bella's two older children, Megan and Timmy, loved playing with the pup. She could drop in on her parents, or on Nana, who lived with them. Fran and Nick De Luca were the kind of parents who were always glad to see their children and had an open door policy for family and friends. Besides visiting with her family, Caprice loved spending time with Nana's new kitten, who was growing bigger each day.

As she walked up the path to her front door, the

charm bracelet on her wrist jingled. Seth Randolph, the doctor she'd dated before he'd taken a fellowship in Baltimore to further his training in trauma medicine, had given it to her on Valentine's Day. He'd said he didn't want her to forget him. She wore the bracelet often because she never forgot about Seth. When they'd dated, when he was around, he made her heart flutter, and made her feel special.

Still, more recent in her mind, was a conversation she'd had at Bella's new baby's christening two weeks ago. She had been chatting with Grant Weatherford, her brother's law partner.

She and Grant had an odd friendship. It was more than a friendship really, though neither of them wanted to admit it. When she'd solved murder cases, Grant had helped her. He'd even saved her life once. That was hard to forget. They hadn't yet put to rest what had happened at the Valentine's Day dance. She could recall that night so vividly. When Grant hadn't asked her to dance, she'd been disappointed until Seth had arrived unexpectedly and swept her off her feet. Afterward, Grant had left without a word.

Maybe it was time they cleared the air, though the air was never clear when she was around Grant.

She inserted her key in the lock of her front door. As soon as Caprice stepped inside, Lady was right there, gave a bark, and danced around her.

"Hi, girl, I missed you, too."

Still, she didn't want Lady to become overexcited every time she came home, so she walked by her, inspecting everything as she went.

Lady followed, of course. No accidents were evident. A throw rug was curled up, as if Lady and Sophia had had a chase. Other than that, all was normal.

Caprice's house was a haven for her and her animals.

Sophia, named for Sophia Loren, her nana's favorite actress, sat atop the turquoise carpeted cat tree in the living room. She blinked awake as Caprice went over to her and spread her fingers through the pristine white ruff around the neck of the strikingly colored, long-haired calico.

"Did you and Lady have a good time?"

Sophia's eyes half opened. She emitted a small meow as if telling Caprice her afternoon with Lady had been acceptable. Sophia was nothing if not laid-back. She got to her feet, stretched, and hopped down the cat condo, one shelf at a time. Lady bounded in and touched noses with her.

Having enough of that, Sophia turned and leaped up onto the oversized dark fuchsia chair, catty-corner to the multicolored striped sofa. She sat on the arm of the chair, peering down at Lady.

Caprice patted her hip and Lady followed her through her fifties-style dining room into her kitchen. The buttercup-colored appliances, with their vintage design, always brought a smile to her face. She so liked cooking in here for her family and friends.

Except cooking wasn't on her mind now as she commanded Lady to sit, gave her a special cookie treat and tons of praise. Then she went to the back door, opened it, and let Lady outside.

After Lady scampered off the porch, Caprice took her cell phone from her slacks pocket.

Putting trepidation and better judgment aside, she speed-dialed Grant's number.

He answered after the first ring, his deep baritone doing funny things to her equilibrium. "Hi, Caprice."

Tongue-tied for a moment, remembering the night that the two of them had delivered a litter of cocker spaniel pups, Caprice took a deep breath. Then, in her confident-woman voice, she asked, "How would you like to take Patches and Lady for a run in the dog park?"

With the sun shining all day and the wind dying down, Caprice was glad to be outside with Lady. She'd parked in the lot designated for the dog park and smiled as she opened the gate and closed it behind them. They trotted along the path, where dog crosswalk signs occurred at intervals and paw prints lined the cement path. That path soon turned to gravel.

She spotted Grant instantly. He was crouched down in front of Patches, rubbing the dog's ears. Patches, Lady's brother, didn't look like the other pups in the litter. He had dark brown patches on his ears, around his nose, and on his flanks. His hair was a little curlier, too, and his ears shorter. He was staring up at Grant adoringly.

It had been a surprise when Grant had decided to adopt the last pup left in the litter. Caprice had taken that as a sign he was putting a tragic past behind him and he was ready to care again.

Caprice unfastened Lady's leash and let her run ahead to greet her brother. Grant stood as Lady scampered over to Patches. He was wearing a navy Windbreaker, jeans, and sneakers. The hood on his jacket flapped as the breeze tossed it. He was tall and fit, and ruggedly good-looking.

Now he gave her one of his half smiles as she approached. And, yes, she felt her pulse speed up.

"You're a little dressed up for this outing, aren't you?" he asked, assessing her appearance.

"I had a meeting with a client and didn't want to take the time to change. It's not like I don't get cat and dog hair on everything anyway."

He chuckled. "Isn't that the truth? I use packing tape to get it off. How about you?"

"Lint brush."

As they stared at each other for a moment, even the wind seemed to stop. When they weren't discussing a case or their professions, awkwardness seemed to surround them.

That happened now, until Grant said, "I brought Patches' ball, and I have a Frisbee in the car. Or do you want to just let them run for a while?"

Patches and Lady were already chasing each other around the evergreen garden, which would be bordered with colorful plants—animal safe, of course—come spring.

"Let's let them run. They'll follow us along the paths if we start walking."

As Caprice brushed her hair behind her ear, her charm bracelet jingled. She'd actually forgotten she had it on.

Grant stopped and motioned to it. Maybe he had a must-discuss list for this outing. "Vince told me about that. He said Seth gave you a charm bracelet for Valentine's Day. What does it mean?"

Her throat felt dry and her tongue seemed pasted to the roof of her mouth. Just why did Grant want to know? He'd left the Valentine's Day dance so abruptly after Seth had shown up.

All she could do was be honest.

"Seth gave it to me because he doesn't want me to forget about him. But I don't know where our relationship is going, or what will happen when he finishes his fellowship in the fall."

Maybe Grant hadn't expected her to be so honest because he seemed stymied for a response. He started walking again and so did she.

After a few steps, he said, "I should have asked you to dance at the Valentine's Day dance."

Whoa!

Maybe they were going to get down to the nitty-gritty. Maybe she'd find out exactly what he felt.

"Why didn't you ask me to dance?" She'd been so disappointed that night. She'd been looking forward to spending the evening with Grant, even though they hadn't gone to the dance together. But they *had* sat beside each other. They'd eaten dinner together. Everyone had told her she looked like a million bucks. Yet she'd felt like a wallflower teenager. When the music played, couples had begun dancing and he'd remained silent.

"I guess I wasn't ready to take that step," he confessed.

"It was just a dance, Grant," she said softly.

Stuffing his hands into his jacket pockets, he faced her. "You know my history, Caprice. I haven't dated since my divorce. A dance—Well, it just seemed like it would have been a step in a definite direction."

Grant had been her brother's college roommate, and she'd had a crush on him way back then. But he'd gone his way and gotten married, and she'd told herself she'd forgotten about him . . . until he'd returned to Kismet to be her brother's law partner. Still, when he had, he had tragedy behind him. His daughter had drowned, and he and his wife had divorced. He'd started over in Kismet with Vince because he'd needed a new life.

Caprice was wary of men who were divorced because she'd been burnt once before. Yet her friendship with Grant had just seemed to take hold as they'd worked on murder investigations. Besides . . . when a man saves your life—

"I've missed you the past couple of weeks," he said. "No one else challenges me the way you do."

"Is that good or bad?"

He gave her another one of those half smiles. "I'm still trying to figure it out."

They both needed to figure this out. There was one way to do that—spend more time in each other's company in a low-pressure way.

"You could come with me to the De Luca family dinner on Easter in two weeks."

Now and then, he'd joined them when Vince had invited him. But now *she* was inviting him, and she hoped she'd made that clear.

His brow quirked up as if he was surprised by her invitation. She thought he might make a joke or refuse, but he didn't.

He said, "I'll check my calendar. If I can bring Patches, I'm pretty sure it's clear."

"You know my family will enjoy Patches' company, too."

The dogs ran over to join them as they walked a little faster, maybe in anticipation of a family dinner that always seemed to hold surprises.

The Koffee Klatch, Kismet's premier and only gourmet coffee shop, was noisy and busy on Monday morning as workers, passersby, and even tourists stored up on their caffeine for the day. Caprice had told Bella she'd meet her here.

Her sister had started back to work at All About You, a boutique owned by Caprice's best friend, Roz Winslow. Bella sometimes needed space to vent, and these coffee meetings gave them a chance to talk, away from family and the chatter that always seemed to surround them.

The Koffee Klatch not only served up gourmet coffee, but also the best gossip in town. Teenagers with their mobile phones and twentysomethings with their laptops streamed national news while taking in their fill of local news, too. Roy Butterworth, the owner of the Koffee Klatch, even kept a police scanner behind the bar. Not that there was usually that much to scan in Kismet.

Bella was already seated at a table for two with lattes when Caprice arrived. Her sister motioned to her, and to the two blueberry muffins that sat in front of her. She'd already taken a corner from one.

"Your blueberry bread is much better than this."

Caprice put her finger to her lips and shushed Bella as she sat. "Don't say that too loud. Roy might eject us."

Bella laughed, and it was good to see her acting and looking like her old self. She'd had a baby in January and in the past few weeks she'd slowly learned to cope again with an infant. Bella liked to dictate her world around her. She did it pretty well, except for last summer when her life and her husband Joe's had almost been torn apart. That was behind them now, Caprice hoped.

"How many hours are you working this week?" Caprice asked as she took the latte thankfully and warmed up her hands with it.

"Only twelve. I'd like to be putting in more, but Joe and I made an agreement—only twelve to fifteen hours a week for the next couple of months. The day care provider I found through the church mothers' group is caring and responsible. But I don't think she wants to care for Benny more than part-time. Mom said she'd babysit for me this summer if I want to work more hours. Do you think I should let her?"

"What are your concerns?"

"First of all, she won't accept any payment. You know how Mom and Dad are. And Joe isn't going to stand by and let her do it for nothing."

"Maybe Joe could help Dad with a summer project. Or maybe you could get her a discount at Roz's boutique."

Bella ran her hand through her black curls. "Hmmm, I hadn't thought of that."

"Any other worries?"

"Mom isn't getting any younger. A baby requires a lot of energy."

Even though their mother was fifty-seven, she was young at heart, exercised, and usually had plenty of energy.

"You know Mom loves babies, and I bet Nana would like having Benny there, too."

"Are you saying I'm worrying about nothing?" Bella seemed a little defensive.

"Pretty much. I'm not sure you want to be away from Benny more hours, and this is your way of putting up roadblocks."

Bella took a few more sips of her latte and then eyed Caprice. "Leave it to you to tell me how you think it is."

Caprice leaned forward and patted her sister's arm. "You can always try it, Bee, and see how it goes. If there's a problem, you can change your plans."

Bella was thinking that over, and Caprice was about to tell her that she'd invited Grant to their Easter family dinner. Suddenly, from behind the bar, Roy Butterworth called, "Breaking news."

Roy was in his forties, but had already gone bald. His black-rimmed square glasses made him look more like a professor than a coffee shop owner. He was leaning over the shelf where the scanner was located.

"A unit was dispatched to Ace Richland's place," he announced. "My brother's on the force. He's on duty this morning. I'll give him a call and see what he knows."

Caprice and Bella sipped their lattes until he waved his phone and said, "Got a text back. He doesn't know much. Something about stolen guitars."

Stolen guitars. Ace had a couple hanging in his office, but the valuable ones were in his secure room.

"Didn't you say he keeps them in some sort of safe room?" Bella asked.

"There's a security code to get into the estate, and a security system on the house. The safe room has a code of its own. I'll give him a call and see what's going on."

Ace answered on the first ring. "How did you hear?" he asked.

"The Koffee Klatch."

"Jeez, already? I'm learning all about small-town chatter channels. The police just got here, asked a few questions, and now they're examining the secure room. But there's no doubt in my mind how this happened."

"How?"

"I had a party last night and some of my friends brought guests. I don't always keep that room locked. I mostly keep the guitars in there because of the temperature control."

"What's missing?"

"Two of the most valuable ones. They're insured. I have bigger problems than the stolen guitars," he complained.

She wondered if his problems had something to do with Alanna.

"One of my band members just quit last night, and

I have to find a replacement for Zeke for the tour," he went on. "It revs up in a few weeks."

"I'm sure you have a line of musicians waiting who want to sign up."

"I still have to interview them, hear them play, see how they fit in with the rest of the guys. Just when I thought I had all my ducks in a row." He sighed. "Alanna tells me you sent her a proposal last night and she accepted. The open house is Sunday?"

"I'm working on it. I'm headed over to Alanna's this afternoon." Last night, she'd managed to get hold of the luxury-real-estate broker she usually used. "A moving crew is going to put some of her pieces in storage. Denise Langford and video cameras are coming in tomorrow."

"Thank you for fitting her in. I know you have a tight schedule."

"You're welcome. Maybe sometime you can meet my nana. She likes your music, too."

"Just name a time," he said with a laugh. "I guess I'll see you at Alanna's open house on Sunday."

"I'll definitely be there. Nikki and I are coming up with a food menu later today."

"Alanna likes cheese grits."

"I'll keep that in mind."

After Caprice ended the call, she made a mental note to tell Nikki about the cheese grits, sure her sister could work them into the menu somehow. Would Alanna appreciate that?

Caprice doubted it.

On Friday, Caprice's morning walk with Lady took them around her neighborhood. Lady had learned to heel quite well, though Caprice still kept a few treats in her fanny pouch as an incentive for Lady to stay in that square beside her. She kept the leash loose and Lady rarely pulled on it.

Caprice was nearing her home, analyzing her mental list to make sure everything was ready for Alanna's open house on Sunday, when she saw her neighbor on her porch across the street.

Dulcina spotted her, too, and waved. "Need me to pupsit?" she called.

Dulcina had become quite fond of Lady and often pupsat when Caprice had an open house or was going to be away for an afternoon or evening.

"Are you free Sunday?" Caprice called back.

"Freer than I want to be. Rod's taking his girls to visit his sister."

Dulcina had begun dating at the start of the new year. Since her new male friend had two daughters, they were taking it slow.

Caprice crossed the street. Lady rushed forward with her, eager to see Dulcina, too.

"I have an unexpected open house. It's from two to six."

"That's no problem at all. I'll bring Lady over here. We'll have a good time." She stooped down and ruffled the fur around Lady's ears. "Won't we, girl?"

Lady gave a little yip.

At that moment, Caprice's cell phone played a Beatles tune—"Here, There and Everywhere." What could she say? She'd been feeling a little romantic when she'd chosen it.

"I won't hold you up," Dulcina said. "I'll see you on Sunday." Then she went inside, as Caprice recrossed the street with Lady.

When she checked the phone's screen, she saw Trista's picture. Why was Ace's daughter calling her?

"Trista! Hi. Are you in Kismet?"

"We sure are. The teachers had an in-service day and I asked Dad about coming up today, but he obviously forgot."

Forgot? Ace? Not where Trista was concerned.

"Isn't he there?"

"Oh, he's here, and so is Mrs. Goodwin. She's still in her nightgown. Oh, wait, she's not anymore. She's leaving. And guess what? Mom and Dad are fighting. Even Brindle's upset."

There were two ways to look at that. Yes, Brindle could be upset by the commotion . . . or Trista was projecting onto Brindle because *she* was upset.

Caprice was at a loss on how to respond to this one. Was Ace so enamored with Alanna that he'd forgotten about his daughter?

She didn't think that was possible. "Maybe your signals got crossed somehow," she suggested.

"Hold on a minute."

Caprice could hear raised voices in the background.

Trista said, "Dad's sure Mom said we were coming this afternoon. Mom's yelling back that we were supposed to be here this morning. Standstill. They'll be at this all day. Can you come over and break it up?"

Wasn't that a new one? Caprice didn't know if peacemaker was on her résumé. But she cared about Trista and her feelings, and Ace was fast becoming a friend. So she had to help, right? Just like she sometimes helped in her own family?

"Okay, honey. I'll be there as soon as I can pack up Lady in the van. She and Brindle can play. Why don't you take Brindle out back, and let your mom and dad handle their differences. They could have it all worked out before I arrive."

"I doubt that," Trista mumbled. "I'll play fetch with Brindle until you get here."

"Is Mrs. Wannamaker there?"

"She's in the kitchen."

"Make sure she knows where you go, so if your parents come looking for you, they can find you."

"All right," Trista agreed, but she obviously didn't want to.

Ace's estate was about a mile out of Kismet proper. The road was deserted most of the time, and that's the way Ace wanted it. After all, the estate was a getaway.

At the gate, Caprice punched in a code. Ace kept her apprised as to what it was. She had the feeling too many people might have that code. That wasn't her problem.

She parked in the wide driveway, let Lady out of her crate, and waited until the pup jumped to the ground. Then they went to the door, side by side.

When Caprice rang the bell, the housekeeper answered. She was frowning. "Trista told me you were coming. Mr. and Mrs. Richland are in the den."

That would be Ace's office.

"Is Trista out back with Brindle?"

"She is. They're having a fine time with a tennis ball. You could let Lady join her."

Five minutes later, after a hug for Trista and praise and affection for both dogs, Caprice wound her way to Ace's den. She could hear voices as she approached the room.

"You don't give us any consideration at all," Marsha was saying.

"Of course, I do. Trista's my daughter and I would

never forget about her. You told me you'd be here after noon."

"I told you *morning.* Who would expect your . . . your *lover* to still be here the day your daughter's supposed to arrive."

Caprice knocked on the door frame. Both Marsha and Ace swung toward her.

"Hi, Marsha," she said cheerily. "Ace. Lady is playing with Brindle and Trista out back." Then dropping all pretense, she explained, "Trista called me. She was upset you were arguing."

Marsha looked embarrassed. Ace just looked stubborn and determined, and his whole body was rigid.

"Did you say Trista went out back?" Marsha asked. "I should go check on her."

Caprice said, "That would probably be good."

After Marsha exited the room, Caprice said to Ace in a calm tone, "You must care for Alanna if she's going to move in. But this happened so fast. Maybe Trista and Marsha need time to get used to the idea."

Obviously still perturbed about his argument with his ex-wife, Ace snapped, "My personal life is none of your business."

Although Ace was bristling, Caprice wasn't going to let that bristle *her.*

"Trista made it my business when she called me. Should I have told her I didn't have time to come, or wasn't concerned about her feelings, or she could handle it on her own? She's twelve, Ace. She looks up to you and her mother. Whether this was a misunderstanding today or something else, she deserves to come first. Isn't that what you decided?"

Ace's lips were still tight and his jaw set. Finally he sighed. "Marsha told me she'd arrive after noon. She's never early. Alanna was here and we were . . . making plans, talking about the open house."

Caprice waved her hand as if she didn't want to know any more, and she really didn't. She said simply, "Trista's upset."

"I'll make it up to her. Maybe I can keep her tomorrow night, too. Even if I miss Alanna's open house."

Ace really did have a good heart. He just had to figure out where Alanna and his daughter fit into his life.

Chapter Three

Caprice knew her open houses sometimes hit snags. It was the nature of the business. However, she didn't expect her client to be a huge impediment.

Alanna Goodwin was a *monumental* impediment.

Never mind that Alanna insisted that when the open house was over, she was wrapping her draperies with the fringed tiebacks once more. Never mind she'd wanted her stamp of approval on all of Nikki's Southern dishes. Never mind she was underfoot and in the way at least half the time Caprice had been staging her house. They'd had a royal battle about moving out the two settees that crowded the room. Caprice had won that turf war by bringing in one love seat from her own storage shed to help de-clutter the space.

The theme of Antebellum Ecstasy was perfect. The only thing that could have enhanced it would have been century-old live oaks with Spanish moss hanging from their boughs in the front yard. There were "oohs and aahs" from prospective buyers about the grandeur of the house, the beautiful white pillars, the expansive veranda around the back, the porcelain knickknacks, and the velvet and brocade fabrics.

Nevertheless . . . Alanna wouldn't stay out of the mix. She was dressed to the nines in pearls and polished cotton, perfume, and hot pink nails, inviting everyone inside as if she had been expecting them for tea. She was talking to prospective buyers and not just talking, but overselling with overkill.

Denise Langford, the luxury-property real estate broker who had listed the house, sidled up to Caprice. "Can't you cage her? She's going to run off clients who are actually interested. When it's a done deal, the buyer sometimes wants to talk to the seller. But not at this stage. What are we going to do?"

"Underneath that pretty lipstick, Alanna isn't all soft-spoken words," Caprice explained, if Denise didn't understand that already. "She'll get what she wants any way she can. I've had to work with her this entire week, and, believe me, it hasn't been easy. The only thing I like about Alanna Goodwin is her cat, Mirabelle. I don't know how the poor thing puts up with her."

Denise actually gave a small smile. "Is Ace coming? Maybe he can distract her."

"He wasn't going to, but then he called me this morning. He asked his daughter if she wanted to stay overnight last night. She did, but then her mom arrived for her first thing this morning. And it *was* first thing. Trista had to be at some sort of youth service today. So now Ace is free to come."

"If he's with Alanna, that could keep her away from the other clients, don't you think?"

"If we both circulate and pull clients away from her when she monopolizes them, we may be able to avert any disasters."

Caprice hadn't been through every room in the house yet today, and she had a question. "Have you seen Mirabelle? She's a white Persian. She followed me around for the past week whenever I came into the house, but I haven't seen her today."

"I haven't seen a cat, but that doesn't mean one isn't here. Don't they like to hide under beds?"

When they are frightened or wanted peace and quiet, they did. Could Mirabelle be hiding? Or had Alanna tucked her away safe and sound somewhere, like in one of the upstairs bedrooms? Yet she hadn't seen her there.

As soon as Caprice checked the kitchen, food, and serving staff, maybe she could find Mirabelle, as well as head off Alanna before she did any damage with prospective clients.

In the huge kitchen, the counters were laden with food servers and warming dishes.

"Are we ready?" Caprice asked Nikki as she looked around.

"More than ready. As we discussed, I concentrated on turkey and pork dishes that were popular from the American Colonial period to the Civil War." She pointed to celery in lead crystal vases and a huge cranberry mold. "I found a description of a plantation dinner and replicated it." She nodded to one of the warming dishes. "Take a peek at the scalloped oysters."

Caprice did. "You've outdone yourself, as usual."

"I know stewed apples don't sound particularly appetizing, but the recipe I found added cream. That should be one of the first desserts to run out, along with the brandy and walnut tube cake. The coconut pudding—" She wobbled her hand back and forth. "We'll see."

"Any cheese grits?" Caprice asked, amused.

"I paired them with braised okra and came up with a baked dish. From the looks of Alanna, she'll be too busy even to taste them."

"It wouldn't surprise me if she came in here and tasted every dish before you serve it."

"I did include biscuits and hush puppies. I would expect most guests would anticipate those being here."

Caprice stopped by the Crock-Pot and lifted the lid. "Now that smells spicy and heavenly."

"Sweet potato soup."

"All of these guests were screened by real estate agents. If nothing else, they're going to be delighted with the food."

A few of the wait staff passed through the kitchen and Caprice had to smile. They were dressed in period costumes. The men wore red waistcoats over close-fitting trousers held up by suspenders. The bodices of the long dresses the female staff wore fastened in front with buttons running up to the high necks. The sleeves were full, widest at the elbow, but narrow on the fore-arm and wrist. Many of them were trimmed with ribbon. Most of the women servers wore their hair parted down the center and drawn back with small buns pinned on each side of their faces.

The blue china on the table resembled early-1800s dinnerware, with country scenes and rose patterns. Pressed-glass goblets were reproductions of an 1850s pattern with tulips. Soon guests would be seated at the huge table enjoying Nikki's concoctions.

Leaving supervision of the kitchen and dining area to Nikki and her staff, Caprice got caught up in wel-coming clients who entered the beautiful house for a tour. Mingling, she answered questions and pointed out particularly intriguing features. As she showed a couple through a sitting room made quaint by French doors opening onto the veranda, she was jolted by what she saw when she opened the doors.

As far as she knew, Ace hadn't arrived yet. His band hadn't been included on the guest list. Nevertheless, one of the members of his band—Len Lowery—was seated outside. Len, with his long blond hair and surfer good looks, played keyboard for Ace—always with a flirtatious eye on the fans. From what she'd heard around town, he flirted with any woman within five miles. At this moment, he and Alanna were huddled on a white wicker settee at the far end of the veranda, speaking in low tones that Caprice couldn't hear.

Just what did Alanna and Len have to talk about?

None of my business, Caprice reminded herself.

The couple behind her took a brief look at the veranda and didn't seem interested in going outside. So Len and Alanna's little confab wasn't disrupted. They were so engrossed in their discussion that they hadn't heard the doors open.

After a last look their way, Caprice asked the couple what else they would like to see and proceeded to direct them to the many bedrooms with their four-poster beds.

Caprice continued to wonder about Len and whether or not he'd come through the front door. The two valets there had checklists. If anyone who did not appear on that list arrived, they weren't admitted.

Had he and Alanna made arrangements to meet on the back veranda?

None of my business, Caprice reminded herself again.

Around four o'clock, with two hours left to go, Caprice realized she still hadn't spotted Mirabelle. She'd been in all the rooms, hadn't she? Was the cat really hiding?

Caprice returned to the kitchen once more. The only place she hadn't explored was the short hall that led to the laundry room, a utility closet, and a back entrance. She stopped by the laundry room, with its high-tech silver appliances that didn't fit in with the antebellum theme. The cupboards and shelves and pull-down ironing board made the space useful. She was about to turn back toward the kitchen, when she heard a faint meow.

Then another meow.

That was Mirabelle. She couldn't be in the utility closet!

But she was. The closet wasn't as large as the laundry room and was cluttered with mops, brooms, buckets, laundry detergent, dishwashing detergent, a sweeper . . . and a luxury pink cat-carrying case, with black embroidery, stuffed on a shelf. There was a litter box positioned near the mops. Poor Mirabelle sat on the tiled floor, pitifully looking up at Caprice.

She meowed again.

Caprice immediately stooped to pick up the cat, cuddling her in her arms. "Were you stuck in here all by yourself?"

The cat meowed as if in answer, saying, *Yes, I was.*

Caprice again took a look at the litter box and glanced around, hoping to see a pillow or blanket for Mirabelle to sit on, as well as food and water dishes. But there were none of those things. She kept petting the cat, who seemed to be sighing with relief as she laid her head against Caprice's shoulder and gazed up at her with eyes more golden than Sophia's.

"I'm going to find you comfort, as well as food and water. We don't want you to get stepped on or let out by mistake, but you need a few conveniences in here, too."

Mirabelle meowed again as if she wholeheartedly agreed.

Since Mirabelle was compliant and seemed to want to stay in Caprice's hold, Caprice carried her into the laundry room and opened a few cupboards. She found two fluffy green towels. Holding on to Mirabelle, she managed to lay the towels in a wash basket. Then she put Mirabelle in it and carried her to the closet.

"Make it your nest. I'll be right back with food and water."

Without bothering Nikki, Caprice found the cupboard that held soup bowls and dessert dishes. She plucked up one of each. She'd seen the pantry closet and now opened that. No cat food. But . . . there were cans of tuna fish. She grabbed one of those. Mirabelle could just have a special dinner today. What cat didn't like tuna fish?

Nikki cut her a questioning look when she saw Caprice dishing out the tuna and then filling a bowl with water.

Caprice merely said, "For Alanna's cat. She's made her a prisoner for the day."

Nikki's understanding look said Caprice didn't have to explain further. Animals were gentle beings who needed care, not isolation. Caprice couldn't do much about the isolation for now, but she could make Mirabelle comfortable.

She reentered the utility room and was placing the dishes near the wash basket when Denise Langford peeked in. "Nikki told me I could find you here. What are you doing?"

"I'm taking care of Alanna's cat because she isn't."

"You could be helping to promote the property. Maybe Alanna doesn't want her cat fed."

"I've been promoting the property for the past two hours."

Mirabelle had already climbed out of the wash basket and was gobbling down the tuna.

"From the looks of Mirabelle, she needed food as well as water," Caprice explained. "There wasn't even a place in here for her to sit."

"She's a cat," Denise said again.

That statement didn't endear her to Caprice at all. Denise obviously wasn't an animal lover.

"Yes, she is, and a lonely one right now. As far as promoting the property, you're the one who sells the houses. I just stage them. I'm going to stay in here a few minutes longer and make sure she's okay. I'm sure you can get along without me."

"Just wait until I spread the word you're becoming a diva."

A diva? Because I care about a cat? She shook her head. "Denise, you do what you have to. For the next fifteen minutes or so, you know where you can find me."

Denise gave a little sniff, took another look at the cat, then left the closet and closed the door.

Caprice sat cross-legged on the floor while Mirabelle ate.

"I know I need to keep good relationships with the real estate agents, but sometimes they expect me to do their job," she explained to Mirabelle. "Sure, it benefits us both when the house sells. But I contract for my work with my clients, and I've already finished it here."

Mirabelle stopped eating and looked over at Caprice as if in total agreement. She blinked and then went back to the tuna.

Caprice sighed.

Maybe March was just a turbulent month for relationships. She thought about herself and Grant. Would he really come to Easter dinner at her parents' house next Sunday as her guest?

Next she considered Seth and his fellowship, his quick visit home on Valentine's Day, and the bracelet on her arm. Could their relationship ever be more than a romantic dream?

Then there was Ace and his sharp comments that his

personal life was none of her business. That had hurt. When she established a friendship, those friends became like family. But maybe Ace, formerly Al Rizzo of Scranton, Pennsylvania, didn't want any more family. He had one of his own, with two brothers and parents who thought he hung the moon. Maybe her friendship with him should just stay a surface one.

Caprice checked her watch, a reproduction of one that Jacqueline Kennedy had worn. It was gold-toned with a rectangular case and a white mother-of-pearl dial. There were black Roman numerals at each hour, and it had an expansion band. Round, clear crystals lined the top and bottom of the bezel. Just like everything else about Jacqueline Kennedy, the watch was classically elegant and seemed to fit today's open house. Yet, sitting on the floor of the utility closet while petting Mirabelle, Caprice knew she wasn't being classically elegant. Time to get back into the fray.

Scooping Mirabelle up in her arms, Caprice gave her a head rub and then set her into the wash basket once more.

"Take a nap," she said. "This will soon be over. I just hope Alanna remembers to let you out. I'll text her and remind her if I have to."

Leaving the light on for Mirabelle—cats liked sleeping under lights—Caprice gave the Persian a little wave and opened the door.

But when she stepped into the hall, closing the door behind her, Ace and Alanna were a foot away, entangled in a lip-lock!

She had no illusions that Alanna had come this way to visit Mirabelle, or give her a bit of affection to help her through the long open house. Ace and Alanna's clinch and her coming upon them was almost funny, really, because Alanna and Ace practically leaped apart as if they were teenagers caught making out when they shouldn't have been.

Ace sheepishly rubbed Alanna's lipstick from his lips. Alanna, however, was wearing a dare-you-to-say-something kind of smile.

Oh, she was going to say something, all right, but not about that kiss.

"You know," Caprice said conversationally, "you could have given Mirabelle one of the bedrooms and plenty of food and water, along with her litter box, rather than stuffing her in a closet."

At that, Alanna looked surprised, but then her eyes shot sparks. "That cat's perfectly fine in there."

"Maybe you should try staying in a utility closet without food and water for four hours," Caprice shot back, having had enough of this Southern beauty and her open house. She didn't know what had gotten into her, but she was feeling smothered by the velvet draperies, the antebellum clutter that Alanna was holding on to, and from Alanna's attitude most of all.

With a look for Ace that might as well have said, *Why are* you *choosing to keep company with* this *woman?* Caprice turned on her heel and left. The house would either sell or it wouldn't. There would be interested parties or there wouldn't be. This was only the beginning and there could be a lot more showings.

Her job as home stager was *done*.

Chapter Four

Caprice hated to admit it, but she felt guilty. It all had to do with parochial school training and Catholic guilt. She was supposed to be a good girl. That sometimes translated into: *Be nice. Don't make waves. Always try to be a peacemaker.*

As she sat on the sofa in her living room staring at the copper silent butler on the coffee table, where she kept affirmations, she realized that she hadn't been a peacemaker yesterday. *Nope.* She'd told Alanna exactly what she was thinking. She'd texted a reminder to her last night about letting Mirabelle out of the closet. She hadn't received one in return. She might feel a little guilty, but she couldn't say she was sorry, because she wasn't. Mirabelle hadn't deserved the thoughtless treatment. If Caprice was sorry about anything, it was about the way she'd left. In her professional life, she didn't fly off the handle. She stayed in a situation and made it right.

However, yesterday, thinking about Grant and Seth, the uncertainty of romantic relationships, the uncertainty of friendships, she'd been thrown a little off-balance.

Centering. She had to center herself. She needed to

put intentions for the week in her silent butler and then repeat them every day.

With Sophia and Lady watching, she wrote down affirmations on slips of paper.

I will be patient with Alanna Goodwin.

I see my relationship with Ace growing healthy and strong.

Whatever romantic relationship forms in my future will feel right in my heart.

But after she was done writing the affirmations and tucking them in the antique, after she'd spent a short stretch in her office working, after she'd finished breakfast and had taken Lady outside to play fetch for a good long time, she'd known what she had to do.

She had to apologize to Alanna for leaving the way she had. It was as simple as that.

Lady had had a good time with Dulcina yesterday and quality time with Caprice and Sophia this morning. So she didn't seem to mind when Caprice filled her Kong toy and her kibble ball, left both beside Lady's bed in the kitchen, set up the pet gates, and told both dog and cat she'd see them later. After a visit to Alanna, she needed to stop at the rental company for her next house staging.

Caprice thought about the unusual glass-walled house and Minimalist Illusion theme she'd chosen for it as she drove to Alanna's.

That was more pleasant than thinking about an apology. She simply wanted to get this visit over with.

Almost there, she realized she should have called Alanna to set up this meeting. However, this visit had been an impulse, and if she didn't talk with Alanna now, she wouldn't. If Alanna wasn't there . . . Well, then, maybe a reconciliation just wasn't supposed to happen. She was a big believer in signs and intuition and things working out just the way they were supposed to. Nana had taught her that.

She usually had tea with Nana every few weeks. Caprice's mother often reminded her that Nana was the only one she'd take advice from. That was an exaggeration, but she did listen to Nana and trusted her judgment on matters of home decorating, cooking, and romance. Nana was an expert on all three. Caprice always smiled just thinking of her grandmother, whose addition onto her parents' childhood home had been a godsend for the family and for Nana. She didn't require much looking after. At seventy-six, Nana was very independent. Still, Caprice's parents liked the idea of looking in on her often. Now that Nana had adopted a kitten Caprice had found in her backyard last month, Nana smiled and laughed even more than she used to. It was a scientific fact that pets helped guarantee a longer life, and she hoped her Nana lived well past one hundred.

When Caprice turned into the long driveway that led up to Alanna's mansion, she noticed a sporty silver car parked there. Alanna drove a black Lincoln. This was a foreign model. If Alanna had company, this would indeed be a short visit.

A warmer wind had blown through Kismet creating a springlike day. Caprice had worn lime green bell-bottoms and a tie-dyed blouse, with a handkerchief hem, in deference to the warmer temperature. Her macramé purse matched her kitten-heeled tan shoes. Even Bella shouldn't complain about this outfit. It was quite respectable. Not as vintage as most of the outfits Caprice wore, but it still had a sixties vibe, just like the lava lamp in her living room and the collection of Beatles vinyl albums in her upstairs closet.

Distraction. She was distracting herself again as she went up to the front door and rang the bell.

She waited a couple of minutes, but there was no answer. Still, as she stood there, she thought she heard the low hum of voices. Was someone on the side in the screened-in porch?

Caprice never meant to be stealthy about her approach. She intended to walk around the side to the back entrance. Yet, as she reached the screened-in veranda, she did hear voices, Alanna's and a man's. It wasn't Ace. Caprice knew Ace's voice. Not that a man's voice meant anything. Alanna probably had other men friends. Maybe it was a repairman of some type.

Caprice was all ready to make a little noise to announce her entrance, but then something she heard stopped her cold. First of all, she suddenly recognized the male voice. It belonged to Len Lowery, Ace's keyboard player. She'd forgotten all about seeing him with Alanna yesterday. What was he doing here again today?

The hairs on the back of Caprice's neck prickled. That was a sign that someone was up to no good. That was a sign that she should be careful. That was a sign that she should keep quiet and listen.

Listen, she did.

Alanna asked, "Are you sure this is going to work?"

Len responded almost too easily, "Sure, it's going to work. I got to Ace's sister-in-law. A little flirting and she was eating out of my hand. It was that night he had the party when he debuted his single. She told me how nervous he is about his upcoming tour. He's afraid he doesn't still have 'it.'"

"So how are you going to make him realize he doesn't have 'it' anymore?" Alanna seemed skeptical.

"All I have to do is sabotage him on the first few

venues. I got Zeke to quit, didn't I? As soon as Ace is unsure of himself and his music, he'll be happy to retire on his fortune in Kismet with you."

Caprice felt the lump in her throat sink straight to her stomach and land there like a bomb. She was horrified by the idea that Len and Alanna were sabotaging Ace. What was she going to do? She had to tell the rock legend what was going on.

However, Ace's words rang in her ears: *"My personal life is none of your business."*

What about his professional life? Should she stay out of it? Is that what a real friend would do? This was going to require thought and lots of it. She wouldn't make another impulsive decision.

As quietly as she could, she backed away from the veranda and scurried to her car in the driveway. She started the Camaro and drove away.

Before she knew it, she was driving through Kismet's business district. Its charm was definitely rooted into its early-1900s heritage. Many of the redbrick buildings displayed white trim around the windows and under the eaves. Several of the shops sported oval signs hung on wrought-iron brackets. The downtown area was a pleasant place to do business.

Soon she pulled into a small parking lot at the rental company, where she chose furniture for her stagings. Minimalist Illusion was a tricky theme, though she thought she knew exactly what she wanted to do. Concentrating on staging that house would put Ace's problem in the background for now. She'd let what she'd learned simmer until she knew exactly how to handle it.

A half hour later, Caprice walked up and down the aisles, a list on her electronic tablet of what she needed to rent. Ralph's Help Yourself Rental was just that. She could pick out what she wanted and have it delivered the same day. Customers here could find everything from giant coffeemakers to ranges, tables to sofas, TVs to computers. As usual, Caprice searched for the unusual, the pieces that would claim her theme, something expensive that could be rented for a pittance. Ralph was a great help because he let her into the back warehouse, where new items had come in and old ones were being shifted to another store. He had another warehouse in Philadelphia and one in Baltimore. Caprice sometimes spent hours going through his inventory online. But she much preferred to choose it in person. Right now, choosing furniture for her staging could keep her mind off Ace, Len, and Alanna.

The house she'd be staging had been designed with glass on three floors. The sun shone in most of the day. She wanted to use that brightness to her advantage. Blinds were enclosed in the windows and an electric mechanism opened and shut them. She found an octagonal black enamel bookcase, a Lucite desk, and white enamel lamps that could seem suspended in midair on glass tables. She added all to her list. Because of Alanna's open house, Caprice was behind on designing and planning, and she was determined to get caught up.

She was filling out paperwork when her phone played its Beatles song. She plucked it from her pocket. Just what would she say if this was Ace calling? Why would he be calling? She was getting paranoid.

Glancing at the screen, she smiled. It was Grant.

"Hi," she said, maybe a little too breathlessly.

"Hi, yourself. Remember that self-defense course you promised me you'd take?"

"I remember. I've been watching for one, really I have."

"I have, too," Grant assured her. "I had a discussion with a client this morning, one of those should-a-woman-carry-a-gun discussions."

"And what did you and your client decide?"

"That's not important. What *is* important is that she told me she signed up for a class at Green Tea Spa that starts next week. Her tae kwon do instructor's giving it. I thought you'd want to know."

"Is it once a week?"

"She said it's a condensed course. There will be three two-hour sessions next week—Monday, Tuesday and Friday. I know you're busy, but this is really something you need to do."

Yes, it was something she needed to do. But there was a lot to think about. She and Lady were still bonding, and she didn't want to leave her alone too often.

As if he read her thoughts, he said, "If you're worried about Lady, I told you I'd pupsit. She and Patches have a good time together."

"That would tie you down."

"Only for a couple hours at a time. I'm okay with it, Caprice. Think about it seriously. The instructor has credentials. She's given the course before. And Green Tea's in Kismet. You don't even have to travel to York or Harrisburg to take advantage of the class."

"You're right. It's something I should fit into my schedule."

"Just call the main receptionist at Green Tea, and she'll give you the information. Oh, and by the way, my schedule is clear for Sunday. Do you still want me to come along for your family dinner?"

Caprice's heart fluttered a little. "Of course, I do."

"What time should I be there?"

"How does five sound?"

"It sounds good. Is there anything I can bring?"

Grant had attended family dinners before, but she couldn't ever remember him offering to bring something. Maybe because Vince always asked him at the last minute?

"I know you usually have the food covered," he went on. "What about if I pick up a basket of fresh fruit."

"That sounds good. I'm going to go over early and cook up my version of chicken cacciatore. So if you want to come before five, that's okay, too."

"I'm looking forward to it," Grant said, and he sounded as if he really was.

Were they turning some kind of corner on their friendship?

When she arrived back home, Caprice was still smiling.

Lady barked when Caprice removed the pet gate and greeted her. Even Sophia ambled to the kitchen as if she were glad to see her.

"My two best buddies. How about a snack before I let Lady out?"

"Snack" was a word that both Lady and Sophia recognized. Lady barked and Sophia hopped up onto a chair at the table.

Caprice laughed, glad she had these two animal friends in her life. She couldn't imagine a house without them.

The following morning, Caprice worked in her office. She e-mailed new clients, scheduled Skype consultations, and examined the layout for the Minimalist Illusion house and the furniture that she'd rent. As Sophia dozed on top of the printer and Lady lounged at her feet, Caprice's cell phone beeped.

She picked up her phone and saw the text from Roz,

Are you too busy for lunch? Can I bring takeout around noon? Thai?

Caprice smiled and texted back, Sounds good. Anytime. She and Roz talked as often as they could, but face-to-face get-togethers were sometimes rare. She knew she'd be seeing her Sunday. After all, she and Vince were dating. She was sure her brother would be bringing her to Easter dinner. But it would be nice to catch up before that.

A half hour later, Caprice was feeding Lady and Sophia their lunch when the doorbell rang. Caprice answered it and hugged her high-school friend. "I was glad you texted. We need some girl chat."

Roz, always model-perfect in hair, makeup, and clothes, wrinkled her nose. "You just want to know what's going on with me and Vince. I know your bottom line."

Caprice laughed. "You got me."

Dylan danced at Roz's feet, and Caprice stooped down to talk to the little dog, whom she'd once rescued as a stray. He was part Shih Tzu, part Pomeranian, and all exuberant energy. When Roz had stayed with her after her husband's murder, her friend had fallen in love with Dylan and now they were a pair. When the little dog yipped, Lady came running from the kitchen, Sophia not far behind. Dylan and Lady touched noses as they usually did; then they rounded each other. Lady was already much bigger than Dylan, but she seemed unaware of that as they bobbed against each other and then trotted into the living room.

"We'd better eat in the kitchen," Caprice said. "With all these little paws around, someone might get the idea they want to try our Thai. It will be easier to guard it if it's on the table."

A short time later, Sophia lounged on the chair

beside Caprice, every once in a while lifting her nose to take a whiff at what was on the table. Dylan and Lady sat between Roz's and Caprice's chairs, hopeful they'd drop something, or have a bite left over.

But Caprice said to them now, "Too spicy, kiddos. I'll give you each one of your cookie treats when we're done." Perky Paws had the best peanut butter cookie treats, and both dogs loved them.

Sophia meowed and Roz just raised her brows.

Caprice told the feline, "Fine, an extra dollop of cream for you."

Roz shook her head. "Vince says we treat them like kids, and he's right."

"He protests a little, but I bet you one day he'll have a dog or a cat, or maybe the two of you will," Caprice slipped in slyly. "How's it going?"

A slight blush colored Roz's face. "It's going. We sure do have fun together."

"Dating prerequisite number one."

"And what's number two?" Roz asked warily.

"That you both have the same idea where you're going."

"That's the tough one, because we don't know. It's only been a year since Ted died. Not even."

That anniversary was coming up for Roz, and Caprice knew it would be a difficult one. She stayed quiet and listened.

"I don't know if I feel guilty because I'm moving on with Vince, or because I made such a mess of my first marriage and don't know if I ever want to try that again."

"Does Vince know where you're coming from?"

"He does, but he's never been married. I don't know if someone who hasn't been married can understand all the implications of it."

Caprice thought about her and Grant. He'd been married. She hadn't. Then she considered Seth. He hadn't been married, but he *was* married to his work.

They were digging more deeply into their Thai food when Caprice's cell phone played.

"I'd better check this," she said to Roz. "Juan is at the house we're going to be staging and he might have run into a problem."

But when she glanced at the screen, she saw Ace's face. Uh oh, just what was she going to say to him? She swiped the screen and put the phone to her ear. "Hi, Ace. What's up?"

"Caprice . . ." Ace's voice sounded strained and very strange. "I'm at Alanna's house," he continued, sounding as if there was something wrong with that.

She was sure he'd been at Alanna's house a lot lately. "Does Alanna need something?"

"No, she—" There was silence . . . absolute silence. "Ace? What's going on?"

"Alanna's here, Caprice, but the thing is—she's not breathing. Her eyes are wide open. She has no pulse. I think she was strangled!"

Chapter Five

"Ace? Are you there?" Caprice was afraid Ace had passed out, shut down, blanked out.

"I'm here," he said in such a low voice she could hardly hear him. "I called 9-1-1. But I can't remember what the operator told me to do. I hung up. I probably shouldn't have. . . ."

He was in shock. She knew how finding a body had rocked her world, and if he really loved Alanna . . .

"Ace, listen to me. Back away from the body and step out of the room, but stay put until the officers or detectives arrive. Do you understand?"

"I don't want to leave her."

"Ace, you have to. That's not Alanna anymore. I'll call Grant and we'll stay outside the perimeter and wait for you. If you feel the police are asking questions other than what you saw and heard when you came in and found Alanna, say you want a lawyer. Just call me back and I'll be there with Grant or somebody to help you. Do you understand?"

"I should call you if they ask questions other than what I saw and what I heard?" he repeated.

"If you feel the police think you're a suspect, call me. I'll be outside."

She heard a long, in-drawn breath. "Okay."

As Ace ended the call, Caprice hoped he could hold together. She hoped Detective Jones wasn't the detective who would appear to take his statement. Detective Jones could be confrontational. Knowing Ace, Caprice realized, he'd be confrontational right back.

"What happened?" Roz asked, knowing something was amiss from Caprice's side of the conversation.

Caprice quickly told her, then pushed her chair back. "I have to call Grant."

Roz said, "Vince is tied up in court. I hope you can reach Grant."

When Grant picked up, she said, "I need you."

Before he could misinterpret those words, she went on to explain Ace's predicament.

With his cool, professional, usual composure in circumstances like this, he assured her, "You gave him the right advice. Are you on your way?"

"I'll stay here with the animals," Roz said. "I have my laptop in my car. I can go over purchase orders. You go."

"Thank you," Caprice said gratefully; then she answered Grant, "I'm leaving now. I'll meet you at Alanna's place in fifteen minutes or less."

Almost fifteen minutes later to the minute, Caprice parked at the edge of the property line leading to Alanna's mansion. Patrol cars zigzagged across the boundary of the property. An ambulance held a prominent position, too, but Caprice was afraid it wasn't necessary. She was sure the coroner was on the way, as well as the county forensics unit.

Before she could open her car door, Grant pulled up right behind her and hurried to her car.

She rolled down the window.

"Stay in your car," he said. "I'll get in with you. It could be for a while and the wind is picking up again."

She didn't think Grant had ever been in her car before. After he opened the passenger door and slid in, he adjusted the seat to accommodate his long legs. His head practically touched the ceiling.

Their eyes met and that unusual awareness that occurred when they were this close in a confined space unsettled her. Yes, they could have a long wait.

Together.

One of the officers standing guard came over to the Camaro.

Before he could tell them they couldn't be here, Grant said, "I'm Ace Richland's attorney. If he asks for me, please tell whoever is on this case that I'm here."

Caprice couldn't see the officer from her side of the car, but she heard him say, "Stay in the car."

"Got it," Grant answered, cooperating.

Again, a heart-thumping awareness overtook the two of them. As always, when she felt disconcerted, she made conversation. "What did you do with Patches?" Since Grant had adopted the pup, he'd been mostly working from his home, taking Patches to his office in the building with Vince now and then.

"Don't worry. My neighbor's taking care of him. What about you?"

"Roz was having lunch with me. She's going to stay awhile. . . ."

"Did you call Vince before you called me?" Grant asked. There seemed to be an underlying message there. They had both done legal work for Ace.

"No." For some reason, she added, "Roz told me he'd be in court all day."

"She's right," Grant confirmed. "They probably know each other's whereabouts most of the time now."

Making conversation, Caprice said, "Vince has been less obsessive about work since he's been dating her. He tries to leave the office at a decent time so they can have dinner together."

"That's what finding the right woman will do. Work just doesn't mean quite as much."

She blinked. Grant's work had seen him through a difficult time. Did Grant feel work didn't mean as much as it once did for him, too?

"Vince needs to have a life as well as his work," she agreed. Then she added, "You do, too."

With one of his shrugs, he confessed, "Patches has saved me from eighty-hour weeks. When I worked in Pittsburgh in corporate law, there were sometimes hundred-hour weeks. That's one of the reasons—" He stopped abruptly.

"One of the reasons what?"

Looking out the window toward Alanna's house, he was silent for a while, and she thought he was going to ignore her question. But then in a gruff voice, he answered, "Work was one of the reasons I wasn't paying enough attention when Sally died. I hadn't taken parenting classes. I hadn't had enough experience. I didn't realize a dad has to be there as much as a mom, for all the everyday things as well as the birthday parties. My ignorance cost us our child."

She turned toward him. "Oh, Grant, you can't blame yourself."

After a moment, he responded, "I don't blame just myself. Naomi and I were both to blame. But if I'd have been awake at the wheel, I could have prevented it."

She doubted that. Sometimes tragedy couldn't be

prevented, no matter how much you wanted to think otherwise.

This was the first time Grant had ever talked about what happened to his little girl. This was not where Caprice would have expected him to do it. But she wasn't going to stop him if he was willing to share.

It seemed, though, that this little bit had been quite enough of sharing because he turned away toward the house again and his mouth grew tight. She knew from the straightness of his shoulders and his erect posture that he didn't want to say more.

A little sharing was better than none.

Two officers were running crime scene tape around the property—up the driveway and across the front lawn. Although she couldn't see them, they'd most likely wrap it around the side veranda and across the backyard, too. Crime scene techs from the York County Forensics Unit would let no square inch of the grid they devised go unturned.

A half hour passed and no one came to the car again, though Caprice had seen Detective Brett Carstead arrive and go inside. Roz had texted Caprice, telling her that Lady and Sophia were fine. Grant received a similar text from his neighbor.

"So Donna's home from school this week for spring break?"

Grant's neighbor was a secretary in the Kismet public-school district. The week before Easter was considered spring break.

"Donna's not taking care of Patches. Simon is. He's really good with him."

Caprice had met Donna when Grant's neighbor had given a home to two stray kittens, who had ended up in Caprice's care. Grant had recommended her and her little girl; and after a visit with Caprice, Caprice had okayed the adoption. But since then, she'd wondered exactly how close Grant and his pretty, divorced neighbor were. Simon Treadwell, his neighbor on the other side, was retired and liked dogs, too.

"Ace just came out," Grant suddenly told her, opening the car door.

They both climbed out.

Ace made a beeline straight for Caprice's yellow Camaro.

Running his hand through his already-disheveled hair, he explained, "They want me to go to the police station. The detectives are going to question me further there. I thought I should have a lawyer with me."

"I'll go with you," Grant assured him. "And Caprice should go home."

"I'm not going home. I'll go to Ace's estate and wait there. The press won't let him alone if they know he's involved in a murder."

As she thought about Alanna's murder, she suddenly remembered Mirabelle. She asked Ace, "Did you see Mirabelle inside?"

He thought about it, but she imagined all he could envision was Alanna's dead body.

"I don't remember, Caprice. Really, I don't."

Caprice didn't hesitate to go to the officer at the boundary tape. Detective Carstead was inside. She had to talk to him.

"Officer, I need to speak with Detective Carstead."

"He's quite busy, ma'am. It will have to wait."

"It can't wait. There's an animal in the house, and I need to talk to him about her. I know I can't go in. Could he please come to the tape and talk to me?"

The officer gave her a skeptical look.

She said, "Give him my name, Caprice De Luca.

I've been involved in other investigations, and he knows me."

"So *you're* the one," the officer muttered, and Caprice had no idea what that meant. He got on his mobile device and not five minutes later, Carstead was walking toward them.

"This better not be a ploy to get inside," he said right away.

"I don't use ploys, Detective. There should be an animal in the house, a white Persian cat with golden eyes named Mirabelle. If you can't find her anywhere out in the open, there's a utility closet down the hall, off the kitchen. Alanna stuck her in there during the open house, so it wouldn't surprise me if she had a meeting— and she apparently had some kind of a meeting—that she might have stowed the cat in there again. There was a cat carrier there. I just want to make sure she's not hurt. I can take her with me."

Carstead studied her for a long minute, then glanced at Grant and Ace, who'd moved toward Grant's SUV for a private conversation.

"I'll check," he said tersely.

A short while later, Carstead walked down the drive, looking a bit sheepish. He was carrying the pink cat carrier. Mirabelle was protesting loudly from inside.

Detective Carstead, who was much more human than Detective Jones, informed Caprice, "The cat was inside the closet." Then after a moment of considering what he should say, he explained, "We've contacted the police in Mississippi to notify Mrs. Goodwin's sister of her death. Once she gets in contact with me, I'll ask her if she'll take the cat. In the meantime—"

Mirabelle was exceedingly upset. Her meow was high-pitched and wailing.

Caprice cooed to her. "Everything will be okay,

baby." Maybe it would be even better than okay because she wouldn't have to stay in a closet, if Caprice had anything to say about it.

She asked Carstead, "Can I take her—until you know whether her sister wants her or not?"

Carstead thought about it. "It's well-known you take care of stray animals in Kismet. I'd just have to call animal control if you don't take her, and who knows where she'd end up? The thing is, Miss De Luca, what if Alanna's sister can't take her? Then what happens?"

"I'll find her a home, one way or another. I promise."

"Don't you already have animals?" he asked.

Just how much did this detective know about her? "What am I, an urban legend?"

"Close to it. You've solved three murders."

That had nothing to do with her animals.

"My cat's going to be put out. My dog will be curious. But I'll keep Mirabelle separated to give her some time to adjust to new surroundings before I introduce her to them. After all, maybe Alanna's sister will want her. What's her name again?"

"Her name is Twyla. Twyla Horton."

Grant and Ace were already getting into Grant's SUV to drive to the police station.

Caprice took the carrier from Detective Carstead. "Do you have my number?" As soon as she asked the question, she knew how stupid a question it was. "Of course, you do," she murmured.

She thought she saw Carstead's lips quirk up a bit, and he looked amused for a moment.

He said, "How is it that when there's a murder in Kismet, you're somehow involved?"

She shrugged. "Kismet's a small town and I get around."

He rolled his eyes at her quick comeback. "I guess

you do. Believe me, we have you on our Rolodex and on our computer."

After a last glance at the cat carrier, he walked back to the house. As Caprice took Mirabelle to her car and felt the perimeter guarding officer's eyes on her, she decided that these days Big Brother *was* watching.

Grant waved as he drove off and she waved back. He or Ace would let her know what was happening, she felt sure.

Caprice texted Roz that she was bringing Alanna's cat home. Roz texted back that she'd take Dylan and Lady to the backyard.

Mirabelle meowed during a good part of the drive, even though Caprice spoke to her. She knew Persians could be talkative. She wasn't sure how Lady and Sophia would like that. She did know she was going to settle Mirabelle in her spare room upstairs, until the cat could adjust to being somewhere new. After all, maybe Alanna's sister would want her. Maybe Ace knew something about Twyla Horton.

Ace—he was going to be grilled. Detective Jones wouldn't waste any time if he was on the case, too. Just how much would Grant let Ace say? The bigger question was: *Would Ace listen to Grant?*

At her home, Caprice exited the Camaro, then carried Mirabelle to the front door. She knew Lady and Sophia were intelligent and was certain their animal instincts would tell them a new feline was in that spare room when they reached under the door, smelled up the sides, just got any kind of whiff at all.

Mirabelle looked healthy, but Caprice would still like to have her checked out at Furry Friends Veterinary Clinic. Marcus Reed, her pets' veterinarian, would give her a true estimation of Mirabelle's condition. She trusted his advice.

Sophia, deep in sleep on her cat tree, paid Caprice no mind when she scooted up the stairs. In the spare room, Mirabelle just seemed tired from the whole day's activities. She jumped up on the single bed and plopped in the middle of the teal blue quilt. She meowed a few times as if to ask guest-type questions: *How long can I sleep? Am I safe here? Is it suppertime yet?*

Caprice sat on the bed beside her, stroking her. She'd make sure Mirabelle felt comforted and loved for however long she was here.

Worried about Ace, she spent a few more minutes with Mirabelle; then she went downstairs and into the garage for an extra litter box. She called to Roz from the back screen door. "I just have to put food and water upstairs for my new boarder and then I'll be out."

Sophia had watched Caprice go up and down the stairs, but she hadn't moved from her favorite spot on the top shelf.

Caprice was no sooner standing on the porch, watching Lady and Dylan chase after each other in the backyard, when her cell phone played. A photo of Ace filled the screen.

"I'm back home," Ace said without preamble when she answered the call.

"That was quick."

"Grant wouldn't let me say much. He's here. I told him I'd like you to sit in on our discussion."

"Discussion about?" she prompted. At least Ace was home and hadn't been arrested.

"You've had some experience with murder investigations. You helped your friend and you helped your sister. So I'd like you to think about helping me. Can you come over?"

"Sure. Do you mind if I bring Lady?"

"You know I don't. She's your sidekick now. Everybody can see that."

"I'll be there as soon as I can."

After Caprice gave Roz thanks for her help and a huge hug, Roz and Dylan left. Caprice patted Sophia, then leashed Lady to take her to the van.

Twenty minutes later, she was sitting in Ace's living room on his black-and-white-striped sofa, where Grant had taken a seat, too. Lady lay between them on the floor. Ace lowered himself into a black leather club chair, his elbows on his knees, his face in his hands. She'd never quite seen him look so . . . tired.

When he lifted his head, he focused on Grant. "I'm their number one person of interest, aren't I?" he asked, obviously wanting a straight answer.

"You are," Grant agreed without embellishment. "I cut the interview short because too much information sometimes can hang you."

Ace winced at that, and Caprice felt a shiver go up her spine.

"But on the other hand," Grant went on, "Detective Jones has a knack for finding out *everything*—everything you want him to know, and everything you don't want him to know. So I suggest you tell what you don't think he should know."

"I wasn't sure what to say," Ace explained. "Alanna and I had a fight yesterday."

"Where?" Grant asked.

"At the Country Squire Golf and Recreation Club. We were having lunch there."

"Was it a serious fight?" Caprice asked.

"Serious enough for Alanna to run out in tears," Ace admitted regretfully. "Everyone in the dining room saw us and saw her leave."

There was silence for a few moments. When Grant didn't ask any more questions, Caprice stepped into the gap. "What was the fight about?"

Ace was silent.

"I can't help you if I don't have all the facts."

Grant pounced on that statement. "You shouldn't be helping. You should stay out of this. If you want to support Ace as a friend, that's fine. But don't get involved in another investigation."

"Ace asked for my help," she said quietly.

Grant groaned. "You're not an expert."

"I helped solved three murders. Maybe not an *expert,* but I might have a nose for this. I'm good at puzzles, Grant, you know that. And if Ace needs my help, I'm going to give it."

Grant glared at her, but she didn't look away. If he didn't understand anything else about her, he should understand this—she was loyal to family and friends and helped them solve problems when she could.

Grant finally sat back against the sofa in resignation. "All right. Ace, what was the fight about?"

Ace looked torn that he even had to talk about this. But then he did. "The fight was about Trista. I'd planned for her to stay with me for two weeks at the end of the summer when I didn't schedule tour dates. I blanked out my schedule for her. But Alanna didn't like the idea at all. She wanted me to tell Trista I had changed my mind and that I was going to be . . . on a honeymoon."

"You were that serious about Alanna?" Caprice asked gently.

"I was. We had a good time when we were together. She could make me laugh. And she had this Southern sweetness that was just so . . . alluring."

Caprice's gaze met Grant's for a moment and she felt herself blush without knowing exactly why. But this wasn't about her and Grant.

Grant looked a bit unsettled, too, and shifted in his seat, stooped to pet Lady, then focused his attention on Ace again. "You didn't know Alanna very long, and I know Detective Jones asked you this, but I want you to think hard. Did she have any enemies?"

"I've been thinking about that since I found her, since Carstead and then Jones asked. No enemies that I know of. But I didn't know much about her business—Goodwin Enterprises. She wasn't involved that much, but she did sit on the board of directors."

Silence hung in the room for a few moments until Caprice said, "She might not have had enemies, but she had cohorts."

Looking confused, Ace asked, "What do you mean?"

Caprice really didn't want to hurt Ace. He was a friend. He might have looked at Alanna as if she were a beautiful magnolia, but underneath that flower were prickles and maybe he needed to know that. After all, the woman had been murdered.

"You're not going to like what I know."

"What do you know?" Ace asked, obviously puzzled.

Grant focused his attention on her, too.

"I left Alanna's in a bit of a huff the day of the open house."

"Right. You found us kissing."

"That wasn't why I left. She'd locked her cat in a closet."

Ace's brows arched.

"But that's not what I'm talking about. I went to her house yesterday to apologize, because it just wasn't professional of me to leave so abruptly. The thing is, when I got there, I heard voices and went around the side porch. She was on the porch with a man, and I recognized his voice. It was Len. He and Alanna were plotting."

"Plotting what?" Ace asked, totally perplexed.

Caprice told him about the phone conversation she'd overheard, as well as yesterday's interchange. She ended with, "They wanted to sabotage you, Ace. She wanted you to forget touring and she was going to make you do it any way she could."

Ace looked as if every blood vessel in his face was going to burst. "Just wait until I find Len. I'll knock his head off."

Grant sat forward on the couch. "Calm down. You have to seriously think about this. You can't have a confrontation with anyone right now. Detective Jones is going to be watching you carefully. Don't even think about an altercation with Len."

"But what if he's the murderer? What if he killed Alanna?" Ace wanted to know.

"Even more reason to keep your distance," Grant determined. "We don't want *you* to end up the same way as Alanna."

Lady had risen to her paws, distressed by the tension in the air, as well as from the upset in Ace's voice. She went over to him, whined, and then sat on his foot.

When Ace looked down at her, he inhaled and calmed a bit as he patted her head.

"Just because Len and Alanna were plotting," Caprice reminded him, "doesn't mean Len has anything to do with her murder. After all, Alanna could have been plotting with someone else other than Len. About something else. And *that* person could be the one who murdered her."

Whether Ace knew about enemies or not, Caprice guessed Alanna might have had a few.

But how was she going to find out just who would make that list?

Chapter Six

Caprice leaned over the examination table at Furry Friends Veterinary Clinic the following morning and wiggled a toy mouse at Mirabelle.

"Come on. Come on out for Marcus. He has to examine you."

Marcus chuckled and shook his head. "You really think that's going to do it?"

"She's scared. I'm not sure how well taken care of she was at Alanna Goodwin's. I think she has a pedigree, and I think Alanna kept her more as a status symbol than anything else. Just my opinion, mind you."

Marcus glanced at the computer screen on his laptop on the counter. "Everything's in order in her medical records that were e-mailed to me. She's two years old. She was last seen six months ago by a veterinarian for her yearly rabies shot. Are you sure you don't want to keep her with the veterinarian she had?"

Caprice had called the two veterinarians in Kismet, one of whom was Marcus, to find out if they had treated Mirabelle. They hadn't. She'd spread her search to York, explaining she was now taking care of Mirabelle in case the veterinarians hadn't seen an account of

Alanna's death. There weren't any HIPAA laws with animals. To have Mirabelle's records transferred, all she'd had to do was have Detective Carstead call the vet and verify that she was the one who now had custody of the cat.

"I trust you, Marcus, you know that. Mirabelle could become my new permanent adoptee."

"Are you sure you want to take on another animal?"

He gently upended one side of the carrier so Mirabelle had no choice except to step onto the table. She looked up at Caprice and meowed.

Caprice protectively curled her arm around her and petted her, cooing, "It's okay, baby." Then she addressed Marcus again. "Two cats and a dog. I can handle that. I put another litter box beside Sophia's in the laundry room. Upstairs, Mirabelle has one in the spare room and Sophia has one in the sewing room under the eaves."

"That should do it . . . *if* the animals all get along."

"You know they eventually will. It's just going to take time."

"And patience. But you have that."

Marcus Reed was big, burly, and black, with a wide smile and a buzz cut. In his forties, he was an experienced vet and had helped out Caprice on many occasions. Now he gently but confidently examined Mirabelle from teeth to ears, from coat to heart.

"From her records and from what I've observed here," he said, "she seems in good health. I couldn't see a flea treatment in her recent past, but since she was an inside cat, that doesn't surprise me."

As soon as Marcus was finished with Mirabelle, the cat curled up close to Caprice again and huddled under her arm.

"Do you know what food she was on?" the vet asked.

"No, I don't. I'll put her on Sophia's diet and see how she does—a good wet food and crunchies in between."

"If Detective Carstead helped you with the records transfer, it sounds as if you two are getting along."

All of it had been businesslike. "He wants me to focus on the cat and keep my nose out of the investigation."

Marcus's brow inched up. "But you won't, will you?"

"Ace could be their number one suspect. I know he didn't kill Alanna."

Now Marcus appeared worried. "Are you sure? Maybe they had a lovers' quarrel gone wrong."

"Ace can be a hothead, but I just can't see him hurting somebody he loves," Caprice responded with a confidence she felt in her soul.

"I bet the press is having a field day with this."

"Ace had to hire extra security to keep them away from him and his property. He's going to feel like a prisoner until this is resolved."

"Where are you going to look first?"

"I need to learn some background on Alanna. I think that will be a good place to start."

"Google?" Marcus asked with a quirk of his brow.

Caprice shook her head. "This time, I think I need to talk to those who knew her best. I just have to figure out who they are."

An hour later, Caprice was at home again with Mirabelle ensconced in her guest bedroom. After her outing, the cat just wanted to sleep. With Marcus's okay, Caprice knew she could introduce her to Sophia and Lady soon.

After Caprice gave Sophia petting attention and took

Lady outside for the necessities—a game of fetch, as well as training on all her basic commands—she settled at her computer to work on floor plans, purchase orders, and rental agreements. She was hardly aware of time passing as Lady played with her kibble ball, and Sophia washed herself in a patch of sunlight.

When her cell phone played, she picked it up and sat at complete attention when she saw the name—*Twyla Horton.*

"Hello," she answered quickly. "This is Caprice."

"Miss De Luca, this is Twyla Horton."

The deep Southern accent was very much like Alanna's. Twyla went on explaining; her voice was a bit husky now. "Your number came to me in a roundabout manner. A detective from Kismet, Detective Carstead, notified the police department here about what happened to Alanna." Twyla stopped, as if she'd gotten choked up by the news she'd received.

"I'm so sorry, Miss Horton."

After a moment, Alanna's sister said, "Oh, please, call me Twyla. Our local police chief came to the house to inform me about what happened, but he gave me Detective Carstead's contact information so I could find out more about it."

"Have you spoken with Detective Carstead?"

"I have. He was very kind. He told me what he could. He has questions for me, personal information he wants filled in, I guess, about Alanna."

"Detective Carstead is very thorough."

"I imagine he has to be. I told him I'd be flying into BWI Airport tomorrow and can meet with him."

"Again, I'm so sorry for your loss."

Whether or not Alanna was liked in Kismet, she'd been this woman's sister. Caprice knew all about sisters because of her two, Bella and Nikki. They'd always been her best friends. She couldn't even contemplate what losing one of them would be like.

"Thank you," Twyla responded. "I can hardly wrap my mind around this. I just saw her over Christmas. I had off from work and stayed over the holiday vacation."

"What kind of work do you do?"

"I'm an account manager with an office furniture store in Biloxi. Since I used my vacation days over Christmas, it's not easy for me to get off. But I have no choice, of course. Alanna's lawyer wants to make her last wishes known. Apparently, the police need that information, too. I'll call Mr. Travers next." She stopped. "Sorry I'm rambling. I can't seem to think in a straight line."

"When I spoke with Detective Carstead," Twyla went on, "he said I should give you a call because you have Mirabelle."

"Yes, I do. Will you be taking her, once everything is settled?"

"That's why I had to call you. I'm afraid I can't. I'm allergic to dogs and cats. Whenever I stayed with Alanna, I had to take allergy medication. Oh, I didn't mind. It was worth it, of course, to spend the time with her. But I wouldn't be able to handle Mirabelle twenty-four hours a day."

"I understand that." Caprice couldn't imagine being allergic to animals. What a terrible loss. "Do you know if Alanna had any good friends who might want Mirabelle?"

"No, I don't. Alanna had friends she played tennis with and had lunch with. But since Barton died, she kept to herself a lot. So I don't know that she had a best friend or anything like that. Detective Carstead said you were quite fond of animals. Are you interested in keeping Mirabelle? I want her to go to someone who will really care for her. She's such a beautiful cat with a sweet personality."

That she was.

"I am fond of animals. Right now, I have a cat of my own and a cocker spaniel pup, who's less than a year. I think Mirabelle will fit in, once she gets used to them and they get used to her."

"I don't want to see her going to a shelter," Twyla said with a catch in her voice. "That would be just too awful, because then if she wouldn't get adopted—" She stopped abruptly. "Well, you know."

Yes, Caprice did know, and she wouldn't want to see that happen, either, not to any animal.

"I'll be glad to keep Mirabelle and start acclimating her here. In the eyes of the law, animals are considered possessions and I didn't want to overstep my bounds. Ace is a good friend and I want to help him any way I can, too."

"Mr. Richland is a hoot. I met him when he picked up Alanna to take her to a New Year's Eve dance. Of course, I Googled him and downloaded much of his older music. Alanna was happier with him than I've seen her and heard her in a long time. She had so many plans for them."

That was the problem, Caprice thought. Alanna's plans might not have been Ace's. And if the police got wind of that, Ace could even be in more trouble. But she didn't want to delve too deeply in her first conversation with Twyla. After Twyla Horton arrived in Kismet, she could get to know her better.

Then maybe she could figure out who had killed Alanna Goodwin.

* * *

As Caprice pulled up in front of her childhood home, she realized it was always a haven when she was unsettled, mixed up, and had to think something through. That's why she'd driven here this evening.

Her parents had invested in the house when she was almost too young to remember moving in. Its architecture was unusual for Pennsylvania. It was a Spanish-style home, with casement windows, yellow stucco, a red-tiled roof, and more repairs and upkeep than any house should have. But that's how her parents had been able to afford to buy it, and they all loved it. Even more now, since her parents had added an addition that Nana lived in.

The house was on a corner. Its double-bay detached garage, matching the house architecture, stood to the rear of the property. Her parents and visitors had the habit of parking along the curb, across the lawn from the side porch, and that's where she parked now.

Caprice didn't recognize the green sedan that was parked in front of her dad's truck advertising his business, DE LUCA MASONRY. He was handy around the house and took on a lot of the repairs himself. To her mother's relief, he mostly spent his time in his company's office now and let his crews handle the brickwork contracts. But he still knew his way around a saw, hammer, and trowel.

Lady trotted beside Caprice as they approached the side porch and the dark brown, ropelike pillars, which supported it. This entrance led into a foyer. The living room, a sunroom, and a library stretched on the left. To the right, a staircase with a landing led upstairs. Straight ahead was the dining room. It had always been the center of the house, but there was an eat-in area off the kitchen, too.

After Caprice opened the door and unleashed Lady,

she heard voices coming from the dining room. Lady headed that way and so did Caprice. However, the moment she faced the large mahogany table, the antique china cupboard, and the casement windows along the dining-room wall, she knew there was trouble.

The tension in the air was so thick, even Lady stopped, sat beside Caprice, and looked up at her, instead of going to one of the adults sitting around the table as she usually did.

Caprice didn't know what was going on, but she hadn't seen her uncle Dominic in a very, very long time. He was seated at the table with her mom and dad and Nana. But no one looked very happy.

Spotting her, her dad rose to his feet. "Caprice, come on in."

Hmmm, she wasn't sure that was a good idea.

In his late fifties, her father was still a handsome man, and he cared very much about his family. His black hair was laced with gray now and had receded a bit at his forehead. Putting in more time at his desk at work, he'd added a few pounds over the past couple of years. But he was still fit and strong, a quiet leader in their family. Now he forced a smile and motioned her to the table, where coffee cups and the remains of a pie sat.

He said jovially, "Look who's here."

He, of course, meant Uncle Dom.

Out of the De Luca family habit, Caprice went to her uncle, with Lady following close behind, and gave him a hug. He wasn't quite as tall as her father. Once thin, he had now added more pounds than her dad. Lots of lines creased his face. His thick tortoiseshell-framed oval glasses sat high on his nose.

He hugged her back with the enthusiasm that she remembered as a child.

When the hug was finished and she caught a glimpse of her mom's face, as well as Nana's, she definitely knew all was not well.

Past history or new?

Uncle Dominic was her dad's younger brother who lived in Baltimore, about an hour and a half from Kismet. But he was the black sheep and the family never talked about him. Even Caprice knew not to bring up his name.

Twelve years ago, Uncle Dom had fallen in love and accepted the money Nana Celia had given him for his wedding. Nana had hoped for a grand celebration with her son and his new wife. But Uncle Dom's fiancée had convinced him to elope and take a honeymoon around the world instead of having a wedding. On top of that, Ronnie hadn't liked the big-family smothering feel of the De Lucas. She didn't want anyone knowing her business or barging into it, as Caprice's relatives were wont to do. With the wedding rift and Ronnie's attitude, Uncle Dom had cut himself off from the rest of the family for all these years.

Yes, her dad visited him once in a while, but he didn't talk about those visits. Caprice had gotten the feeling that Nana had never forgiven Dominic for cutting the whole De Luca family out of his life. To Nana, family *was* life.

Lady scampered to Caprice's mom and wiggled around at her feet. Fran made a big fuss over her, and Caprice recognized it for what it was, a defensive stalling maneuver, not to have to deal with the situation at hand.

Nana, however, was looking straight at Caprice. "Your uncle Dom is visiting . . . for a while." Nana's lips pursed shut in a tight line. Her hands fluttered in agitation as she picked up her napkin and folded it, as if there was something final in the gesture.

Caprice had rarely seen Nana unsettled. Nana Celia was a ballast for the family. She weighed in on every issue, but never dictated. Her advice was wise and practical. Tonight, though, she looked every one of her seventy-six years. She wore her long gray hair in a controlled bun at the nape of her neck, usually securing it with her favorite combs. The hairdo gave her a regal appearance. Yet, tonight, her shoulders seemed to slump a little in her high-collared blouse, and her smile was nowhere to be found.

Caprice made her way around the table to sit next to her mom, across from her father and Uncle Dom. She suddenly felt as if she had dropped into the middle of warring factions.

Since no one else was talking, she wanted to be clear on what her nana had said. She asked her uncle, "So you'll be staying in Kismet?"

"Yes," her uncle answered. "Your father has generously invited me to stay here."

Uh oh.

He studied Caprice for a moment. "You've really grown up. You were still in college the last time I saw you."

"I was," she agreed, feeling every bit of the awkwardness of the situation.

Her uncle was looking at Lady now. "Is she friendly?"

"She is. A little shy, though." Lady was a good judge of character and it would be interesting to see what happened with her uncle.

Dom came around to where Fran sat and crouched in between her and Nana. He held out his hand to Lady.

She sniffed it and looked up at him with her big brown eyes.

He smiled. "Can I pet you?"

Lady cocked her head as if she were inviting the action. So Uncle Dom slid his hand under one of her ears and around her neck and gave her a scratch. She sidled up to him and rolled over on her back for a belly rub.

He laughed. "She's great. I haven't been around dogs in a long time, not since your father and I were kids."

When he rose to his feet, Lady followed him around the table. She'd made a new friend and wanted more of those belly rubs.

Soon he took his seat once more, but he lowered his hand to ruffle Lady's fur. "Your father told me how you've solved a couple of murders."

"I seem to have a knack for it," she said lightly.

"You helped out Bella and Joe. Your dad told me all about that."

So her uncle was making it clear that he wasn't altogether out of the loop.

"I couldn't let members of my family be suspected of murder," she explained.

"You like to help."

"Don't we all?" she returned.

He shrugged. "I guess that's why I've come to your father. I might as well lay it out on the table. I've fallen on hard times."

"I'm sorry." That just seemed to be the right thing to say.

"I was the manager of a branch of Wood Hill Financial Services."

Caprice recognized the name. It had been big news when the company folded.

Her uncle stopped petting Lady to pick up his mug

and have a sip of coffee. When he set it down again, he admitted, "I couldn't find another job when Wood Hill closed. As it was, Ronnie and I were living paycheck to paycheck. So without mine coming in, we couldn't pay our bills. Because we couldn't pay our bills"—he raised his hands in an I-didn't-know-what-to-do gesture—"we had problems. We got a divorce. All my resources have run out."

Caprice wondered if her dad had lent her uncle money and if he'd been living on that. Her mother still had not said a word.

Caprice wondered what her mom was most upset about. Her uncle Dom staying for a while? No, she loved having guests. The fact that Nana would be upset if Uncle Dom stayed? Possibly. Or, the possibility that there was no time frame for which her Uncle Dom might stay.

Caprice canvassed her dad's face and could see the affection he felt for his brother. But she could also see that her nana and her mom were disconcerted by it all. They'd been terribly hurt at being cut out of his life for so long. She felt like she was in the middle and no step in either direction would be a good one.

She rose to her feet. "I think maybe I should go."

But her mother took her arm. "Nonsense. You're part of this family. You deserve to know what's going on . . . just as we all do." Fran seemed to give a pointed glance to her husband.

Nana spoke now, too. "We'll make another pot of coffee. You must have a piece of pie. Nothing's going to get solved here tonight. We all just have to get used to the idea that Dominic actually wants to be part of his family again."

Ooh, that was a barb, and so unusual for Nana, who

made a point of being kind and generous and helpful.
She was really upset.

Maybe it would be a good idea for Caprice to stay
for a little while and let Lady work her animal magic.
Maybe some of the tension would ease. Maybe the dis-
cord between her uncle and the rest of his family would
diminish.

She could only hope.

The following morning, Caprice thought about the
apple pie and coffee that she'd had with her parents,
Nana, and Uncle Dom last night. In her own kitchen,
readying her blueberry scone recipe for a meeting she
was having in half an hour to discuss reunion plans
with high-school classmates, she popped the tray into
the oven. Sophia was sitting at her dish, licking up odds
and ends of her breakfast. All exuberant energy, Lady
pushed her kibble ball across the kitchen, left it in a
corner, then found a pull toy, which she brought to
Caprice.

"I thought I tired you out playing catch and fetch in
the yard this morning."

Lady shook her head, the pull toy flapping back and
forth as she did, as if to say, *That wasn't nearly enough.*

Crouching down, knowing a few minutes wouldn't
make any difference in her schedule, she eyed Lady,
held out her hand, and then said, "Let go."

Lady didn't. She just shook her head more, and Caprice knew the dog wanted her to take hold of the pull
toy and try to pull it from her. Instead, Caprice was
trying to teach her the "let go" command.

She made eye contact with Lady, held out her hand
again, and said, "Let go." Already sitting, Lady looked

confused for a moment, studied Caprice's hand, and then opened her mouth. The toy fell into Caprice's palm.

She made a great big fuss. "What a wonderful dog you are. You learn so fast. I'm so glad we're best buddies."

Caprice placed the toy on the floor and took a step back. Lady snatched it up and shook her head with it again.

Caprice laughed and held out her hand. "Let go."

Lady didn't hesitate this time. She let the toy drop into Caprice's fingers. Caprice again praised her from here to next year.

Sophia was done eating now and washing herself in her pristine, catlike manner.

Caprice said to Lady, "She might be ready for a chase."

Lady heard the word "chase." She ran over to Sophia and barked.

Knowing that signal, Sophia took off for the living room, with Lady at her back paws.

After washing her hands and drying them, Caprice chose colorful mugs from her mug tree and set them on a hydrangea-patterned tray on the table.

Thinking about last night all over again, she hoped her uncle could figure out a solution to his problems without causing more family tension. On the other hand, she hoped her mom and Nana could accept him into the fold again. Still, twelve years of separation and hurt feelings were hard to overcome.

Caprice was removing the scones from the oven when her doorbell rang. She set the cookie sheet on the counter and hurried to answer it, grinning when she saw her friend Roz and Dylan. The dog yapped at Caprice and then trotted inside.

Caprice's downstairs was one big circle—living room to dining room to kitchen to utility room to bathroom to her office, around the stairway to upstairs and back to the living room. Lady now stuck her head out from the office. When she spied Dylan, she barked. Dylan yapped in return.

"Go play," Caprice said. "That will give Sophia a break."

As if the dogs agreed, they both ran into the office.

"Lady has toys in there she'll share," Caprice called.

Roz had no sooner come inside, when two more cars parked at the curb and three women emerged. Fifteen minutes later, after greetings and hugs, Caprice and her friends chatted while they enjoyed coffee, tea, and Caprice's fresh-baked scones, which had been brought into the living room and arranged on the coffee table.

"I can't believe it's been fifteen years," Alicia Donnehy said. "We can suggest everybody turn off their smartphones for the night so we can all chat and concentrate on each other."

"That might not go over well," Connie Miller said. "Especially if they have pix of their kids on their phones."

"It's only a suggestion," Tara insisted. "Hopefully, we'll all get involved in conversation and won't even listen for our phones. Speaking of phones," Tara continued, focusing her attention on Caprice, "I have a friend who works part-time at the police station when they need clerical help. She told me she heard your name mentioned."

Uh oh. She had to find out more about this. "Did she know why it was mentioned?"

"Something about you taking Alanna Goodwin's cat. Paperwork had to be filled out or something. Did you take her cat?"

Having Mirabelle here wasn't a secret. In fact, later

today, she was going to introduce her to Sophia and Lady. It was time she had more room to roam than the spare room.

"I do have Mirabelle. She's a sweetie. She's up in the spare room. After we're finished eating, if you want to go up and meet her, we can. I'm going to let her out with Lady and Sophia later."

"A sweetie, you say?" Alicia asked with a frown. "Very unlike her mistress."

Hmmm. Maybe this group could talk about something more than the high-school reunion. "Did you know Alanna?" Caprice asked them all.

"Not 'know her' know her. Whenever she came in to have her teeth cleaned, she'd act as if she owned the place."

Alicia worked as a dental hygienist for a local dentist.

"That would be kind of hard with her mouth opened and your hand in it," Tara said with a laugh.

Alicia laughed, too. "You're right about that. But she managed."

Now Roz weighed in. "She was a frequent customer at All About You and very hard to please."

"Harder than me?" Caprice joked.

Roz applauded Caprice's vintage look, but often didn't have much to suit her. Caprice had, however, found a fabulous dress there for the Valentine's Day dance, and it had wowed Grant and Seth.

"Much harder to suit than you. When something's right, *you* know it. Alanna . . ." Roz shook her head. "She had this biting sarcasm she often used. Bella wouldn't wait on her if she could help it. I tried to be patient with her—but sometimes she was so critical of everything she looked at, I really didn't care if she was a customer or not."

"She used to come into the Blue Moon Grille, but she acted as if she was slumming," Tara revealed.

Tara was a waitress at the Blue Moon, one of Caprice's favorite places to eat. She and Seth had dined there on the outside deck under the moonlight, and it had been so romantic.

"She was picky about her food?" Caprice guessed.

"Not only that. She'd ask if we had a really expensive wine, and you know we're kind of middle-of-the-road. Or she'd complain there were crumbs on the table that had to be wiped off before she could eat. I mean, crumbs she made. The sweet tea was too sweet. The coffee was too bitter. The cream was too thin. You get my drift."

"But she should have tipped well," Alicia chimed in.

"She did do that," Tara acknowledged. "But I have a feeling that was to make an impression more than it was to show appreciation for service. I just don't know anybody who liked her."

No one in the room contradicted that statement. Still . . . Caprice considered the fact that Ace and Len had seemed to like her.

"Maybe she only made friends with men," Caprice wondered out loud.

All the women nodded in agreement.

Just how did that fact play into Alanna's murder?

Chapter Seven

A short time after her high-school classmates left, Caprice set up the puppy gates at the kitchen doorways. Now the fun should begin. She had introduced pets to each other before, but every situation was a little different. Mirabelle was meeker than some cats. There was no telling what would happen when she met Sophia and Lady. The best thing to do in a case like this was to keep Mirabelle separated from the other two, but let them *see* each other. A screen would be the best strategy, but she didn't have a spare one right now.

Lady and Sophia had watched her set up the gates, curious about the whole endeavor. Lady was particularly curious because, in the past, she'd had to stay *in* the kitchen, not outside the gate in the hall or on the other side in the dining room.

After the gates were secure, Caprice went upstairs to fetch Mirabelle. The cat had to be getting cabin fever. Still, she seemed to like sprawling on Caprice's guest room bed the best and never went to the door to be let out. She enjoyed sitting on the table by the bedroom window, too, peering out at the birds filling the yard again, now that winter was over. She seemed happily comfortable in her seclusion, yet Caprice knew she could be much happier with housemates.

"You're going to meet your sisters," Caprice told her as she lifted her from the bed, gently deposited her in her carrier, zippered it up, and took it downstairs. Lady and Sophia were still nosing around the gate between the dining room and the kitchen so Caprice stepped over the gate that led from the bathroom and hall on the other side.

"Okay, everybody, this isn't going to be a once-and-done deal. I'm just going to let Mirabelle roam about in here and get used to the place. Lady and Sophia—you can sniff at her through the gate, but you're just going to get to know her slowly. Even Marcus agrees that would be best."

After all, she hadn't had any problems after she'd found Sophia and brought Dylan into the household. Last year when she'd taken in two kittens, they'd been fearless and hadn't hesitated to play with Sophia, once they'd gotten to know her. Even Dylan had joined in their play.

But an adult cat was a little different.

When Mirabelle meowed from her carrier, Sophia's ears flopped into what Caprice called airplane position. Her tail puffed up. With her long hair, she looked like one big calico fluff ball.

Lady backed away from Sophia, but it was obvious she wanted to see what was going on in the kitchen. Back legs up, front paws down, she nosed her way to the gate.

Caprice unzipped the front of Mirabelle's carrier. The feline stepped out. However, as soon as she did, Sophia hissed, Lady barked, and Mirabelle went wild. Her tail grew as big as Sophia's. Her whole body seemed to be in backward motion. Sophia ran toward the living room and up the steps. When Lady barked again, Mirabelle ran in the other direction, somehow managed to jump the gate, and ended up in the living room under the sofa.

Caprice sighed—so much for the well-laid plans of an animal lover who thought she knew what she was doing.

She removed the gate. She should have known better than to think a gate would work with cats. Too late now. Everybody had sort of met everybody.

Moments later, she crouched down in front of her sofa. To her amusement, Lady was right there beside her, doing the same. She could pen Lady in the kitchen, but at this point she didn't think that would solve anything. She extended her hand farther under the sofa. The small sofa legs were too short for her to stick her head under. Somehow Mirabelle had gotten under there, though.

Lady wiggled and pushed her nose under, but that was as far as she could go, too.

Caprice's hand finally came upon soft fur. At least she didn't think the fluff was a dust bunny. No, that was definitely a tail.

She ran her fingers through Mirabelle's coat and talked to her softly. "Hi, baby. I know you're scared, but this is a really nice bunch out here. You'd have a lot of fun."

Mirabelle meowed and rubbed her head against Caprice's hand. This was going to take patience, cat treats, and a lot of coaxing.

"I'll be right back," Caprice said to Mirabelle, intending to dip into the jar of cat treats and maybe even open a can of tuna. But as she opened her pantry door, her phone in her pocket played. She quickly took it out and saw Twyla Horton's name and number.

As she grabbed a can of tuna, she answered. "Hello?"

"Caprice, this is Twyla Horton."

"How are you?" Caprice asked, thinking immediately of Twyla's sense of loss and the grief that would be with her for a very long time.

"I still feel a bit shell-shocked. I'm at White Pillars, trying to absorb the fact I won't see Alanna again. When I landed in Baltimore, I had a text on my phone from Detective Carstead saying they'd finished at the house. I've spent the last hour cleaning up. I suddenly realized I don't really know anyone in Kismet, and I thought of you. Could we possibly get together, maybe have breakfast or something? Maybe you could fill me in on professional services in the area, the most economical place to get good food, that type of thing? Would you mind?"

Caprice found that she wouldn't mind at all. Twyla was very different from her sister, not at all haughty or condescending. "How about breakfast tomorrow at the Sunflower Diner? It's near Country Fields Shopping Center."

"I've never been there. When Alanna took me to brunch, we usually went to the Country Squire Golf and Recreation Club."

"That's a white-napkin brunch. The Sunflower is more paper place mats and fake sunflowers on the tables."

Twyla gave a little laugh. "That sounds perfect. What time should I meet you there?"

"You name the time. Do you need directions?"

"No, my rental car has a GPS. I'll just plug in the address. Is eight-thirty too early?"

"No, that's fine."

"I have that appointment with Detective Carstead tomorrow and I'd like to talk to you about that, too," Twyla added.

"Sure. I'll see you at the Sunflower at eight-thirty."

"Sounds good. Thank you, Caprice."

Caprice pocketed her cell phone, eager to pick Twyla's brain tomorrow morning. Maybe she could recall something Alanna had said or done that would help Caprice find the murderer.

Until then, she had a cat to lure out from under the sofa, another cat to reassure she was still queen of the house, and Lady to take outside for a bit of exercise.

Her life was never dull.

Although March had turned the corner into April, a morning bite was still in the air as Caprice pulled open the Sunflower Diner's glass door. The diner was busy this morning, since many people had a work holiday the Friday before Easter. She knew several of the patrons at the diner. After waving to a former client, and stopping by a table to ask about the health of a friend of her mom's, she spotted the woman in the back booth who looked as if . . . as if she didn't quite belong.

Caprice approached the booth, more confident with each step. The woman's hair was light brown and cut short, and it had a natural wave that framed her face as if it hadn't taken much care. She'd been studying the place mat menu, but now she looked up and Caprice could see her eyes were as green as Alanna's had been. She had high cheekbones like Alanna's, but that was where the resemblance seemed to end.

She smiled tentatively at Caprice, and it was a genuine smile.

"Twyla?" Caprice asked as she stood at the table.

Twyla rose to her feet and extended her hand. "Caprice, it's so good to meet you."

Caprice seated herself across from Twyla and motioned her to the booth seat once more. "I never thought to give you a description of what I looked like."

"Me either," Twyla said. "I'm so glad we could get together. I feel kind of lost. When I visited Alanna, I spent most of my time with her and didn't get around the town much."

"It's not that big. You'll soon find your way around." Taking a folded sheet of paper from her purse, she handed it to Twyla. "This is a list of all the businesses I frequent. I thought that might come in handy."

"Just what I need."

"You feel comfortable staying at Alanna's house? Maybe 'comfortable' isn't the word I want. Do you feel safe?"

"Alanna had an alarm system. From what Detective Carstead said, it hadn't been breached. She must have known whoever killed her." Twyla rubbed her arms. "That thought gives me chills, but it also means as long as I have that alarm system on, and I check who's at the door, I should be perfectly fine."

Caprice, of course, knew about the alarm system, but it didn't do much good if you let someone inside who you knew and they murdered you.

So she asked Twyla, "Are you sure you don't know anybody who would want to hurt your sister?"

"I thought about it and thought about it. I suppose someone associated with Barton's business, or his board of directors, might have held a grudge. After Barton died, Alanna had to make decisions about the company. She had meetings over the holidays about expansion into China. From what I understand, she was going to vote for it. Half of the board was against it. In those meetings, other board members were trying to change her mind. Apparently, she was going to be the deciding vote. So there might have been some bad feelings there."

Caprice hadn't thought much about the business end of Alanna's life. Though with a company like Barton Goodwin's, where millions of dollars were involved, money *could* lead to murder.

The waitress came to take their order. Caprice and Twyla both ordered the breakfast special. That was another way Twyla was unlike her sister. Alanna watched every morsel she put in her mouth. She might have liked cheese grits, but she mostly ate salads, along with a small portion of protein. Caprice learned a lot about a client while she was helping one stage his or her house. But Twyla's order of the special, with its two eggs, hash browns, and bacon or sausage, wasn't for a dieter.

"I'm nervous about meeting with Detective Carstead," Twyla admitted. "Will they put me into an interrogation room with folding chairs and a scarred table?"

Caprice had to smile. "It's not far from that, but it's not too gritty. Just answer Detective Carstead's questions truthfully and you'll be fine. He's not so bad. Detective Jones . . . he's got an edge."

"The reading of the will is on Monday, and I know Detective Carstead's interested in that," Twyla said.

"He's looking for a motive."

After staring out the window for a moment, Twyla turned back to Caprice, her eyes misty. "I still can't believe she's gone."

Caprice remained silent. Sometimes the best sympathy was just presence, not words that couldn't convey condolences well enough.

"Did you know much about Alanna?" Twyla asked, her voice still thick with grief.

Caprice shook her head. "I gather you were close?"

"We were close when we were young, maybe because we were poor, maybe because we missed our dad. After he left, he only saw us once or twice a year, then not at all. When Mama died, I was just out of high school and Alanna was working at a local TV station. She was so pretty and talented. I expected her to be another Diane Sawyer someday."

"She gave up her career?" Although Caprice had used search engines to research Alanna, she hadn't found much. Mostly photographs with Barton Goodwin.

"Oh, after she met Barton, he became her world. It was certainly a different world than we'd grown up in."

"You mean because Barton Goodwin was wealthy."

"Oh yes. He could provide Alanna with everything she'd never had, anything she could ever think of wanting—furs, cars, jewels. But more than that, as his wife, she had a carte blanche ticket for acceptance in social circles that before were closed to her."

"Did she change because of all that?"

Twyla's nose crinkled. "Alanna was always sure of herself and confident, or at least she pretended to be."

Caprice suspected that married to Barton, Alanna had gained more assurance and arrogance and haughtiness, and maybe even a sense of entitlement.

Twyla didn't seem to possess those qualities.

The waitress brought their orders, and Caprice settled in to enjoy her breakfast with Twyla Horton. If she listened carefully, she might learn more that would lead to a clue that would help with the investigation.

* * *

Caprice opened her mom's oven door on Easter Sunday and delicious smells rushed out. As she peered at the two casseroles of her version of chicken cacciatore—tomatoes, peppers, and spicy sausage, along with chicken thighs—the dishes produced the aromas that always made her parents' house smell like home. Good foods were constantly simmering or baking. Their lingering scents gave the house its character.

She read the meat thermometer she'd used to test the chicken. "It's looking good," she told her mother, who was tossing a salad in the huge glass bowl on the counter. "Fifteen more minutes should do it."

"The water for the pasta's boiling. I'll drop it in." Picking up the pasta jar on the counter, her mom opened the lid.

No one else was around for the moment. Joe and the kids, her dad and Uncle Dom, were outside flying a kite. Bella and Nana were huddled in the living room discussing Bella's latest costume creations for kids. She was selling them online now. Her christening outfits were all special order and were really taking off. Between making those and working at Roz's, she was a busy woman.

Caprice took this opportunity to ask her mom, "So, how's it going with Uncle Dom?"

Looking troubled, Fran De Luca sighed. "It's going. He mostly sits at his laptop, trying to find a job. With school closed for spring break this week, I kept busy with cleaning and preparing the house for Easter. But Nana has spent more time in her rooms this week than she usually does so she can avoid him. She's loving that kitten you found, by the way."

Valentine was sleeping on Nana's lap right now as she talked to Bella in the living room.

"I'm glad she's bringing Nana some joy."

"She is. Your uncle isn't."

"Everything that happened, happened a long time ago," Caprice suggested.

"Maybe so. But consequences from it are still rippling. He cut us out of his life. How could he just do that? Your father seems to understand a whole lot better than I do."

"They're brothers, Mom. Think about me and Bella and Nikki and Vince. Wouldn't we forgive anything?"

Her mom dropped the pasta a handful at a time into the huge pot of boiling water. "I suppose you would. We *could* blame the whole disaster on Ronnie. We could blame it all on love. Apparently, Dom made her the center of his world, and he wanted to make her happy. But he should have stood his ground, even if she didn't want contact with us. He should have made an effort to unite us all. After all, your aunt Maria is in Montana, but she sends us pictures. She invites us to come stay with them. She visits us every couple of years. We understand the distance. We understand the expense. But e-mails go a long way. So do texts and phone conversations. Your uncle cut himself off completely."

Aunt Maria, her father's sister, had always lived across the country and they rarely saw her. But she did keep in touch. "Do you think he cut himself off because he didn't want to deal with Ronnie's reaction?" Caprice guessed.

"Most probably. He doesn't like conflict. None of us do. But family is worth fighting for."

Family *was* worth fighting for. Caprice knew that to be true.

The doorbell chimed.

Fran's fierce expression, and her conviction about

family, eased into a knowing smile. "You'd better answer that. It could be somebody you want to see." Her mother knew she had invited Grant.

"You mean Vince and Roz or Nikki?"

Her mom's smile broadened. "Hardly. They wouldn't have rung the bell."

Caprice hurried from the kitchen, then through the dining room, with its long mahogany table now dressed with a white tablecloth and her mother's good china. The cuckoo clock, which had hung in the dining room for as long as Caprice could remember, emitted a small cuckoo bird. It cuckooed five times.

Grant was right on time.

When she opened the door, they both just stood there for a minute or so, unsure of how to proceed. He'd never come here as her guest before.

In his arms, he carried a basket with fresh fruit. Noticing Patches wasn't at his feet, she used that as a stepping-stone. "Didn't you bring Patches?"

Grant chuckled. "He's already playing out back with Lady. I stopped to say hello to your dad and Joe, and they introduced me to your uncle."

Caprice lowered her voice. "There's tension around all of them that they're going to have to work out."

"Your uncle Dom said he's been searching the job sites, looking for work. Do you think he'll stay in the area?"

Caprice gave a shrug. "Nobody knows what's going to happen. But that doesn't mean we can't enjoy the meal and conversation and everybody's company. I'm glad you came."

She was, and she might as well be honest about it.

Grant hefted the fruit basket he had in his arms from one side to the other. "Where would you like me to put this?"

"Let's put it on the buffet in the dining room for now. It looks so pretty. I hate to tear it apart."

"I ran into Detective Carstead yesterday at the police station. I had to stop in to pick up some paperwork on a client."

"Did you talk to him about Alanna's murder?"

"You know how closemouthed he is. He soaks up information like a sponge, but he doesn't give any out. He did say they hope to have some movement in the case after they know what's in the will."

"Does he think Alanna changed it to leave everything to Ace?" Caprice asked, wondering if she had.

"That's certainly a possibility."

"He doesn't need it," Caprice said.

"Do you know that for sure? He has a tour coming up that's going to be costing a pretty penny. Half a million is what I heard. Until money starts flowing in, he has this estate he just bought in Kismet and a condo in L.A. He might have expenses you wouldn't even think of. He could be in the hole. His divorce could have put him in debt."

"So we have to hope he's not the beneficiary."

"I don't think hope is going to have much to do with this," Grant said with a grimace.

"I had breakfast with Twyla Horton—Alanna's sister—on Friday. She called me after she got to town. Since I took Mirabelle, she feels I'm a contact of sorts."

"Did you learn anything from her?"

"Not a lot. But she did bring up the possibility that Alanna had some enemies from Barton Goodwin's business dealings. She was a member of the board, and some of the other members didn't like the way Alanna was going to vote on an expansion project."

"So there are lots of leads."

"Yet nothing concrete. The truth is, Len and Alanna's association bothers me a lot."

"Yeah, it's still under Ace's skin, too," Grant agreed. "He can't very well stay away from Len, with Len in his band, and them having rehearsals together and picking a new band member. But I told him to pretend he knows nothing. His freedom could depend on it."

Caprice felt so comfortable talking to Grant like this, about the ins and outs of an investigation. Grant was dressed in khakis and a black oxford shirt, with its sleeves rolled up his forearms. Her pulse quickened because she was aware of her attraction to him. Was he attracted to her?

Suddenly the door flew open and Vince and Roz walked in, followed by Nikki. They were all carrying something to contribute to dinner. Vince brought wine. Roz carried a bouquet of tulips and a huge box of candy. Nikki had hold of a Crock-Pot wrapped in a towel.

"Cream of cauliflower soup," she said. "I just have to plug it back in."

With the bread her mom had baked, and the cannoli Nana had filled, this meal would be another feast.

Grant moved to take the Crock-Pot from Nikki. "Next to the fruit basket?" he asked Caprice. "I saw a receptacle there."

"That would be perfect." She exchanged a look and a smile with him that the others couldn't help but catch.

Vince's brows arched.

Roz winked.

And Nikki?

Nikki had an absent expression on her face that was unusual. What was up with her?

As Grant strode with the Crock-Pot into the dining room, Roz and Vince followed him.

"Mom will have a vase for those," Caprice called after Roz. "They're gorgeous." She turned back to Nikki.

After removing her Windbreaker, Nikki laid it across a ladder-back chair, which sat against the wall.

"What's wrong?" Caprice asked, because she knew something was.

Nikki didn't even think twice before she blurted out, "Drew Pierson is going to open his own catering business. He's going to be in direct competition with me here in Kismet."

In February, Nikki had decided to look for a partner for her business so she could get more time to herself, more time to live a normal life instead of working sixty hours a week. Among the chefs she'd interviewed was Drew Pierson. At first, they'd seemed to work well together. He went along on a couple of Nikki's catering jobs, one of the open houses Caprice had planned, and the Valentine's Day dance. But there had seemed to be a spark between him and Nikki that had gotten in the way of work. Nikki had wanted Drew to work for her for a while to see if their association could hold up. But he'd wanted a partnership or nothing, and she hadn't been ready to commit to that. So she'd decided on nothing.

Vince returned to the foyer, obviously overhearing their conversation. "Why are you worried? You have a good business going now. Why should that change?"

"Drew's food is good. I'm afraid he's going to take a huge bite out of my business. Scuttlebutt is he has connections at the Country Squire Golf and Recreation Club."

"Don't you have connections there? You've catered events for them."

"It's not the same. I know some of the staff. They

helped me make inroads. But apparently he knows members of the club. He knows the influential people, and the ones who hold the purse strings."

Vince settled his arm around Nikki's shoulders. "Come on, sis, really. If you do your best work, you'll be fine."

Caprice saw that Vince was trying to be the supportive brother. But the reality was—both she and Nikki didn't know if that was true.

Would Nikki's Catered Capers be fine if Drew Pierson's company was in direct competition?

Chapter Eight

Caprice didn't know what to expect when she arrived at Alanna's house early Monday afternoon. Twyla had called her around 10:00 A.M. and asked her to stop over.

"I know what's in the will now," she'd said. "I'm probably a suspect, along with everybody else. But there's someone else on the list, too."

"Who?" Caprice had asked.

"Archer Ford."

"Who's Archer Ford?"

"Barton's illegitimate son."

Caprice had asked Twyla if she wanted to talk about it, and Twyla did. For her side of it, Caprice wanted to know who this Archer Ford was and what his connection to Alanna could be, so she'd accepted Twyla's invitation to stop at White Pillars.

Twyla greeted her at the front door in jeans and T-shirt, her feet bare. She said, "Let's go into the parlor. I can't stand being in the living room. It creeps me out."

Caprice could see how it would, staying in a house where someone had been murdered. On the other hand, Caprice had staged the smaller parlor to be a comfortable sitting area. She'd added aqua to the dark greens, off-white pillows to the settee. She and Twyla both sat there.

Twyla motioned to the glasses of iced tea and short-bread cookies on a tray on a side table. "It's sweet tea," she said. "The way we make it down home."

"The cookies look home-baked."

"I needed something to do last night, and I wanted to fill this place with good smells. Do you know what I mean?"

Caprice did know. Every house had its own unique aroma as well as ambience. Cinnamon and sugar added pleasantly to the mix. She sampled one of the cookies. "These are good." After she took a sip of the tea, she realized it *was* sweet.

Twyla had folded her hands in her lap and looked a little lost. "Alanna left me this house. I never expected that. I never expected anything, really. Actually, I thought Alanna might leave her estate to charity. She and Barton donated to several foundations."

"She was your sister."

"Yes, she was. But we weren't so close in our adult years. Our lifestyles were very different. Alanna spent her teenage years trying to get away from our home-town. And Barton finally took her away. But I made a life there, a good life. I have a boyfriend and a little bungalow with a yard."

"From what I understand, Alanna had a hefty estate."

"She did. She left a third of it to charity, a third of it to me, and a third of it to Archer Ford. The business was a separate entity."

"So tell me about this man, Archer Ford. Besides in-heriting Alanna's estate, did he have any other reason to want her dead?"

"He might. After Barton and Alanna moved to

Kismet, Archer approached Barton, claiming he was his son."

"Why wait until Barton moved here? Was Archer Ford from around here?"

"He lived in D.C. When his mother died, she left him a letter with the information that Barton was his father. Apparently, Barton flew to the D.C. area a lot because of government contracts."

"How old is Archer Ford?"

Twyla thought about it. "He must be around thirty. Barton supposedly had the affair early in his first marriage."

From what she'd learned online, Caprice was already familiar with the basic facts. Barton was twenty years older than Alanna and had been married and divorced before he met her.

Twyla confirmed that info when she said, "Barton was two decades older than my sister. She thought he was stable and faithful. But when Archer came out of the woodwork, then she found out that Barton had cheated on his first wife."

That would be a shock *if* a woman believed the man she'd married adhered to the same values *she* did. Then Caprice considered another aspect of this family drama. "Alanna was Archer Ford's stepmother, so to speak." She couldn't imagine the Southern beauty liking that idea.

"Not exactly his stepmother. Barton denied paternity to Archer. He didn't want a scandal to damage his reputation."

"Would that matter to a businessman?"

"Maybe not in the old-fashioned sense, because infidelity is more common today. But it might have changed the terms of his divorce settlement if his ex-wife found out about it."

"What if Archer went to the press?"

"Without a paternity or DNA test, Barton would still have denied it and probably would have convinced his connections to squelch it."

"Barton sounds like a hard man."

Twyla took a bite of one of the cookies and nodded. "He was. When Alanna told me about it—in confidence, of course—she said she felt sorry for Archer. She liked him. He even moved to York so he could be close by Barton, hoping he'd change his mind. After his mother died, he didn't have any other real family. So Alanna kept in contact with him. I think she felt Barton would eventually soften toward Archer and accept him. But Barton never did. When he died, he didn't leave anything to him. He left his fortune to Alanna. That had to be a disappointment to Archer that his father wouldn't even acknowledge him in death."

Was that motive for murder? If Archer knew he'd inherit if Alanna died . . . Caprice guessed there was more to this story. After nibbling the rest of her cookie, she sipped more tea. She could get used to the sweetened iced tea.

"This feels like a soap opera," she said. "What happened next?"

Twyla glanced away for a while, as though thinking better of telling Caprice all of this. Family matters were sacred to some families. Then again, most families didn't have to deal with murder.

After a long lull in their conversation, Twyla admitted, "I looked you up on the computer."

That could be good or bad. "And what did you find?"

"Everything about your success as a home stager, of

course. I can see why Alanna wanted to use you to sell the house. But I also read about the murders you've solved."

"I sort of fell into doing it by accident."

Twyla canvassed her face as if trying to decide about her trustworthiness. Finally she said, "I want you to know all this so you can find out who killed Alanna. That's what you're going to do, aren't you? Because Ace is your friend?"

"I won't get in the way of the police investigation, but if I can give them more information, I will. And if you have anything they should know—"

"I'm not sure if I should tell them about Archer or not." After a bit more hesitation, Twyla confided, "After Barton died, Alanna and Archer had a fling. I asked her about it at Christmas, if it was still going on. She told me she'd just ended it before Christmas. Archer just didn't move in the right circles, or have the clout of a man like Barton—or Ace Richland."

Caprice didn't act surprised, because she wasn't. "Alanna liked her lifestyle."

Twyla shrugged. "She had enough money to keep her lifestyle with what she inherited from Barton."

After considering what Twyla said, Caprice shook her head. Maybe she knew Alanna better than she thought she did. "Yes, she had Barton's money. But she didn't want to be alone and she wanted a man who could bring to a relationship or marriage as much power as she did. If she dumped Archer for Ace . . . that could definitely give Archer a motive for murder. I wonder if Archer knew he'd inherit when Alanna died."

Twyla shrugged. "I have no idea. Sometimes Alanna was like the wind. She'd change direction in a matter of minutes. I thought she really felt something for Archer, but then she just dropped him."

Caprice suddenly wanted to meet this disappointed lover. Jealousy was a powerful motive for murder. Most likely, he'd attend Alanna's funeral.

Her mind and Twyla's must have run in the same direction, for Twyla said, "I made arrangements for Alanna's funeral. It's on Wednesday. I have another appointment with the funeral director this afternoon."

To move away from that morbid topic, Caprice asked, "Do you think you'll be staying in Kismet?"

Twyla looked a little lost again, as if she was overwhelmed by all of it. "I just don't know."

Caprice understood her confusion. Maybe after Alanna's funeral, Twyla could make up her mind whether to stay . . . or return to her life in Mississippi.

There was no way for Caprice to know whom the police considered their main suspect for Alanna's murder. Two suspects headed the top of *her* list—Archer Ford and Len Lowery. Hopefully, she could meet Archer Ford at Alanna's funeral. And Len . . .

She needed to know more. She wouldn't mess with Len himself. That might be too dangerous. But she *could* have a talk with Zeke Stoltz and find out why he'd quit Ace's band.

Dulcina worked at home as a medical transcriber, so Caprice phoned her to see if she could puppysit Lady for a couple of hours. Dulcina assured Caprice she could. With the holiday, her workload had been lighter.

After Caprice handed Lady into Dulcina's care, after she tucked Mirabelle into the guest bedroom for safe-keeping, she drove her Camaro to Harrisburg's west shore, where Zeke lived. He and his wife rented a town house there.

Caprice had phoned Zeke to set up a meeting and

he'd tried to shut her down. But she'd played her best card. "This is a murder that happened, Mr. Stoltz. If the police haven't talked to you yet, they will. Ace is my friend. I'm trying to figure out the best way to help him. I promise I won't take up much of your time. I have to be back in Kismet by six for a class I'm taking tonight." Her self-defense course began this evening at seven and she didn't intend to be late.

Zeke had set their meeting time for three o'clock.

Zeke's reluctance to talk about Ace had been obvious in her phone conversation with his former bass player. Now when he opened his door, she could see that reluctance in his eyes and on his face. He was a tall guy, maybe six-three or six-four, lanky, with a scruffy black beard. He wore his thick black hair short. His jeans were worn. His oversized T-shirt had seen many washings. From the scowl on his face, Caprice surmised he was obviously not happy to see her.

She extended her hand anyway. "I'm Caprice. You're Zeke Stoltz?"

"I'm Zeke. I was hoping something would come up and you couldn't make it."

That was a welcome if she'd ever heard one! "I promise this won't be painful."

"Maybe not for you."

What did *that* mean?

Although he apparently didn't want her to come in, his polite nature took over and he motioned her into his living room. This was a high-end town house in a gated community. The furniture Zeke and his wife had chosen was modern in style, with sleek pieces and clean lines. The boxy sofa was a saffron color. An orange lounge chair complemented it. Black enamel tables held lamps and substantial stone sculptures.

Zeke gestured her to an armchair. "You said this would be short. I don't have much time."

She sat and met his gaze directly. "I'll get right to the point. Ace is a suspect in Alanna's murder. I want to make sure he doesn't get charged."

Suddenly a black Labrador retriever bounded into the living room. He stopped when he saw Caprice, but then ran to his master.

Zeke rubbed the dog's flank. "We have company, boy. Be on your best behavior."

Caprice laughed. "Don't we always tell them that?"

"You have a dog?"

That was the first softening of Zeke's expression that she'd seen. "Yes, I do. Lady's a cocker spaniel. What's his name?" she asked.

"His name's Woofer, because his barks sound like they come straight from a speaker."

She sat very still and smiled at the dog.

His ears perked up and he looked at Zeke.

Zeke said, "Go ahead. I think she's friendly."

Caprice couldn't hide her smile. She hoped she'd given Zeke that impression, since she believed he'd open up more easily if she had.

Woofer trotted over to her and looked up at her. She held out her hand to let him take a sniff. He did and then sat at her feet.

"You're a well-behaved guy."

"My wife spends a lot of time with him. That might change a bit when the baby's born."

She'd asked Ace why Zeke had quit. Zeke had told Ace that since his wife was pregnant, he just didn't want to go out on the road right now. The pregnancy hadn't been planned.

But Caprice knew he'd turned down good money to

make that decision and she wondered if it was the truth. If what she'd overheard panned out, it wasn't.

Woofer sat at her feet as she asked, "So this was your first touring gig with Ace?"

"Yep. It was going to be."

"And you moved here from L.A. to be part of the tour? To be part of the band?"

"I did."

"Then it doesn't make sense that you'd quit. Your wife is early in her pregnancy, right?"

"She still needs me," he said defensively.

"I'm not questioning that."

"What are you questioning?"

"The reason you quit. I have information that led me to believe you might have been persuaded to quit."

"You mean offered money? That's not true."

"Then tell me what is true, Zeke."

He looked away and finally made eye contact once more. "The truth is, I'm going to be a family man. Instead of touring, I'm setting up a sound studio in Harrisburg for musicians who want to make demos. I took a tour of a couple of studios in this area and they're okay, but I can do better. I'm going to give workshops, too, in songwriting and marketing. It will be a different life, but it's what my wife and I want."

"Did you want to set up a studio when you moved here?"

His shoulders slumped a little. "No, I wanted to tour. I wanted to be part of the band that played with the great Ace Richland."

"So, what changed?" she prodded again.

He studied her hand petting his dog. He studied her. "I didn't tell you anything."

"Of course, you didn't."

After some hesitation, he finally admitted, "One of

the other band members let it spill that Ace was different on the road than he was here in Kismet. Supposedly, while on the road, he's into drugs and women. When I signed on, Ace assured me that kind of life was over. I don't want to be a thousand miles from my wife when she's hearing rumors. I don't want her worried about them . . . or me."

Caprice knew Ace was clean—no drugs. His daughter meant too much to him to become involved in that again.

"Tell me something, Zeke. Which band member gossiped about Ace?"

Zeke shook his head. "I can't tell you that."

"It was Len Lowery, wasn't it?" she asked quickly, firmly, with determination.

Although she didn't expect an answer, she saw from his expression, the way his eyes widened and his brow furrowed, that the gossiper had been Len Lowery.

Hoping she could do Ace a favor—and Zeke one, too—she said, "Len has an ax to grind, though I'm not sure what that is yet. I just don't think he's being straight with anyone. So don't close your door on your relationship with Ace. Okay?"

"I'm going ahead with the sound studio," Zeke insisted stubbornly.

"If that's what makes you happy, and that's what will help your new family, go do it. But if you really want to tour with Ace's band, and your wife can deal with that, don't reject the idea because of what Len said."

Caprice didn't know if her words were going to make any difference. She didn't know if Len was the murderer or not.

But she intended to find out.

* * *

That evening, Grant picked up Lady and her crate and took her and Patches to the dog park while Caprice attended her self-defense course. This was the first of three two-hour classes held at the Green Tea Spa this week. Eight other women were taking the class. The instructor, a tall blonde in her forties, explained what the participants in the class would learn. The physical or tactical part of the instruction was the smallest part and would be taught last. Women had to learn other skill sets along with the tactical to remain safe. A crisis situation messed up thinking, as Caprice well knew already. So there would be instruction on using every tool at her disposal, including what her gut told her and what her morals told her. She would learn what negotiation could get her, how and when to use force, and then lastly how to apply it. Tonight was the beginning and she listened carefully, especially about options, quick thinking, and flexibility.

She was glad Grant had encouraged her to do this.

After the class was over, she drove to Grant's town house. When she parked out front, she couldn't help but wonder if his neighbor Donna was home next door. Donna and Grant seemed to have a friendship, but Grant had assured her on more than one occasion that was all there was—a friendship. She believed him.

Still, the little green-eyed monster inside her wondered what kind of friendship they had.

When she rang Grant's doorbell, she heard both dogs bark.

He answered, looking good in jeans, T-shirt, and some evening beard stubble. *But then again,* she thought, *he always looks good.*

"They knew it was you," he said as he opened the storm door.

"Lady might know the sound of my van, but I don't know about Patches."

"He read Lady's mind."

"Right. Males read women's minds so easily."

Grant just cocked his eyebrow at her at that. "Would you like coffee, soda, a Rolling Rock?" he teased. He'd once accused her of being a beer snob, until she'd told him her grandfather had taught her to like Rolling Rock.

"It would be easy to settle for that beer, but I'm tired and I want to stay clearheaded."

"Did the course take a lot out of you?"

"Not physically. Not yet. But she gave us so much information that I'm not sure I absorbed it all."

Grant nodded. "I know what you mean. I took a couple of courses like that when I lived in the city. You need a refresher every once in a while. You not only forget, but your reflexes seem to get slower as you get older."

The dogs wound about their feet, greeting Caprice, looking for her praise and attention, which she always gave them freely. After a few minutes of pouring affection on them, she sat on the sofa and Lady stretched out on her foot. She ruffled her dog's ears and scratched her under the chin. Then Patches sat on her other foot. She laughed and did the same to him.

"If you're involved in a murder investigation again," Grant said, "you need to put your safety first."

"I am. I will. And this time, if I have any evidence of who committed the murder, I'll call Detective Carstead. And if I can't get him, I'll call Detective Jones, even though he probably won't believe me . . . even though he'd probably brush me off."

"You've been right before. I don't think he'll do that."

She shrugged. "I wanted to talk to you about something."

Grant was sitting beside her, and his elbow brushed hers as he leaned a little closer. "What?"

There was an anticipation in his eyes that made her wonder if he expected this to be personal.

"It's about Ace," she quickly said so he didn't get the wrong idea.

She was a little confused about who she wanted to be personal with. Seth was still in the picture. She hadn't worn her charm bracelet tonight because she hadn't known what they'd be doing at the self-defense class. She still wasn't exactly sure what that charm bracelet meant. She wore it often and she thought about Seth even when she wasn't wearing it. But Seth wasn't here. With his schedule as demanding as it was, they couldn't even have regular phone conversations.

What did Seth expect of her? And what did she expect of him? Just what was going to happen when his experience at Johns Hopkins was over?

All were important questions, and all questions she couldn't answer.

She and Grant had always seemed to have a connection—ever since he was Vince's roommate in college and Vince had brought him home on weekends. However, she'd been younger than Grant, and he'd been more experienced. He'd gone on to get married, and she'd found a career and then a new road with it. When her decorating business had started collapsing because of the economy, she'd had to find a way to stay afloat, and she'd done that with home staging and unique themes. She always thought if she had enough information, she could analyze her way out of anything.

But matters of the heart were difficult to analyze. When Grant had moved back to Kismet, he hadn't been ready for even friendship. But over the past year, they'd become friends—maybe more.

Sitting here with Grant, with their two dogs at their feet, she felt safe and secure, yet a little bit giddy, too.

Very confusing.

So she settled on the subject she wanted to talk about. "I went to see Zeke Stoltz, Ace's band member who quit."

"You suspect him?" Grant asked, sounding puzzled.

"Oh no, not Zeke. But I found something out, and I don't know if I should tell Ace this, either. It has to do with Len and Alanna's sabotage."

"I think Ace has a short fuse on a good day. He's had a lot of bad ones lately."

"I know. That's what I mean. I found out that one of his band members, and I think it was Len Lowery, told Zeke that once Ace is on the road, he expects him to use drugs and hop from woman to woman."

"Ace says that's all behind him," Grant reminded her.

"I know, and I believe him. But Zeke doesn't know if he should. His wife's expecting a baby and he doesn't want her to worry. He doesn't want her to have those concerns when he's on the road with Ace. That's why he quit. He's opening a sound studio in Harrisburg, plans to write music, and maybe even teach. It sounds like a good life if that's what he truly wants. On the other hand, if he wants to be playing and on the road, I hate to see somebody like Len shoot down his dream."

"You said you think it was Len who spread the rumor. Zeke wouldn't confirm it?"

"No. He's a good guy. He doesn't want to get anybody in trouble. And besides the whole rumor-spreading aspect of this, Len could be the one who stole Ace's guitars."

"That's a leap," Grant warned her.

"Maybe so. But I'm thinking about talking to Detective Carstead and informing him about the conversation I heard between Alanna and Len."

Grant nodded. "That's probably the best way to handle it." After a moment, he asked, "So, why did you want to talk to me about this?"

"Because I'm asking for your advice. Should I tell Ace?"

Grant ran his hand over his jaw and his stubble. "As his friend, I understand that you don't want to keep anything from him. But as his lawyer, I don't want to see him get into any more trouble than he's already in."

"So you don't think I should tell him?"

"You don't know for sure that Len's the one who told Zeke. So I'd say for now, just keep it under wraps. If Zeke decides to go to Ace and talk it out, that's a different story. But I think you should just stay a little removed from that right now."

"Ace has his performance at the community theater coming up on Saturday. He has to work with his band . . . with Len. I hope he can find someone to replace Zeke this quickly."

"Ace has connections. He'll find somebody."

"In Kismet?"

"If not in Kismet, in Baltimore or maybe D.C. Harrisburg and Philly aren't that far away. You have to stop worrying about everybody in your life, or you're going to get gray hairs."

She could see he was teasing her, and that was unusual. She laughed. "I think I see a few at *your* temples. I guess you worry about a few of the people in your life, too."

"*You're* the one who's caused most of those gray hairs lately."

They studied each other for a long moment, and then

Grant said, "I had a good time with you at your parents' house yesterday."

As usual with Grant, she tried to say what was on her mind. "It felt different having you there as my guest rather than as Vince's friend."

"Different how?"

"I felt everybody was watching us."

He smiled again. "They just wanted to see if any fur would fly. You and I don't always have smooth sailing."

"Is that bad?"

"Not necessarily bad. I'm just trying to figure out why it is."

She nodded. "Me too."

If he leaned toward her a little more, if she leaned toward him, they might just find out how compatible they really were. But neither of them seemed ready to make that move.

Lady bumped her head against Caprice's leg and yawned. Caprice took that as a sign.

"I'd better be going. Mirabelle's alone in the bedroom. I'm going to try to broker friendships again when I get home. If they're all sleepy, maybe they'll be more mellow."

"Good luck with that," Grant said in a wry tone. "You know they'll all wake up and want treats as soon as you get home. They're just like kids."

Kids. That brought up a subject that she and Grant would have to talk about someday. He was still grieving over the child he'd lost. He'd only shared a bit of his regrets with her. If he ever shared his grief— Grief was so personal and raw and stirred up everything in that bottom point of your heart that turned you inside out and upside down. But if Grant ever shared that with her, she knew a closeness would grow between them that they'd never shared before.

He stood, and Patches came to attention as if he thought Grant might take him for a walk. Grant said to him, "We'll take another run around the yard in a little while. We have to send off Caprice and Lady first. You'll see them again tomorrow night."

"Three nights this week is a lot of puppysitting time. Are you sure you're okay with that?"

"Knowing that by the end of the week you can possibly toss me on the floor will be worth it."

Caprice laughed, unable to imagine that scene. She gathered Lady's fuchsia leash, which was lying over the coffee table. She clipped it onto her collar. After he put Lady's crate in Caprice's van, Grant leashed up Patches, too, only his leash was, of course, brown. Afterward, Grant and Patches walked Caprice out to her van. He stood on the sidewalk while she led Lady into her crate inside the van, praised her for being such a good dog, and then closed the door.

As she stepped back, Grant was close by her side. She opened the driver's door and hiked herself up onto the seat. "Thank you for watching Lady."

"You'd do the same for me."

Yes, she would.

As she closed her door, started the van, waved, and drove away from Grant's town house, she saw him watching her from the rearview mirror. She *would* watch Patches for him. In fact, she'd do a lot more . . . if he ever asked.

Chapter Nine

It was ten-thirty at night when Caprice returned home, let Lady outside for an end-of-the-day run around the yard, and gave Sophia a dollop of cream.

When she entered the spare room, Mirabelle was nowhere in sight. Caprice guessed where she might be. She'd left the closet door open.

Heading for it now with Lady at her heels, she pushed the door open wider and spotted the beautiful but shy cat.

"Come on, Mirabelle, come out. Everything will be all right. I promise."

Mirabelle had made a bed for herself on an old quilt on the floor. She seemed quite contented there, especially when the door to the room was open.

Since Lady was right by her side, Caprice said to the cocker, "I think you scare her."

Lady looked up at her as if she had no idea why that might be.

As Caprice considered the past few days, she realized Sophia never seemed to venture near the room when the door was open. She seemed to be under the impression that if she ignored Mirabelle, the Persian might go away. If she turned her back on her, the other cat wasn't there.

Caprice knew patience was important in a situation like this, but she also had to use common sense, too. If what she had done so far wasn't working, she had to change what she was doing.

So patting her hip, she said, "Come on, girl" to Lady, then walked out of the spare room and into her bedroom. Lady followed. She didn't close the spare room door. She knew Lady was ready for a good night's sleep because she settled in her bed on the floor beside Caprice's bed.

Caprice's bedroom, like every other room in the house, brought a smile to her face when she entered it. There was the yellow armoire with hand-painted hummingbirds and roses, the pastel braided rugs in blue, pink, and yellow. With the yellow-flowered swag valances topping sheer pink panels, which coordinated with colors in the valance, Caprice had given the room a light, airy feel.

"I'm about as ready for bed as you are," she said to Lady as she changed into draw-stringed pajama pants printed with kittens and a pale pink matching T-shirt. "But I'm going to read for a while and see if Mirabelle joins us."

She had decorating magazines she wanted to page through, as well as a few on her e-tablet. She tried to keep up with the trends, though they didn't dictate how she decorated anything. It all depended on the person-ality of her client and his or her likes and dislikes.

However, before Caprice could even page through two magazines, the day took its toll. She fell asleep with the magazine open on her lap, her e-tablet beside her, and Lady snoring in her bed on the floor.

To her surprise, when she awakened around 2:00 A.M.,

Mirabelle was on her bed! She'd snuggled close to Caprice's leg.

"You came out," Caprice said, delighted.

Mirabelle blinked her golden eyes and didn't twitch a whisker.

"And you expect me to protect you," Caprice added.

Just then, there was a meow from the top of the chest of drawers by the window. Sophia perched there.

"Hey, there," Caprice said, stifling a yawn. "There's room on the bed." But Sophia just blinked her eyes, swished her tail, and stared at Caprice and Mirabelle accusingly.

"You all sleep where you want. I've got to get some shut-eye. See you in the morning."

With that, Caprice turned out her light, closed her eyes, and easily fell back to sleep.

In the morning, Mirabelle stayed upstairs. She seemed perfectly content on Caprice's bed. To her relief, Lady didn't jump up on the bed to rout her out. The cocker simply put her paws on the edge of the mattress and sniffed a couple of times. Mirabelle moved to the middle.

When Caprice called to Lady, her dog followed her downstairs, as did Sophia, who must have spent the night on the chest of drawers. Her feline complained loudly before she ate her breakfast.

"We'll get used to this," Caprice assured Sophia as she opened the door to take Lady outside.

The early-April morning was cold, though "cold" was a relative term. The temperature had dropped to the forties and Caprice's light jacket didn't seem warm enough.

Lady, of course, was just fine as she snuffled among

the daffodils, which were popping up, and sniffed at the crocuses in the corner.

Caprice took her cell phone from her pocket, hesitated only a moment, then called the Kismet Police Department. When she asked for Detective Carstead, she was advised she could leave a message on his voice mail. She did.

To ignore her chill, Caprice exercised with Lady, running across the yard with her, throwing her ball over and over again. Lady never tired of bringing that tennis ball back to Caprice's feet. Lady was hunched down, her head on her front paws nosing the ball, her hind end still raised, when Caprice heard her name called from beyond the yard's gate.

"Caprice?"

It was Nikki's voice.

The gate opened and her sister stepped into the yard, bundled in her red winter jacket and jeans.

Lady ran over to her immediately and rolled over at her feet.

"I wish everyone greeted me that way," Nikki said wryly, crouching down and rubbing Lady's tummy.

After a few minutes of that, she stood and Caprice could see something was on her mind. "You're out and about early," she prompted.

"I had to talk to somebody or I'd burst." Nikki's hands were balled into fists and she looked more agitated than Caprice had seen her in a while.

"What's going on?"

"Drew Pierson is what's going on."

Nikki was usually fairly unflappable. Right now, she looked as if she was ready to strangle someone; and from her statement, that person was Drew Pierson. Her sister's hair was disheveled, appearing as if Nikki had been running her hand through it, and she couldn't seem to stand still as she shifted from one sneakered foot to another.

Stooping, Nikki picked up Lady's ball and tossed it. Lady ran after it, happy to be playing again.

"What did he do? Call you and tell you he wants to combine your businesses? Or did he call you and ask you for a date?" Caprice suspected that sparks between Nikki and Drew had been the real reason she'd turned him down as a partner. She definitely did not want to mix business with pleasure.

"Either of *those* two I could have dealt with," Nikki muttered. "But since he started up his catering jobs, I've lost two clients to him. One was a wedding reception for a couple I'd met at one of your open houses. The other was a cocktail party for Melba and Colin Brown."

Melba and Colin practically ran the entertainment agenda for the country club. That couple was influential and a definite loss.

"I met Melba when I catered a luncheon at Country Squire Golf and Recreation Club," Nikki explained. "She liked what I offered and the way I presented the food. And I thought I had the party locked down. I followed up with a call to her and discovered she'd signed on with *Drew*."

"Did she say why?"

"No, but I got the impression that someone had talked down the way I prepare food. Also, she did say Marlow Bernstein and his wife recommended Drew."

The Bernsteins were also patrons of Country Squire. "In fact, don't they run the social calendar, like scheduling bridge club events and garden society dinners?"

"Exactly. I asked Mom if she knew them. After all, many of the St. Francis of Assisi parishioners do attend Country Squire shindigs."

"What did she say?"

"She said she thought Drew's mother's maiden name was Bernstein, so that could be it—a family connection. But those were two important clients to lose, and not catering their parties will leave a hole in my budget."

With a rush of motion, Lady brought the tennis ball back to Nikki, dropping it before her sneakers.

Another caterer in town was definitely going to cut into Nikki's profits. On top of that, the fact that her competition was Drew, whom she'd cooked with and talked with and joked with and considered taking on as a partner, made this situation that much worse and even galling.

"You could try talking to Drew," Caprice suggested.

With a sigh, Nikki snatched up the ball and tossed it in a different direction than the last time. "What good would that do? He's not going to close down a business he started because I can't cut it."

"That's not true. You *can* cut it. You're acquiring catering jobs in York and even Lancaster. You need to expand those markets."

Caprice had learned a lot since she'd started her own home-decorating business and now home-staging business. Nikki couldn't just sit by and rely on clients in Kismet if she wanted to continue catering and make a living doing it.

Watching Lady race after the ball, root it out, and snatch it up, Nikki agreed with Caprice's assessment. "You know, that's exactly what I was thinking. If Drew and I are going to be in competition, then we're really going to be in competition. He'd better watch out, because I'm not going to let him cut down my business. I stewed about it all day yesterday and all last night. I don't think I got a wink of sleep. But coming over here today, I came up with a few ideas. I need the name of your Web site designer."

Caprice smiled, liking the way Nikki was revved up now. "Going to revamp?"

"Exactly. Instead of the basics, my site is going to have buttons and newsfeeds and maybe even a video of me cooking. I'm going to create a whole new Web presence."

When Lady plopped the ball at Nikki's feet again, Caprice had to smile. This is what the De Lucas did. They didn't take adversity lying down. They got up, shook themselves off, and figured out what to do next.

"If you want social media feeds, then I imagine you're going to get involved and post a few times a day? We can cross-post."

Nikki had often scoffed or pooh-poohed the time Caprice spent on her social media pages, but she'd found communicating with clients any way she could mattered, and Nikki was going to find that out, too.

"You're going to have to teach me about sharing and liking and tweeting and retweeting."

"It's really not complicated. But it *can* be a time sink. You'll have to figure out the best way to do it effectively, and you're not going to build a following overnight. It will take time. I can help you with that, putting out calls on my pages, but you still have to put the time in."

"Oh, I'll build my following, all right. At our house stagings, I'm going to make a concerted effort to have promotional materials ready, not just my business card. I'm thinking about having a pamphlet printed."

"A rack card might be more economical to begin with. I know a good online site you can use. We can either design it together, or my webmaster can do it for you."

Lady hunkered down with the ball, expecting another toss.

"That's enough for this morning," Caprice told Lady. The tone of her voice, as well as her words, informed her pup that play had ended. Caprice snatched up the ball, patted her hip, and said, "Come on, we have to try and entice Mirabelle downstairs for breakfast."

Nikki asked, "Do you have time to go over the best venues to place ads?"

"Sure. You ought to see if you can link to local businesses and their Web sites."

"Link?"

"I'm sure Isaac would let you link to his Web site."

"You think somebody looking at an antique shop Web site would care about a caterer?"

"You never know. You get your nails done at the Nail Yard. Maybe Judy would link with you, too. And what about the Cupcake House? We sometimes use Dana's cupcakes at our open houses."

"You're full of ideas."

"I try."

Once inside the kitchen, Caprice started a pot of coffee and fed Lady her breakfast. Sophia had finished hers long before and was already lounging on her cat tree in the living room.

Caprice took a small can of cat food from the pantry, spooned half of it onto a dish, then went into the stairs and called, "Mirabelle? I have something for you to eat. If you don't come and get it, Lady will eat this, too."

There was silence.

"Mirabelle?" Caprice called again.

Suddenly she heard a thump and Mirabelle appeared at the top of the stairs.

"Come on. Meet me halfway. Then you can decide if you want to take an after-breakfast nap upstairs or downstairs."

Mirabelle's nose twitched.

Caprice had cheated with the food. Instead of Sophia's usual diet of chicken or turkey, Caprice had chosen a can of cat food with tuna in it. Most cats couldn't resist tuna, and Caprice knew Mirabelle liked it from the hungry way she'd eaten the real thing on the day of Alanna's open house.

Caprice called into Nikki, "Keep Lady occupied for a few minutes, will you?"

"Will do."

She glanced into the living room at Sophia, who didn't seem to give a hoot what she was doing with Mirabelle. Yet, Caprice knew better from the swish of her long-haired calico's tail. Sophia was attuned to exactly where Mirabelle was sitting and the attention Caprice was giving her.

"Come on," she coaxed Mirabelle again, waving the dish a little. Then she set it on the sixth step.

Mirabelle came down the top step slowly, one paw at a time.

"We're good," Caprice cooed. "Lady's in the kitchen with Nikki. Nobody's going to bother you."

After looking all around just to make sure, Mirabelle tentatively stepped down another step, then another, then another. Soon she was on the step with the dish, lapping up the food eagerly.

"Aha!" Caprice said with satisfaction. "Hunger and tuna help every time."

In no time at all, Mirabelle had lapped up all the food. She sat on the step, washing and licking her lips. Every once in a while, she glanced up at Sophia to see if she'd moved a whisker or a paw. But all was quiet.

Still, when Caprice lifted the dish, Mirabelle meowed. Caprice petted her, rubbed her under the chin and behind her ears. "Are you going to stay down?"

Mirabelle took another look at Sophia and then scampered back upstairs.

Progress. That's what mattered.

On her way back to the kitchen, Caprice heard her cell phone play. She snatched it from her pocket. "Hello?"

"Miss De Luca?"

She recognized the voice. "Yes."

"This is Detective Carstead. I understand you wanted to talk to me."

"I'd like to discuss the Alanna Goodwin investigation."

"You know I can't do that," he said firmly.

"I know you can't tell *me* anything, but I might have a few things to tell you."

Was that a sigh she heard?

He responded, "I'm on my way out now. But how about if you meet me back at the station around noon?"

"That sounds like a plan."

"I'll see you then." He didn't say good-bye; he just hung up.

At least he hadn't dismissed her. At least he was willing to listen to her.

At least . . . she hoped so.

Caprice had been at the Kismet police station many times before, under more stressful circumstances. She'd sat on that hard bench in the reception area for hours. But today she went right up to the desk and said, "Caprice De Luca to see Detective Carstead."

The on-duty officer, whose name tag read, OFFICER CARSON MENDEZ, looked down at a printout on his desk and nodded. "He's back. I'll buzz him." He did; and a minute later, Detective Carstead was in the doorway motioning to her.

Generally speaking, she knew how this meeting was going to progress. He'd be terse and gruff and he'd want her out of there fast. That was just fine. She'd say what she had to say and leave. He could either take the information and do something with it . . . or not.

The detective didn't lead her to the interrogation room, but rather to his office. It was small and messy. Folders topped two file cabinets and also straggled across his desk. Binders filled a bookcase, but the top shelf held a photograph of an older couple. She imagined they were his parents. In another photograph, she recognized a younger Brett Carstead. His arm circled a boy about the same age as he was. His brother, maybe? She didn't know much about Detective Carstead, just that his attitude wasn't as arrogant and terse as Detective Jones's. She'd seen compassion in his eyes more than once, and she was glad of that.

He motioned to the wood-and-fabric chairs in front of his desk. She settled into one and watched him as he sat across the desk from her. His gaze seemed to see everything about her in a glance, from her Beatles T-shirt (she had several) to her russet flared slacks, from her tapestry vest with the copper-colored fringe to her pocketbook. When his gaze fell upon her macramé purse, she wondered just what he was thinking. Some guys thought the way she dressed was strange.

Seth didn't.

She didn't think Grant did, either. He'd come to accept it as part of who she'd come to be. But she'd seen the looks and stares about her clothes, not about her. She walked to the beat of a different drummer. What could she say?

"You've never come here before to share information," he said.

"Before, I never felt I had information that I needed to share."

He shook his head. "Are we going to go round and round?"

"Absolutely not. I have something to tell you about Alanna Goodwin and Len Lowery."

Carstead shuffled over his desk and found a folder. He opened it. "Lowery is one of Ace Richland's band members. What does he have to do with Alanna Goodwin?"

"That's the whole point, Detective Carstead. When I went to Alanna's house for the staging, I found Alanna and Len huddled outside on the veranda, away from everyone else. I couldn't hear what they were talking about and I had prospective buyers with me, so I backed off, backed away, and forgot about it."

"And why did you remember it again?" He picked up a pen and was playing with it now, switching it on, then off again.

Her moments were numbered if she couldn't get him interested. "I didn't leave the open house with as much professional aplomb as I would have liked."

His eyes assessed her once more. "Do you mind if I ask you why?"

This was why she was here. "I don't like to speak ill of the dead, but Alanna was not taking care of Mirabelle, at least not in the right way. Her cat," Caprice reminded him.

He nodded and waited for her to go on.

Caprice did. "Sure, Mirabelle had a roof over her

head. She had shelter and food. But I'm not sure how much loving she got, or what else went on when Alanna was and wasn't there. I got the feeling that every time she had a meeting or women in for afternoon tea and she didn't want to bother with Mirabelle, she stuffed her in a closet. That's where I found her the day of the open house. This tiny cubicle of a closet, with no food or water and no place to nap, not even a towel crumpled on the floor. Did you ever hear of such a thing?"

He looked impatient, not as if he was thinking about whether or not he had. "Caprice, I don't have animals. I don't deal with animals."

"Learning curve in a nutshell. They need tenderness, love, and care as much as they need food, water, and a safe place to be with a human who will give them the attention they deserve. Stuffing a cat in a closet isn't giving him or her any of those things."

"So, what happened after the closet?" he asked with an obvious attempt at patience.

"I left in a huff. I didn't stay until the end of the open house. I didn't wish Alanna a happy sale. I felt she was all wrong for Ace and he couldn't see it."

"And what does that have to do with who murdered her?"

She cut to the chase, since that was what he wanted. "I went by the next day to apologize. After all, my relationship with real estate agents, as well as their clients, is important to my business. One client leads to the next. But I never apologized. I heard voices on the screened-in porch, so I went around the side. Then I recognized the voices—Alanna's and Len's."

Caprice went on to tell Carstead how the two of them were planning to sabotage Ace's tour. However, as soon as she said it, she had the feeling she shouldn't have. Was this giving the detective even more reason to go after Ace? This was what she got for sharing information; she could tell from the look in Detective Carstead's eyes, he was thinking about all of it.

To encourage him to be motivated to think on a different track, she said, "I bet Alanna was paying Len to do the sabotaging. Have you made any headway on who stole Ace's guitars?"

As soon as Carstead was going to open his mouth, Caprice held up her hand. "I know what you're going to say. You can't share any information because you're still investigating. Well, maybe Len stole those guitars. Have you at least looked into his financial records?"

Detective Carstead's eyebrows rose. "We have a competent police department, Miss De Luca. You shouldn't worry yourself about any of this. We're investigating. We'll find out who killed Alanna Goodwin. Why don't you just concentrate on taking care of her cat."

If that wasn't patronizing, Caprice didn't know what was.

Coming here had been a mistake. "Oh, I'll take care of Mirabelle, better than Alanna Goodwin ever did. I came here today because I thought my information could help you . . . because it was the right thing to do. But you obviously don't care what I think."

She stood and turned to go, but suddenly the tall detective was blocking her path.

"Caprice, your information could help. I'll admit that. But even though you're *more* than competent at ferreting out clues, you shouldn't be involved."

More than competent. At least that *wasn't patronizing.*

When she remained silent, he shook his head, then sighed. "We prefer our private citizens go about their business and not set foot in ours. That's safer for you and a lot less complicated for us. Understand?"

Oh, she understood. But she didn't like it. Staring directly into his dark brown eyes, she asked, "So if I find anything out, do you want to know, or should I just keep it to myself?"

He scowled. "You won't stay out of this?"

"Ace is my friend. How can I? I could learn something just from being around his band. I could learn more about Len."

"If you hear something you think is relevant, leave me a message."

"I'll do that," she said, then maneuvered around him and left his office. But she could feel his eyes on her back as she walked down the hall. She could feel his disapproval.

His disapproval didn't matter. She wouldn't let Ace be railroaded for a crime he didn't commit.

Chapter Ten

Caprice showed her driver's license to the security staff at Peaceful Path Cemetery on Wednesday morning. A big, burly guy, with an electronic ear gadget, checked the list on his smartphone and gave her a nod.

"You can take a seat under the canopy in Mr. Richland's row," he directed her.

Late last night, Ace had called her and asked her if she was coming to the funeral today. It had sounded as if he needed moral support. He told her his parents were driving down from Scranton, but he'd like her there, too. He also explained that Trista and Marsha wouldn't be coming.

No surprise there, she thought. But then she wondered if the police had talked to Marsha. After all, wouldn't she be a viable suspect? An ex-wife who could be jealous?

Unless Marsha had an airtight alibi. Ace had also told her that he and Twyla had consulted on today's funeral arrangements. They'd decided on a graveside service and then a reception at Alanna's house.

After her second self-defense class last night, she'd picked up Lady at Grant's. They'd discussed her meeting with Detective Carstead. Grant had assured her Carstead would pursue every lead. Today, Caprice was going to do the same. Scanning the group under the canopy, including two patrol officers who appeared to study everyone, Caprice spotted Ace, Twyla, and Ace's parents in the front row. Len was seated in a row farther back, with Ace's band members. He looked subdued in a brown suit. Out of the corner of her eye, she caught sight of Ace's two brothers to the rear of the ten rows of chairs; they were deep in conversation. Caprice was glad Ace's family had shown up for him.

In contrast, Twyla sat next to Ace in a black jacket and skirt, looking pale and fragile. Alanna had been her only living relative. How lonely today must feel.

An older woman in a navy pants suit was openly crying. Who was she, and what had Alanna meant to her?

The seats were filling in fast now, and it was almost time for the service to begin. Caprice gave condolences to both Twyla and Ace, hugging them, giving them an extra-hard squeeze. Ace's dad motioned her to a seat next to his wife and moved down one.

He leaned close to say in a low voice, "Women do this so much better than men. She's going to get all teary-eyed because of how this death hurt Ace. You can most likely say a few words of comfort better than I can."

Caprice had had a couple of conversations with Mrs. Rizzo. The truth was, Ace's mom reminded her a lot of her own mom. She was glad to sit next to her and be of help if she could. Some people were uncomfortable at viewings and funerals; apparently, Mr. Rizzo was one of them. When Ace's two brothers came to sit on the other side of their dad, Caprice felt honored to be able to sit in this row with them.

Alanna's casket was burnished copper and there were lilies and roses and mums everywhere, from the huge spray atop the casket to the baskets and arrangements of flowers circling it.

Mrs. Rizzo leaned toward Caprice. "I was so happy Ace found someone. We weren't too thrilled that Alanna was going to move in without the benefit of a wedding. But they were planning one at the end of the summer, so I was just going to look the other way until then."

Caprice knew her own mom would probably think the same way. She remembered Ace and Alanna in the lip-lock at the house staging.

"He really cared for her," Caprice said, sad for Ace, too.

"I only met her once," his mom whispered. "She did have Southern charm." Then Mrs. Rizzo said something interesting. "I think she and I would have clashed at some point, but if she made Ace happy, that was what was important."

Caprice had a feeling Alanna would have clashed with anyone who didn't see things her way. Ace's mom had probably sensed that from the outset. After all, moms just knew those kinds of things.

The service was a combination of Bible verses, sermon, and personal tidbits both Twyla and Ace must have relayed to the minister. He talked about Alanna's Southern style, her charitable donations, the boards she sat on, as well as her bridge club friendships.

What friendships? Caprice wondered. From what she'd learned, Alanna didn't have friends. She might have belonged to a bridge club and the garden club and the country club, but as far as personal friendships, Caprice hadn't heard about a single one.

At the end of the service, Reverend Springer said,

"Miss Horton and Mr. Richland invite all of you to White Pillars to share more memories and break bread together." After those words, he crossed to Twyla and Ace and murmured in somber tones, probably giving them more comfort and sympathy.

Caprice didn't know most of the crowd. However, she did spot Gail Schwartz, who was an acquaintance of her mom's. Gail was the head of a headhunter agency and might have had business associations with Alanna. Floating around the reception could give Caprice some clues as to who these people were. She might also unearth a tidbit that could lead to the killer's identity.

Alanna's house was everything Alanna had always wanted it to be. Twyla had ordered fresh-flower arrangements, and the spread on the dining-room table was nice, even though Nikki hadn't catered it. Everything looked deli-prepared. Kismet had an excellent deli, located near Vince's condo. He often went there for takeout.

Unlike Alanna, Twyla was hands-on, arranging food on the table, asking the housekeeper if she needed help in the kitchen. Ace looked a bit forlorn as he sat talking to his parents and his brothers in the huge living room.

Caprice wondered if Twyla still wanted to sell the house. They'd have to talk about that. Caprice had rented furniture for the staging. If for some reason Twyla was going to stay in Kismet, all of that would have to go back. For now, though, the house was in ready-to-sell condition.

After sitting with Ace and his family for a bite to eat, Caprice excused herself and wandered about a bit, merely to see who was there. Len Lowery and two other band members had straggled out on the veranda and were conversing. Maybe about their performance at the community theater this coming Saturday?

Wandering into the small parlor, where she'd seen Alanna study that photo in her desk, Caprice straightened a painting on the wall.

"Always on duty?" a woman's voice asked from the doorway.

Turning, she saw Gail Schwartz. "I suppose. If Twyla wants to sell the house, we have to keep it in tip-top shape."

Entering the room, Gail looked around. "So very Alanna, isn't it? The whole place, I mean."

"I didn't know Alanna very well."

"Are you being discreet?" Gail asked with a wry smile.

"I try to be. But I do know Alanna certainly did have her own opinions about things."

Gail rolled her eyes. "That's putting it mildly."

It sounded as if Gail knew Alanna better than any of the other women Caprice had spoken with. "So *you* knew her?"

"We were on a committee at the Country Squire. We served many of the same charities. I couldn't help but run into her now and then."

"It doesn't sound as if you enjoyed those times."

Hesitating, Gail picked up a porcelain dish displayed in a rack on one of the marble-topped tables. "I don't know many people who *did* get along with Alanna. To tell you the truth, women just didn't like her."

"And men?" Caprice prompted.

"There were rumors."

"What kind of rumors?" Caprice hoped with all her heart that Alanna hadn't been cheating on Ace. She hoped even more fervently that if Alanna was, he wouldn't learn about it.

"Alanna's husband was much older than she was. She was an attractive, stylish woman, disliked by other women. There were bound to be catty remarks."

"Twenty years older, I understand," Caprice prompted.

"Yes. Under normal circumstances, she never would have met him. She was a no-name journalist from a town in Mississippi when she interviewed him. After that, they became an item. Once they married, she shared his fortune . . . and his power."

"Power?"

"Sure. They were always giving dinner parties with influential guests. Alanna made her own contacts among them."

"I heard that Barton had an illegitimate son, Archer Ford," Caprice said. "Do you know if he's here today? I haven't had a chance to ask Twyla."

"Archer Ford." Gail said the name with much disapproval. "Yes, he's here. He's in the reading room down the hall, looking over the shelves of books. My guess is, he's the most broken up about Alanna of anyone here."

"I don't understand."

Gail made sure no one was in the doorway or strolling down the hall. Then in a low voice, she revealed, "Well, among those rumors that flew about concerning Alanna . . . One day at the Country Squire, a bridge club member told me in the strictest confidence, of course, that she'd heard Alanna and Archer were having an affair while Barton was still alive. After Archer came to Kismet to tell Barton he was his son, he decided to stay in the area and got a job managing a York hotel. I think Alanna had something to do with him finding that job and staying near Kismet."

"Really?" Caprice wanted to keep Gail talking. This was information she hadn't heard before.

Gail stepped even closer. "Supposedly, Alanna cut off the affair and went on a European tour for six months to get over Archer and save her marriage."

Suddenly footsteps sounded in the hall. Gail moved away, obviously afraid she'd be overheard. Then she waved her hand as if none of it mattered anymore and shrugged. "Those were the rumors."

Caprice thought about the funeral again and everyone there. She said, "There was an older woman in a navy pants suit at the funeral who was terrifically upset. Do you know who she was?"

Gail nodded. "That was Muriel Fink. She was Barton's private secretary for years. He brought her here from Mississippi. She retired after he died. Maybe she had a soft spot for Alanna because Barton loved her."

As Caprice absorbed that, Gail moved away. "I've got to go. I have a meeting back at the office. It was good to see you again, Caprice."

When Gail left the room, Caprice had questions—questions she hoped she could find the answers to. Why would Alanna go away for six months if she wanted to put her marriage back together? Had Barton joined her in Europe and they'd enjoyed a second honeymoon?

Did Twyla know all about Alanna's supposed affair with Archer Ford while Barton was alive? She hadn't mentioned that. Then again, Mississippi was a long way from Pennsylvania. Not all sisters were as close as Caprice was to Bella and Nikki. Maybe the rumors had only traveled in Kismet.

So Archer was studying the books in the library. What better opportunity would Caprice have to meet him?

Caprice hadn't worn black today. Black just wasn't her thing, not even for funerals. After all, a funeral was supposed to be a celebration of a life. She'd worn a dark blue suit, reminiscent of Jackie Kennedy's style, though without the pillbox hat. And because of navigating the lawn at graveside, she'd worn her Capezios, which were flat and soundless.

She hurried down the hall to the library. She'd re-arranged bookcases and furniture in there herself. As with most of her suggestions about the house staging, she'd had a tug-of-war with Alanna about stowing away a lot of her knickknacks.

Archer Ford—tall and broad-shouldered, with light brown hair—didn't hear her come into the room.

He was standing at one of the bookcases, a leather-bound book in his hands. His shoulders shook.

Maybe she should just turn around and walk out again. Maybe she shouldn't intrude on this moment.

Whether she'd made a movement or whether he simply became aware he wasn't alone, he turned her way. Caprice got a firsthand glimpse at the tears in his eyes.

He cleared his throat and closed the book.

She said, "I'm sorry. I can leave."

"No, don't leave," he responded quickly. "I just came in here for a few moments of . . . I don't know, solitude. I wanted to remember without the crowd around me."

She extended her hand to him. "I'm Caprice De Luca. I staged the house for Alanna."

When he shook her hand, his grip was firm, though a little stiff. She sensed he was embarrassed. He shouldn't be, if he was expressing emotion. Was it honest? Was it guilt?

"I'm Archer Ford," he said. "Alanna's husband was my father."

At her raised brow, he shrugged. "It's a long story. If you live in Kismet, I'm surprised you haven't heard it."

"Gossip is ten percent truth, ninety percent possibilities. I wait until I know the facts to really put any store in it."

"I can see why Alanna chose you to stage her house. No nonsense and get rid of the frills. I noticed changes since the last time I was here. House stagers de-clutter, right?"

"That's one of the things we do."

So he admitted to being here. As a guest? As a lover? She nodded to the book in his hand. "Alanna told me she'd read most of the books in here."

"Hemingway," he said, raising the book. "He was one of her favorites, especially his novel *The Sun Also Rises*."

"Maybe Twyla will let you have the book," she posed, watching his expression.

His brow furrowed. "I've never met Twyla before today."

"Really?"

"With Alanna living here and Twyla in Mississippi, it just never happened. I suppose she was shocked when she learned I'd inherited a third of Alanna's estate."

"She might have been," Caprice agreed noncommittally. "Were *you* surprised?"

"I never imagined Alanna would do that. But it's part of that long story. Barton Goodwin never recognized me as his son. He didn't acknowledge me in his will. So I would guess that's why Alanna acknowledged me in hers."

Considering herself a good judge of character, Caprice studied Archer as he talked. Most of all, she watched his eyes. He seemed to be sincere about his grief, as well as about his surprise at being an heir. But she could be wrong. He could be a very good actor. Because if he'd known about that will, he had a very strong motive for Alanna's murder.

After a few more minutes of conversation, Caprice left Archer and mingled once more. She dropped in on the conversation the band was having, but that had been all about music and what they were going to play at the upcoming concert. Soon guests began to depart. Ace and his family were the last to leave. Caprice watched as Ace gave Twyla a hug and thanked her. She thanked him for all his help.

After good-byes all around, Caprice and Twyla were left with the housekeeping staff cleaning up. Twyla looked wrung out and Caprice understood how she felt. Funerals did that, emotionally and physically. It was good to have other people around who remembered loved ones, but it took a lot of energy to deal with them, too.

"Let's go in here," Twyla said, motioning to the small parlor. "I need to unwind if you have the time."

"I have the time." They could compare notes and Caprice could possibly learn something new.

"Ace's parents are very nice," Twyla said. "His mom put her arms around me as if she'd known me for years."

"He comes from a good background."

As they settled on a settee, Twyla revealed, "Ace told me a little about his family and that he felt left out when he was growing up because of his music. Nobody else understood it."

Ace had told her that, too. She was glad he felt comfortable enough with Twyla to confide in her.

"One person I couldn't have more than a stilted

conversation with was Gail Schwartz. Were she and Alanna friends?" Twyla asked.

How to delicately answer that? "They knew each other through clubs and charity organizations."

"She seems to have a real edge. She told me she's a headhunter. Maybe her attitude comes from her job."

Or maybe it came from a relationship with Alanna that might not have been a smooth one. Were there more details there?

As Caprice thought about her conversation with Gail in this very room, her gaze fell on the desk, the one where Alanna had taken out the photo of the little girl. She might as well just jump into a discussion about that.

"When I had a meeting with Alanna, we were in this room. Or rather we were going to talk in this room. I'd been taking a look around the house. When I came in here, Alanna was at the desk and had taken out a photo of a little girl. Do you know anything about that?"

"A photo of a little girl?" Twyla looked puzzled. "No, I don't." She stood quickly, as if glad to have something to do, and went over to the desk. "In the drawer?" she asked.

Caprice nodded.

"I have to go through all of Alanna's things. I haven't gotten to this room yet."

After she pulled out the drawer, she shuffled through an envelope or two and then she found the photo. She lifted it out.

Joining her at the desk, Caprice studied it with her. It was a photo of a child who appeared to be around six. She was wearing a dance recital costume, with a pink leotard and a long tulle skirt with matching satin toe shoes.

After studying it, Twyla shook her head. "I have no idea who it is."

Caprice asked, "May I?"

Twyla handed her the photo without hesitation. After another look at the child, Caprice turned the photo over. She noticed the name of a dance studio in York on the back.

She asked Twyla, "Do you mind if I hold on to this?"

"I don't mind. If you think it will help find out who killed Alanna, I think somebody should look into it. From what I understand, the police had a warrant to go through the house, so they sifted through everything."

"I imagine they're still talking to everyone, too. You mentioned that Gail Schwartz has an edge. She shared a rumor about Alanna with me."

"Rumors in small towns are like grits and okra. They just seem to go together. Alanna let rumors roll off her back for the most part. She said people here started them because they were jealous."

"That could be true, but this rumor was very personal. Gail told me Alanna had had an affair with Archer Ford *before* Barton died."

Twyla's eyes grew big. "You're not serious!"

"Gail seemed serious. She said Alanna broke it off to save her marriage and she went to Europe for a while."

Twyla thought about it. She seemed to be sorting through the years in her mind. Finally she said, "About seven years ago, Alanna went to Europe without Barton."

"He didn't join her there?"

"I don't think so, but I don't know for sure. We weren't in touch while she was there. In fact, before she left, she'd simply sent me a brief e-mail saying she needed to get away for a while. When she returned, though, I came to visit, and she and Barton looked as if they'd missed each other a whole lot. Very lovey-dovey. But that's all I know. In a lot of ways, Alanna was a very private person. I don't know if she confided in anyone."

Though Alanna *had confided* her favorite novel to Archer Ford. Did that count as a confidence? Just what part *had* he played in Alanna's life?

At some point, Caprice might have to talk to him again. But not today when he truly seemed to be grieving. No, not today. After she finished up with this visit with Twyla, she'd be grateful to go home to Lady, Sophia, and Mirabelle and delve into her pile of work.

That evening, Caprice sat on her sofa with her legs stretched out, a tablet of graph paper in her hands. Mirabelle lay lengthwise between her legs. Every once in a while, from her perch on her cat tree, Sophia looked down at them disdainfully. Her golden eyes targeted Caprice now.

Caprice smiled at her. "Don't be a grump. I have plenty of love for you and Mirabelle and Lady. We're a family." After a little wave at her cat, she returned her focus to the room design on the graph paper. Sometimes she liked to get away from the computer and just do furniture placing the old-fashioned way.

Lady, who had been sleeping on the floor beside her, looked up and gave a yip to remind Caprice she was there, too. Caprice rubbed the dog's neck. She had thought about lighting a fire in the fireplace. She enjoyed these evenings with her furry crew. But the weather had warmed up a bit and she was short on wood.

Studying the graph paper, she erased the placement of a library table, checked the measurements for a curio cabinet, and placed that there instead. She had to admit she wasn't accomplishing as much as she'd like. She was distracted by everything she'd learned at the funeral reception. What was true and what wasn't? Who were the villains, and who were the friends?

She was pondering that when her cell phone played "Here, There and Everywhere." She'd placed it within easy reach on her mosaic-covered coffee table. She seriously thought about letting the message go to voice mail. Still, the caller could be Ace or Grant . . . or Seth. She hadn't talked to Seth since the Valentine's Day dance.

But when she picked up her phone, she saw her mom's photo. Maybe her mother just wanted to know how the day had gone.

"Hey, Mom. Did you and Dad go out to dinner tonight?" Her parents often did that and called it "date night." They needed that time together even more, now with her uncle in the house.

"No, Caprice. I'm calling about Nana. She's been taken to the hospital. She was having chest pain and we were afraid she was having a heart attack. Can you come?" Her mother's voice was unsteady and she sounded close to tears.

Caprice lifted her legs over and away from Mirabelle and swung them to the floor. "I'll be there as soon as I can."

"Oh, honey, I'm scared."

"I know you are. Hold on to Dad until I get there. Do you want me to call the others?"

"Will you? We're on our way, following the ambulance, and I can't even think straight."

"Is Uncle Dom with you?"

"Yes, he is." It seemed that was all her mother was going to say on that subject.

"Vince might be with Roz. But don't worry. I'll get in touch with everyone."

"Thank you, honey."

Caprice brushed her mom's thanks aside. She would do anything for her nana and her mom, and her mom knew it. "I'll say some prayers in between phone calls. You know how Nana believes in the power of a Hail Mary."

Right now, Caprice wanted to believe in that power, too.

Chapter Eleven

By the time Caprice drove to York Hospital, she was practically hyperventilating. If anything happened to Nana . . .

Nothing was going to happen to Nana. If anything was wrong, the doctors were going to fix it. If only Seth could be here. She could ask him questions. He'd have contacts. Maybe she wouldn't feel so alone.

Medical emergencies with family members were always traumatic—maybe because they were such a close-knit family; maybe because they all cared so much.

Caprice drove around the large hospital to the emergency room entrance. No point parking in the visitors' garage. Nana would have to be evaluated. Then if she was admitted, they'd assign her a room. At least that's the way the process had gone when her mom's good friend Louise had been whisked to the hospital this winter.

When Caprice thought about Louise, the whole month of February seemed to flash before her eyes as she'd solved a murder and Lady had saved her life. She shook her head to concentrate on the here and now.

Before she'd left home, she'd taken Mirabelle into her spare room again. Her three furry friends seemed to be getting along, at least when she was looking. But she wouldn't take the chance of something disastrous happening when she wasn't there. She wanted Mirabelle to feel safe. Everyone needed to feel safe.

Even at this hour, the hospital was a busy place. Nikki was waiting for her in the reception area. When Caprice had called her, she'd been returning from a catering gig in York. Vince could be here already, too. He had a lead foot on the accelerator when he needed to be somewhere.

"Come on," Nikki said. "Vince is here. Bella's on her way. Joe's going to watch the kids while she drives over here."

The siblings had decided separate cars were best so they could come and go as they needed.

"What's happening?" Caprice asked.

"For now, they took blood, and Nana's hooked up to monitors and an IV. They said something about a calcium CT scan of her heart."

"The blood work should show whether or not she had a heart attack," Caprice said.

"How do you know that?" Nikki asked.

"I read a lot," she said simply. "When Louise was in the hospital, I downloaded articles about heart conditions, since she had an arrhythmia."

Nikki directed Caprice through doors that led to the emergency room cubicles. "I don't know how many of us are supposed to be back here. Maybe Dad and Uncle Dom and Vince will take a walk when we go in."

"What do you think of Uncle Dom?" Caprice asked.

"I think he got caught up in a situation he didn't know how to deal with. What would you do if you married someone and he didn't like your family or want anything to do with them? How would you choose?"

"I wouldn't marry someone who didn't like my family." Caprice was certain of that.

"We're a lot to handle sometimes," Nikki reminded her.

Yes, they certainly were. But wasn't anybody who you cared about?

When Caprice stepped into the cubicle, her mom came over and gave her an extra-tight hug. Her dad patted her on the shoulder.

Uncle Dom said, "I'll go out to the waiting room for a while. Somebody should be there when Bella arrives."

Caprice's dad agreed. "I'll go with you."

Vince gave Caprice's arm a squeeze as he passed her and then stopped in the doorway. "How about coffee all around? I should be able to find some somewhere."

"Sounds good," Nikki said.

Caprice went straight to Nana. "What are you doing here?"

"Isn't that a good question?" Nana asked, trying to tuck wayward strands of her hair back into her bun. "Your mom and dad panicked. Before I knew it, a man and a woman were at the house taking my pulse, giving me oxygen, carrying me out on a gurney. Do you know how uncomfortable that thing is? And that ride in the ambulance. My back will never be the same."

If this hadn't been so serious, Caprice would smile. "They wanted to bring you here quickly to figure out what's wrong. Chest pain isn't anything to ignore."

Nana looked down at her hands, which were folded on top of the sheet. "I suppose not. I got scared, too."

Caprice pulled the vinyl chair over and sat next to Nana, taking her hand.

Not five minutes later, Caprice's dad brought Bella into the cubicle. But he didn't step back inside.

"There are too many of us. If we make too much of a ruckus, they'll throw us out," he assured them all.

Bella rushed to Nana and gave her a hug; then she stood on the other side of the bed from Caprice. "How come all the guys are out there and we're in here?"

Nana, who was pale, gave her a weak smile. "For the same reason women go through labor and men don't."

"You mean there's a constitutional difference?" Fran asked.

Nana shook her head. "There's an emotional difference. You and Bella and Caprice and Nikki can sit here and tell me how worried you are. You understand when I say I'm afraid. These men of ours don't want to hear it, because they can't deal with it. At least not outwardly."

"Now, Nana," Fran began. "You know Nick would listen to whatever you had to say."

"Maybe so," Nana conceded. "But Vince and Dom . . . I don't know."

"I think Roz is helping Vince get in touch with his softer side," Bella suggested. "Did you watch them at dinner on Easter? He hardly let her out of his sight. I think those two are getting serious."

"I hope it's not too soon," Fran worried. "It's only been a year since Roz's husband was murdered."

"Yes, but Roz and Ted were on a collision course long before that," Caprice mused. She wasn't telling secrets out of school. Everything had come out after Ted had been murdered.

"How long do you think they're going to keep me here?" Nana asked. "I want to go home."

"And we want you home," Fran assured her. "But we want you well. As soon as the doctors figure out what caused that pain, then maybe you can go home."

This was going to be a long night, Caprice suspected.

She'd have to drive home in a couple of hours to check on her pets. They weren't used to being alone at night, and she really didn't know how they were going to react. Mirabelle was safe in the spare room, but she might wonder where Caprice was since she'd been sleeping on her bed lately. Although Lady had a crate in the kitchen, Caprice rarely penned her in it. However, she had erected the pet gates before she left. In the house with Sophia at night, she might get scared. What she should do was install one of those pet cams. Then she could keep track of what was happening, at least in one of the rooms.

Two hours later, the cardiologist had determined that Nana hadn't had a heart attack. But she was taken to the cardiac lab and a calcium CT scan was performed. The test results on that were good, too. However, they were going to admit Nana for observation and keep her overnight. Soon she'd be settled in a room.

The family had taken turns keeping Nana company. "You all have to go home," she said. "They'll settle me in a room, and I'll try to get some sleep. Who knows what they have in store for me tomorrow?"

Nikki immediately said, "I'll stay. Bella needs to be with her kids. Caprice has to check on her pets. Mom has school tomorrow, and Dad and Vince have work. Nana would probably prefer that Uncle Dom not stay, so I'll stay and report what's happening."

"I should stay too," Caprice's father volunteered.

"And do what?" Nana asked him. "Stand guard over me? Do you think I'll get any rest with all of you around?"

Caprice had to smile, because that was probably true. If Nikki stayed, she could be a calming, quieting presence.

"I'll go, Nikki," Caprice agreed, "If you promise to call me if anything changes. Anything at all. Text me after Nana's settled in a room and let me know if you leave."

"I'll do all of the above," Nikki said. She took Nana's hand. "I promise I'll take good care of her, everyone. I'll be her advocate, and I'll make sure they treat her right."

Even Seth agreed that when a family member was hospitalized, another family member should be his or her advocate and be there as much as possible. She and her family would take turns. They would protect Nana and speak up for her if she didn't feel up to doing it herself. But knowing Nana, she'd ask about every little pill, every little service, and every little beep.

That was Nana.

When Nikki called Caprice the next morning, Caprice found out that Nana was having more tests.

Nikki said, "There's no point coming to the hospital when she's not in her room. I'm going home now. Mom took a personal day and is staying here. She'll call you as soon as Nana's settled back in her room or we know something. Distract yourself with solving Alanna's murder."

Taking her sister's advice, Caprice was determined to do just that.

Even though she'd been around Alanna a few times, she hadn't gotten a sense of who she really was. She thought about Muriel Fink, Barton's former secretary, who had been extremely upset and seemed to be grieving deeply. Maybe she'd been like a mother figure to Alanna? Who knew? But that was the point. So Caprice decided to visit her.

After taking Lady on a good long walk that let Sophia and Mirabelle have some time alone together, she returned home and carried Mirabelle to the spare room again. Mirabelle seemed to like being closeted by herself, and Caprice wondered just how much Alanna had put her in that utility closet. That wasn't fair, she supposed, but cats were good companions. They were social animals, even though people thought of dogs in that way. The only time cats preferred being closeted in a room alone was when they wanted to feel safe . . . or if that had been their way of life. Caprice suspected it was a little of both for Mirabelle.

After filling Lady's Kong toy with kibble, and giving Sophia a dab of cream, she headed out.

When Caprice had looked up Muriel Fink's address in an online directory, she'd found an *M. Fink,* who lived at an address near Country Fields Shopping Center. Caprice decided not to call first. Sure, she might get there and nobody would be home. However, after being part of three murder investigations, she'd decided face-to-face contact was usually best. Plus a phone call about something like this was always complicated. An unexpected visit usually produced more information.

As Caprice parked her Camaro at the curb in front of Muriel's house, she assessed the one-floor ranch-style home and calculated that it was even smaller than Bella's. As she'd learned while talking with her sister at the hospital, Bella and Joe were coming closer to the decision to list their house and look for something bigger. They'd been pricing possibilities online, unlike Grant, who was sporadically touring houses that could possibly suit him.

Thinking about Grant right now would muddle her thoughts.

She climbed out of her car and walked to the front door. Daffodils poked up out of the ground in front of

the living room's picture window. Blue and yellow
crocuses were blooming on the other side of the porch.

She rang the bell.

When Muriel answered the door, she looked as if she
were dressed for an exercise class in pale green knit
slacks and shirt. In her late sixties, Caprice guessed,
Muriel's gray hair framed her face in an attractive short
cut, and her blue eyes sparkled with curiosity as she
eyed Caprice speculatively.

"Miss Fink, I'm Caprice De Luca. I was a friend of
Alanna's." She was using that term loosely. "Maybe
you recognize me from the funeral?"

Muriel studied her again. "Why, yes, I think I do,"
she responded with a Southern accent thicker than
Alanna's and Twyla's. "You were sitting in the front row
with Mr. Richland. And Alanna's sister."

"That's right," Caprice agreed. "Could I talk to you
for a few minutes?"

"What about?" Muriel asked, obviously not going to
allow a stranger to set foot in her home without a good
reason.

"I'm trying to figure out who might have wanted to
do Alanna harm. Unfortunately, Mr. Richland is a suspect, and I'd like to give the police other avenues to
pursue. Could we talk?"

At that explanation, Muriel opened the screen door.
"I just returned from my yoga class. The place is a
mess."

"I promise I won't look around," Caprice assured her
with a smile.

As Caprice entered the living room, she realized
Muriel must not know what a mess was. True, there
were folded towels on a corner of the sofa, and a
newspaper spread over the coffee table. A coffee mug
rested on a side end table and a pair of shoes lay by

the recliner. But the room was bright with rose floral fabrics on a cream background. A porcelain vase holding a few daffodils sat on a clover-shaped occasional table at the plate glass window.

"I became quite emotional at the funeral, I'm afraid," Muriel admitted. "When you get to my age, losing one more person just seems to be too much. Barton's sudden heart attack and death was a shock. Now Alanna's murder. It was all just too much."

"I understand," Caprice assured her.

"Please sit," Muriel said, motioning to the sofa. "Would you like a cup of tea? I just put water on to boil."

"That would be lovely. My nana and I share tea at least once a month."

"How about orange spice?"

"Sounds good."

Ten minutes later, they were both seated on the sofa, mugs of tea in their hands. They'd been making small talk up until then, but now Caprice said, "I'd like to know more about Alanna. I staged her house to sell, but we talked mostly about business."

"Alanna was a complicated woman," Muriel acknowledged. "I know she had a reputation for being icy and unbending, but she wasn't always that way. When she and Mr. Goodwin first married . . ." Muriel shook her head.

"She changed over the years?" Caprice prompted.

"Oh yes! Understand, I was Mr. Goodwin's secretary in Biloxi. He brought me up here when he moved the company here. He trusted me that much, and it's a good feeling."

"Yes, it is. You must have been very valuable to him."

"A good secretary's hard to find," Muriel said with a wink. "I knew how his mind worked, at least where business was concerned. He was smitten with Alanna. And she seemed smitten with him."

"I see. So theirs was love at first sight?"

"It seemed to be," Muriel agreed. "They married quickly after just a few months. I'm not sure how well they knew each other, though. Barton could be quite genial and charming when he wanted to be. But he had a ruthless underside, too, and I don't think Alanna saw that at first."

"But she did after they were married?"

"I don't know for sure," Muriel admitted. "But after the first year they were married, she stopped calling as much while he was at the office. They didn't go to lunch together as often. Of course, by then she'd settled into his lifestyle."

"And that lifestyle consisted of . . . ?" Caprice prodded.

"Oh, she worked on the boards of foundations for charities. She spent time giving dinner parties for Barton's associates. They could be quite elaborate, almost like a state dinner. She ran his house in a way the first Mrs. Goodwin never could."

"The first Mrs. Goodwin?" Caprice asked.

"Oh, she was a scatterbrain. She couldn't even keep the menu straight for dinners. Once Barton made his fortune, all she wanted to do was shop. And the truth is, I think she drank a little too much. I think that's what broke up his marriage."

"I see. But Alanna was different."

"Oh yes. Alanna was very organized and she paid attention to detail. She could have run her own company. She's one of those women who could have broken any glass ceiling. She was a happy woman back then, even if she was strong-willed."

"Back then," Caprice mused. "So, when did she change?"

After a few moments of consideration, Muriel answered. "We had all moved here to Kismet. Alanna and Barton had settled in, giving dinners and parties in that fabulous house he built for her. They were enjoying their life. But then, something happened."

Caprice could guess what that was, but she wanted Muriel to tell her. "Something drastic?"

"That depends on the way you look at it. A man came to see Barton. His name was Archer Ford. He was at the funeral, too."

"I met him."

"He claimed to be Mr. Goodwin's illegitimate son."

"I imagine that shook up Barton's life."

"Well, Mr. Goodwin's first marriage was long over. But he confided to me that he didn't want to be immersed in scandal . . . or have his ex ask for more money because she could hold an affair over his head. Mr. Goodwin simply hadn't wanted to admit he was unfaithful to his first wife. He refused to take a DNA test, claiming Mr. Ford was greedy and only wanted to take his money. Like many rich men, he could be suspicious and paranoid at times. So he denied everything."

"Did he feel Alanna would think less of him?"

"Possibly. Barton was a proud man, with lots of ego. After all, he was an inventor. He'd created something out of almost nothing. He didn't want to deal with the repercussions of accepting Archer Ford into his life."

"How did Alanna react?"

"I wasn't around her that much then. But I do remember a Christmas party after Mr. Ford came forward. Mr. Goodwin and Alanna didn't know I was in hearing distance. Apparently, Alanna thought Barton should include Archer in his life, but Barton was vehemently against it. After that, there seemed to be a tension between the two of them, which hadn't been there before."

"And you think Alanna changed after that?"

"No, not then, though I think her relationship with Barton changed. Maybe she was disappointed her husband wouldn't accept his son, no matter what the cost. About a year later, she and Barton separated for six months. Just before they separated, there seemed to be a defiance in Alanna that hadn't been there previously. It was like she was determined to be happy, no matter what she had to do. That's when *she* started shopping a lot, just like the first Mrs. Goodwin had. The jewelry she bought . . ." Muriel rolled her eyes. "That woman had the best taste. Not flashy, but classic. But I knew what that double strand of pearls with the sapphire clasp cost."

"So when they were separated, Barton didn't join her in Europe at all?"

For a man who had millions and could jet-set anywhere, why wouldn't he visit his wife if he wanted them to get back together? If he wanted to save his marriage?

"Europe?" Muriel repeated with an odd look on her face.

"Isn't that where Alanna went?"

"That's what Alanna told anyone who asked. But I saw the receipts for the trip. She flew to Vermont. As far as I know, that's where she stayed the whole time. I could be mistaken about that, but credit card statements don't lie."

No, credit card statements didn't lie.

So, just why had Alanna told everyone she'd gone to Europe?

* * *

Caprice was still pondering that question, as well as her whole conversation with Muriel Fink, as she drove home. Halfway to her house, her cell phone played "Here, There and Everywhere." Just why did she like that song so much? The haunting melody? The words? The sentiment? That if you loved someone, they would be there for you?

Shaking those thoughts away, she picked up the phone and saw her mom's number and picture. "Hi, Mom. How's Nana?"

During the time she'd spent with Muriel Fink, she'd managed to push her worry aside, but now it came roaring back.

"Nana will be back home in about half an hour. They're putting her discharge papers together now."

"Do they know what's wrong? Do they know what happened?"

"Nana had gastric tests this morning, which she wasn't too fond of, an endoscopy among them. Apparently, she's suffering from acid reflux and a hiatal hernia rather than a heart condition. She's relieved about all that, but most of all sorry that she scared us. I keep telling her we couldn't take any chances, and we won't in the future, either. As we get older, there will be many more of these kind of crises for all of us."

That was a pleasant thought! But Caprice imagined as one aged, one had to think about all that. It was a daunting prospect really.

"I want to come over and see her."

"That will be fine, honey, but give her a couple of hours to settle back in. You know, let her decompress from being at the hospital."

"Can I bring her anything?"

"Just yourself. I'm making chicken soup for supper."

"Why don't I bake your cinnamon apple recipe, which she likes so much?"

Her mom thought about it. "That dish probably would go down easily. She has medication now that should help her."

"I'll be over about three. She should probably stay in bed for the day."

"You know she won't. We'll watch over her in shifts. I'll see you later."

Time flew by as Caprice took care of her animals, caught up with paperwork on new proposals, researched prices for a living room and dining room a client wanted her to redecorate, and checked in with developer Derrick Gastenaux to see if any more of his model homes might have sold. Another one had a contract on it, and he thought prospects of closing the deal looked good. In fact, he was so pleased with the sales of the homes since they'd become available before Christmas, he was planning to build three more. He wanted Caprice to stage those, too.

Contracts with developers like Derrick made her feel solvent. This kind of business was money in the bank, which let her know she'd have enough to pay expenses until the end of the year. She was never sure clients would sign with her, even if they called for a home-staging consultation. All she could do was keep up a good reputation, helping to sell houses fast so that one seller or buyer recommended her to another seller or buyer.

When Lady whined at Caprice, Caprice decided to take her along to see Nana. If Nana wasn't up to the company, her mom would take Lady under her wing or maybe outside for a romp in her gardens. Caprice's dad would be using the rototiller soon. At the beginning of the month, her mom had planted heirloom tomato seeds. She cared for them by using a heat pad and a grow lamp in the basement. In a couple of weeks, she'd move them to shelves in the house's sunroom and then finally outside under the porch so they grew a little hardy before they were planted. Today was sixty degrees and sunny, so her mom could take Lady outside to examine the gardens and see just how much work had to be done before planting.

Since Caprice was taking Lady with her, she opened the door to the spare room. "Come on out, Mirabelle. I'm sure Sophia will like the company."

On the bed looking totally content, Mirabelle just crossed one front paw over the other and gave a little mew in response.

Maybe Mirabelle would come out, and maybe she wouldn't. Maybe Sophia would go upstairs, and maybe she wouldn't. Caprice would find out when she got home. Having Lady out of the house would make the atmosphere conducive to two stranger cats becoming friendly cats.

She hoped.

When Caprice arrived at her childhood home, going to the back entrance where her Nana's suite of rooms was located, she rang the bell with one hand, holding the casserole of warm cinnamon apples in the other. Her grandmother had definitely not gone to bed. She answered the doorbell's ring herself, dressed in spring blue slacks and a flowered shirt. Blue-and-pink sneakers covered her feet.

The first thing she said to Caprice was "I took a shower to wash that hospital smell off me. I didn't need a doctor to tell me I had acid in my throat."

Caprice asked, "Are you going to have a cup of tea with me?"

Fran, who had been hovering in the living room, said, "That would be a terrific idea. Enjoy some tea and baked cinnamon apples, while I take Lady outside to examine my tomato bed. I can tell her the story of when her mom was found there."

"You should wait until Patches is around to tell him, too," Nana said slyly with a sideways glance at Caprice.

"I'm sure Grant has already told Patches that story," Fran responded, taking a sweater from the back of an armchair. "Don't get into trouble while I'm gone."

Both Nana and Caprice wrinkled their noses at her while she led Lady out the door.

Nana and Caprice didn't talk as they brewed tea and dished out the still-warm apples.

As they sat at the small table in Nana's apartment and stirred their tea, Caprice asked, "Does your throat hurt?"

"The doc said it would be a little sore for a week to ten days. But I've hurt worse. I'll just stick to smooth and soft for the next few days. Thanks so much for bringing the apples."

Nana was wise, with a lot of experience, and Caprice didn't claim to know more than she or her doctors did. But she had a question she wanted to ask her, and she hoped it didn't make Nana angry.

"Can we talk about why you're feeling so poorly?"

Nana's golden brown eyes studied her. "It's a stomach thing," she said.

"I know," Caprice assured her. "But when did you start feeling bad? I don't mean the chest pain, but before that."

"It's been the past week, more often than not. I had episodes before now if I ate too many sweets or a dinner that was too rich. But never regular like this."

"In the past week, Uncle Dom has been here."

Her grandmother looked at her with what almost seemed like surprise. She hadn't connected those dots.

"No matter what you eat, more tension means more acid, don't you think? That riles up the hiatal hernia."

"I don't know if that's scientific," Nana grumbled.

"Maybe if you and Uncle Dom resolve your differences, everyone would feel better."

At first, Nana frowned. But then she reached over and took Caprice's hand. "*Tesorina mia,* you'll understand someday when you have children of your own. When you have a child, you give them your entire heart. They're born of your heart. They're born of you. There's a connection that can never be cut, no matter what anybody tries to do. Mothers know this. When a child tries to pull away, it hurts."

Caprice waited, suspecting Nana had more to say. She hadn't used *"tesorina mia,"* her "my little treasure" endearment, in a long while.

Nana finally spoke again. "If Dom had been pulling away to establish his independence, I think I could have understood that. But that wasn't the case. He was letting a woman manipulate him. Ronnie didn't care two figs about us, only about what Dom could give her. But that also included one hundred percent attention. Sure, we understood that. They were going to be newlyweds. But to take the money your grandfather and I had saved for him and splurge it on a world trip, and then come back and actually tell me they wouldn't be visiting very often . . . how do you think that made me feel? And your grandfather? And your mom and dad and Maria? We loved Dom. We wanted to love Ronnie. But she wanted no part of us, so he wanted no part of us."

Caprice could tell Nana's voice sounded thicker the longer she talked. She was probably straining it and she shouldn't be.

"I probably shouldn't have brought this up today, but it's just something that I thought you should think about. If you and Uncle Dom could find some peace, maybe you'd feel better."

"Dom was in the wrong and he's never admitted that. Not ever. He's never said he's sorry. So, what can a mother do but hurt?" Nana put her hand over her heart. "Right here."

This had to be settled one way or another for all their sakes. Nana was a loving woman and all she wanted to do was love her family, including Uncle Dominic. Maybe it was time someone talked to him. Maybe he was the one who could bring this family back together again.

Chapter Twelve

There were empty seats!

On Saturday evening, as Caprice stood inside the entrance of the community theater where Ace's concert was being held, she couldn't believe that he didn't have a full house. But then this was Kismet—small town, big gossip. In a place like Kismet, suspicion, rumor, and innuendo could ruin a career.

Of course, Ace's career wouldn't be ruined by this. He had a much bigger audience across the country, maybe even across the world, now with digital downloading. Still . . . if Alanna's murder didn't get cleared up, suspicion was a nasty shadow to brush away.

Caprice suddenly realized she wasn't alone. A shoulder brushed hers. She turned her head to see . . .

"Grant!" she said with surprise. When she'd picked up Lady last night after the last session of her self-defense course, he hadn't mentioned he was coming tonight.

"What? You didn't think I could afford a seat when the money goes to charity?"

The seats tonight had cost five hundred dollars a

head. But the band was giving half of the funds to a children's charity.

Grant added, "I wasn't sure Simon would pupsit Patches until this afternoon."

"Our seats are probably rows apart."

"It's two minutes until concert time, and there are plenty of empty seats. What row are you in?"

"Eight."

"There are even empty seats there. Come on, I'll join you. If whoever bought the seat next to you arrives, I'll move."

This was a side of Grant she hadn't seen much before—more casual, flexible, maybe even ready to have a good time.

"Is any of your family coming?" he asked.

To her surprise, he laid his hand gently on the small of her back as they walked toward their row. Caprice almost tripped.

She wasn't sure why Grant was having this effect on her, but he was. "Mom and Dad and Uncle Dom are trying to stay close to Nana. They're still worried about her."

"How's she feeling?"

"I called her this afternoon. The acid reflux medication is helping, and she's adjusting her diet somewhat. But the truth is, I think a big part of the problem is anxiety over Uncle Dominic being there. I talked to Nana about it, but I think I want to talk to Uncle Dom, too."

"The peacemaker," Grant murmured close to her ear, right before they entered their row.

His minty breath had tickled her earlobe and she felt positively weak in the knees. She had to buck up. She had to clear her head. She was here to listen to Ace's music . . . and to watch Len Lowery. Grant was here to listen to music, too, and maybe . . .

"Did you come to keep your eye on Len and Ace?" she asked.

"I did," he admitted. "When I talked with Ace earlier today, he confessed it's been hard to act as if everything's the same when he's rehearsing with the band. They found a new bass player, and that's been keeping Ace occupied as they bring the new guy up to speed. So he's stayed away from Len. But I don't know how long that will last."

"I thought Vince and Roz might come tonight."

"I had to stop in at the office for paperwork. Vince said Roz bought a ticket, but he was taking her to a wine tasting somewhere near Lancaster instead. I guess they feel time alone is more important than the concert."

"I'm still afraid Roz is going to get hurt."

"What about Vince?" Grant asked.

"It depends if they're both serious. I think she's becoming more serious. Has Vince said anything?"

"Vince talk to me about his love life?" Grant scoffed. "Not going to happen. But I can tell whenever he talks about Roz . . . he has a different attitude about her than about other women he's dated."

Caprice's elbow brushed Grant's as the community theater manager appeared onstage to talk to everyone gathered. The theater darkened and the spotlight targeted him.

Roger Canfield considered himself a connoisseur of the arts—books, plays, literature, and music. He was quite stuffy to talk to. His comb-over didn't do the trick over his bald spot. Short and stocky, he was wearing an expensive suit. She could tell that from the glow of the fabric under the lights. It fit him superbly.

He said, "Welcome, everyone, to our Ace Richland concert. Usually, our policy is no photographs and no video. Still, no video, please, but we know we can't keep you from taking photos with your cell phones. Just remember, those flashes from regular cameras can be distracting. So without further ado, let's pull the curtain up on Ace Richland."

Ace didn't come up to the mike and say a few words as he usually did, and Caprice wondered if that was a mistake. Or maybe Ace was just going through the motions tonight. He was grieving.

The band started right in on one of Ace's first hits. However, from the opening notes, Caprice could tell the audience wasn't totally involved. In fact, there seemed to be an awkwardness over the whole theater. Maybe if Ace had welcomed everyone . . .

Grant nudged her. "Do you think the audience will get into it?"

"I don't know. I sure hope so for Ace's and the band's sake."

As if Ace's band could feel the tension in the theater, the camaraderie they usually shared among themselves didn't come across, either. Their jokes between songs fell flat. It wasn't that the band didn't give the audience their money's worth. They played long and hard. They played song after song. But it was difficult to get the audience to clap along, difficult to have the give-and-take Ace usually enjoyed with his listeners.

And one of the causes . . .

Len was looking sullen. The newest band member seemed to be feeling his way, glancing at the others for approval or the go-ahead. The drummer and the other guitarists were doing their best to make this an evening full of music. But there was a pall and everyone could feel it.

Suddenly the atmosphere changed when Ace stepped forward as if he'd made a decision. He made eye contact with each of his band members . . . except for Len. He carried the mike close to the edge of the stage and spoke to the audience as he normally did after every song.

"This next tune originated when our bus was rolling through Tennessee," he said with one of his famous smiles.

Finally the tension in the audience thinned. During the upbeat melody, folks clapped to the beat of the music.

When that tune ended to a round of applause, Ace introduced his new bass player, Caleb Jacobs. While Caleb played a solo, Ace took a few swigs of water from a bottle on a stool. Midsong he picked up his guitar and joined in, and he and Caleb dueled it out on their guitars.

A burst of applause again came from the audience, and Caprice breathed a sigh of relief. Maybe everything was back on track.

By this time, Ace had introduced all of the band members, except for Len.

Grant leaned close to Caprice and in a low voice said, "Len hasn't stopped scowling since he started playing. Do you think Ace is cutting him out somehow?"

"It's possible. Len usually has his own solo at some point. Maybe Ace has just decided he doesn't deserve one and hasn't clued Len in."

"More trouble brewing," Grant predicted.

So without Len giving a solo, or even being introduced, Ace wound up the evening of music by saying, "Thank you all for coming out tonight. I just want you all to know I feel at home here in Kismet. Since I moved here, I've made some good friends." He looked straight at Grant and Caprice.

But before Ace could continue with his remarks, either what a terrific place Kismet was to live in, or more about the charity or his music, a heckler from about three-quarters of the way back in the theater shouted out, "Did you kill Alanna Goodwin?"

A hush swept over the theater. Ace's face reddened and his fingers gripped his guitar hard.

Caprice didn't know what to expect out of him next. She found herself clutching Grant's arm.

Ace stepped close to the mike and said in a low voice, "Thank you all again for coming out tonight." Then he turned and left the stage.

Caprice was still holding on to Grant's arm. He wasn't moving away.

"Maybe I should go after him," Caprice suggested.

"No. You go home. I'll see if there's anything I can do."

She relaxed her grip on his arm and let go, realizing how strong Grant felt . . . how very masculine.

"He's probably embarrassed about what happened. I'll find him and make sure he's all right," Grant assured her.

Uncertain, Caprice realized she trusted Grant to do what he could. Maybe Ace would confide in him . . . vent to him if she wasn't around.

"All right," she agreed reluctantly. She and Grant stood, exited their row, and moved to the aisle.

She was about to head in the other direction, but then she stopped and turned back to him. "If you need me, call me. Ace doesn't really have that many friends here."

Grant nodded and hurried toward the stairs and the door that led backstage.

Caprice watched him mount the steps and remembered the feel of his arm under her fingertips.

It was 1:00 A.M. when Caprice got the call. She'd been answering e-mails in her home office. Mirabelle and Sophia were already asleep on her bed upstairs, a bed's length apart. When she'd gotten home and changed clothes, they'd been there, and they hadn't moved. At her feet, Lady slept as Caprice made sure all her pressing correspondence was taken care of.

Her cell phone played on the desk, where she'd set it to charge. Multiple docks helped her keep it revved up.

"Are you awake?" Grant asked.

"I was just answering e-mails. What's going on?"

"Can you come to the Blue Moon Grille?"

"Now?"

What was this, a late-night date? Though the idea thrilled her a little bit. The Blue Moon Grille was open until two on weekends. Late hours for a restaurant in Kismet, but it worked. Maybe because it was the only restaurant around that was open so late.

"I need your help with Ace."

"He's there?"

"Oh yeah, he's here. The whole band is. Ace wouldn't talk to me backstage. He put on a disguise and snuck out to a low-profile car he had his bodyguard rent for him. I made sure he drove off without being followed. But he must have gotten in contact with his band members and they all ended up here—including Len. He called me after he broke Len's nose. Can you come?"

"*Broke Len's nose?* I'll be there in ten minutes."

And she was. Even Lady had cooperated with urgency

and made a quick trip outside. Now, hopefully, the animals were in bed for the night.

But she was certainly curious why she wasn't. Why did Grant need *her* there?

She found out when she saw the damage at the Blue Moon Grille. There were a handful of diners and drinkers still there, scattered at tables on the right side of the room and at the bar. A group of men stood outside the French doors on the deck looking in, probably curious as to what would happen next.

It was obvious that the left side of the room had seen a fight. Tables and chairs were pushed aside as if the floor had to be cleaned up for some reason. Grant and Ace sat on two ladder-back chairs near the kitchen.

She hurried over to them. "What happened?"

Grant motioned to the area where they were sitting. "You should have seen this fifteen minutes ago— broken glass, crab pretzels on the floor, not to mention the fries and ketchup."

Ace gave him a glare.

Grant glared back. "Do you want to tell her?"

"I decked Len. There's nothing else to say." He glanced up at Caprice. "I called Grant because I broke his nose."

"Luckily, Len isn't going to press charges," Grant explained. "Apparently, no one saw who threw the first punch. It's a he said/he said situation. But Ace here is ready to go after him again, and I need you to talk some sense into him. Apparently, you're one of the people he listens to."

"I listen to my housekeeper," Ace mumbled, "because she feeds me."

Caprice just shook her head, yanked on a chair, and pulled it over to join the two men. "Ace, go home."

"I can't. I have to talk to the owner about damages.

But what I want to do is go out on that deck and throw Len off it. He killed her. You know he did. Maybe Alanna decided not to pay him what she said she was going to. I just can't believe she'd plot against me."

Caprice wasn't a defender of Alanna by any means; but to make Ace feel better, she suggested, "Maybe she thought she was plotting *for* you. Maybe she thought she was doing the best *for* you."

"*The best?* By ruining my career? There isn't a career any longer without a road show. It's even more important than it used to be."

Caprice glanced toward the deck and spotted Len standing between two of the band members. He was holding an ice bag on his nose.

Ace was still flushed and looked as if he wanted to punch a wall, if not Len. She'd never seen him like this. But being accused of murder so publically, grieving for Alanna, and knowing he had a tour to get on the road—no, those weren't good excuses, but they sure were reasons why he was riled up like this.

Ace was Italian. He came from the same kind of family she did, filled with lots of affection and love and passion.

She reached out to him and touched his arm. "Ace, you have to try to get a grip, and even more than that, you have a daughter to set an example for. Do you really want to wind up in jail? On charges of assault and battery, if not murder? Detective Jones doesn't care how famous you are. It won't take much more than this to prove you have a motive."

"They only have circumstantial evidence," Ace said stubbornly.

"Don't push Jones to search for more." Taking a different tack, she held out her hand. "Give me your phone."

Ace looked at her as if she were crazy.

"Come on," she coaxed. "Give it to me."

He did, and she swiped the screen. Trista's picture appeared. "Take a good look at her, Ace. She wants to respect you. She wants to spend time with you. *Don't mess this up.*"

Ace studied the picture of Trista for a long time. Then he gave a little nod, took three deep breaths, and let his shoulders relax a little. "Okay. No more punches."

Just then, a man dressed in a suit emerged from the kitchen. He was rotund and had a semi-balding head of gray hair. She'd seen him wandering the Blue Moon Grille before, making sure everyone was happy and all the food was prepared exactly the way customers wanted it. His name was Tom Snyder, and he was the owner.

Ace immediately got to his feet and went to meet the man.

Grant started to say, "Do you need me to—"

But Ace just waved his hand at him, indicating he was going to do this on his own.

Grant sighed. "I'm sorry I had to pull you out again tonight. Maybe he would have settled down, but he sure wasn't listening to me, and I could tell his blood pressure was still high, as well as his fury. That scene at the concert was a shame. He told me he's afraid that's going to happen when he goes on the road if Alanna's murderer hasn't been found."

"Oh, Grant." She looked toward the deck. "I want to talk to Len."

"Caprice . . ." There was that warning note in Grant's tone.

She parroted back and stressed his name as he had hers, *"Grant . . ."*

He clasped her elbow. "If he's the murderer, I want you to stay away from him."

"If he's the murderer, that's even more reason to talk to him. But tonight isn't a good time. Maybe tomorrow after he's been to the ER or urgent care and is nursing that nose. Maybe he'll be on pain medicine and tell me the truth."

"If you want to do that, I can go along with you."

She thought about Grant's offer, but she shook her head. "I appreciate your wanting to go along. I really do. But I don't think I'll get as much out of Len if you do. You're Ace's lawyer. You were here defending him tonight. There's no way Len will tell me anything except a bunch of lies if you're along, even if he's on pain medication."

Grant raked his hand through his hair—thick black hair with a slight wave. Caprice was noticing every little detail about him these days.

"If you interview Len, I want you to tell me what time you're going, and I want you to leave your cell phone open to my number. Don't tell me you're a big girl and you know what you're doing, and you finished a self-defense course. Even police officers have backup."

Grant knew her well.

She said simply, "I'll let you be my backup." Then she wondered what it would be like to have Grant as a backup in more than a murder investigation.

Caprice didn't like Len. She knew that wasn't a charitable thought. Nevertheless, as he opened the door to his condo, even though his nose was taped, he still had a look of arrogance. When his gaze wandered over her on Sunday afternoon, sizing her up as if she might be his next date, she shivered. He gave her the creeps. She didn't like guys who thought every woman should drop at their feet. She didn't like guys who had an all-knowing attitude. She didn't like this guy who could be a murderer.

Wearing a denim maxiskirt, paired with a fringed vest, along with a white silky blouse with bell sleeves, she knew she wasn't Len's proverbial cup of tea, or cup of sugar, or cup of whatever. Dipping her hand into her pocket, she felt for her cell phone. She'd texted Grant as he'd asked, and she'd left the line open now.

"This is a surprise," Len said with a smirk. "You're in Camp Ace, aren't you?"

"Could we talk for a few minutes?" she asked politely. She was determined to be polite. She was determined to learn something.

"Come on in," Len said, motioning to the living room.

It wasn't really a living room. Oh, there was a couch, a black leather one. There was a chair in a red-and-black geometric design that was complemented by an ottoman practically as big as a coffee table. But that was where the resemblance to a living room ended.

Two keyboards were positioned side by side. Cords dangled from them to the receptacles. Two speakers sat at opposite ends of the room, with a huge flat-screen TV at the center. An all-in-one computer, with a twenty-four-inch monitor, sat atop an acrylic desk. The ergonomic chair in silver was futuristic, to say the least. Len obviously worked, played, and relaxed in this room.

Once they were both seated, Caprice in the chair and Len on the sofa, he rubbed his temples as if he had a headache. She imagined with a broken nose he might.

"Is Ace still afraid I'll press charges, and he sent you

to smooth things over? That's just like him, not to do it himself."

From what she knew of Ace, that wasn't true at all. But maybe Len had his own agenda here, as he'd had for the past few months. She had no intention of telling him she'd overheard him and Alanna. She was smarter than that. She also didn't want to tip the police's hand if they were looking into Len's bank and phone records. If Carstead and Jones were as thorough as she thought they were, they'd act on the information she'd given them.

"I'm not here to smooth anything over. There were no witnesses. Ace could claim he was defending himself. You two are about the same size, and you're both in good shape."

"I'm in better shape than he is. I'm a heck of a lot younger."

That was true, but she wasn't going to let Len take any points if she could help it. "How did you and Ace originally meet up?" she asked.

Len looked surprised at that question. He shrugged. "L.A. is a big town, yet it really isn't. Circles of musicians know each other."

"Ace had been out of the business for a while."

"I ran into him after he'd just finished up that reality show and was doing all the late-night gigs. He said he was putting a band together again. I was looking for something new, so I hooked up with him."

"You were playing for a band before this?"

"Why all the questions?" he asked suspiciously.

"Just trying to get to know you a little better," she said with a sweet smile. She knew if Grant could hear her, he was probably groaning.

"*Know me better?* Why? What's this about?"

"I'm a friend of Ace's. You're working with him. He's

involved in a murder investigation. Let's just say I'm trying to protect his interests."

At that, Len looked uncomfortable. "He has a lawyer."

"His lawyer isn't investigating Alanna's murder. I am."

He looked skeptical. "You're helping the police?"

"In a way. Do you know anything about me, Mr. Lowery?"

"No, should I?" he asked defensively.

"I've helped solve a few murders. You could say I've been invaluable to the police investigation."

Len now looked downright antsy, shifting on the sofa, crossing one leg over the other, and dropping his leg and sitting straight again. "They haven't questioned me. I'm not even on their radar."

He said that with a bit of smugness, which really irked Caprice. "I'm sure they'll get around to talking to you. You did know Alanna Goodwin, didn't you?"

"Not really. Ace introduced us. That was it."

"But you were at the open house, weren't you? I was the home stager, and I was there, too. I thought I saw you."

He checked his watch. "Look, I've got to take some pain meds. My head's throbbing and so's my nose. Are we about done?"

"We can be. Just one more question. Do you know anything about the guitars that were stolen from Ace's secure room?"

If Len had looked uncomfortable before, he looked a little shell-shocked now. He'd never expected that question. "What do you mean—do I know anything about them?"

"Do you know which ones were stolen?"

"How would I know?"

"Weren't you at the party Ace gave?"

"I was there, loaded to the gills. I don't know anything about his Martin."

Aha! He did know which guitars were stolen. As soon as the words were out of his mouth, Len realized he'd slipped.

"So you *do know* which guitars are missing!"

"No, I just know the Martin's a valuable one. It would make sense someone would want to steal that one."

"And that's *all* you know?"

Len stood, stuffed his hands in his back pockets, and glared at her. "I don't know what you're up to, but I don't know nothin'. I dare you to prove I had anything to do with that theft."

"You know what, Mr. Lowery, I've never been able to turn down a dare."

"Leave," he bit out.

"Gladly. But I imagine the police might want to question you about Ace's guitars, as well as Alanna's murder."

From the furious look in Len's eyes, Caprice knew she had to scoot, and scoot fast.

She rose from the chair and went to the door. "Thanks for your time, Mr. Lowery. I can see myself out."

And she did—quickly.

Then she cut her open connection to Grant before she could hear his shout of disapproval. She might have gone too far. But on the other hand, she might have just gone far enough.

Chapter Thirteen

Caprice had been involved in several murder investigations by now. And even though she'd been in danger a couple of times, she'd never felt anxious about questioning witnesses or suspects. But there was something about Len Lowery that made her wonder if she should have followed Grant's advice and stayed away from him.

This was one of those April days that had grown gray and cloudy. The dampness in the air portended rain—rain that would make her flowers grow, she reminded herself, as she drove home, left her car in the driveway, and went in the front door.

After releasing the pet gate at the kitchen, she was met by Lady, who was all excited to see her.

"It's great coming home to you," she said, dropping down to cuddle and pet her pup. "You always make me feel welcome."

Lady barked, agreeing with her, and then ran to the back door, signaling she had to go out.

"What a good girl you are," Caprice said. "Maybe we can have a game of fetch before the rain starts."

Sophia, who was sleeping on the dining-room table,

meowed, yawned, and stuck out a paw as if to delay Caprice from going outside.

She stopped, reached out, and petted Sophia's silky head, ruffling her pristine white ruff. "Do you know where Mirabelle is?" she asked.

Sophia just gave her a blinking stare.

"I figured as much. You don't *care* where Mirabelle is. My guess is she's up in my bedroom."

Sophia just blinked again.

"We'll find her when I come back in."

Sophia ducked her head down and covered her nose with her paw.

"An attitude like that won't make you friends," Caprice warned her. But Sophia obviously didn't give a darn.

Lady stood at the back door, wriggling. Caprice knew what that meant. She hurriedly opened the door and let her dog jump out onto the porch. When Lady ran down the steps, Caprice followed. She didn't give her "go potty" commands anymore because Lady knew what she was supposed to do. But Caprice still liked to praise her after she did it.

By the time Lady had finished her business, and Caprice had executed the cleanup, a misty rain had begun falling. She went over her to-do list in her mind, prioritizing for the afternoon and evening. She'd developed a new recipe for a chocolate-coffee loaf. She wanted to try it out again to make sure she had the ingredients just right. Maybe she'd whip that up first. The recipe made two loaves and she could take one along to Isaac when she visited his shop. She had questions for him about antique guitars. Besides, she'd like to search through his crystal vases. She was meeting Juan at the glass house tomorrow to make final decisions about staging it. Since they were executing a minimalist theme, Caprice knew crystal vases with the sunshine hitting them would be dramatic and wonderful accents.

She whipped up the one-bowl chocolate-coffee loaf recipe in no time at all. It was one of those "dump everything into the mixer bowl, beat it smooth with the mixer, and pour it into two bread pans" recipes.

The smells of coffee and chocolate laced her kitchen, and she sat at the kitchen table working on her laptop until the baking bread started to make her mouth water.

Through the window, she could see that the spring storm had moved in. Rain pattered on the porch roof. While Caprice worked, Mirabelle had ventured down to the kitchen from the upstairs bedroom, where Caprice had found her napping earlier, and looked up at her new mistress with an expectant expression.

"You want a few crunchies, don't you? If I give you a few, I have to give Sophia a few, and then Lady has to have a treat, too."

All of that seemed to make sense to Mirabelle because she hopped up onto the chair next to Caprice and meowed at her.

After Caprice had served her felines and her pup, and they'd made quick work of eating the treats, she tested the bread with a toothpick and removed it from the oven. *Perfect.*

She'd set it on wire racks to cool just as her doorbell rang. Checking her phone, she wondered if she'd missed a text from Nikki or any of her family. She hadn't.

Opening her door, she was absolutely shocked to see . . .

Seth! He looked a bit damp in a polo shirt and

navy trousers, even though he was standing under the overhang.

"Can I come in?" he asked with one of those smiles that had convinced her to date him in the first place.

"Of course, you can come in. I was just surprised to see you." She opened the storm door.

From behind his back, he produced a bouquet of assorted flowers—daylilies to daisies to mums. "These are for you."

She hadn't seen Seth since Valentine's Day and the dance, an evening that had been special in so many ways. Not the least of which had been the gift of the charm-and-beaded bracelet he'd given her, which she was wearing now.

Before she could ask any questions, he took her into his arms and kissed her, flowers and all. The world spun a little as it usually did when he kissed her. When he broke away, she gazed up at him speechless until her mind started working again.

"What are you doing here?"

"I had a few hours that I could get away and I wanted to see you. Can you go to dinner with me tonight, or do you have plans?"

"No plans," she said. "I could cook something for us here."

"If you don't mind braving the weather, I'd rather take you out. I heard the Purple Iris Bed-and-Breakfast has a wonderful restaurant."

"Are you going to be staying there tonight?" Maybe they'd have more than a few hours together.

"No. I can't do that. I have to be ready for rounds early tomorrow morning. But I want to take you some-place nice and quiet where we can talk. E-mails are fine, but they're not the same as conversation."

"No, they're not," Caprice agreed, excited to see Seth, ecstatic to be with him, yet disappointed that they would only have a few hours together . . . again. She knew what Nana would say: "Enjoy your precious moments for what they are." That's what she was going to do tonight. That's what she always had to do with Seth.

He said, "I brought a duffel, with a nice clean white shirt and a tie."

Lady ran over to Seth now and sniffed the legs of his pants, reacquainting herself with his scent. Then she sat at his feet, looking up at him.

He dropped down into a crouch and petted her until she rolled over so he could rub her belly.

After he stood, he saw Sophia high on her cat tree. He waved at her. She looked at him with her huge golden eyes and then snuggled her head on her paws again. By this time, Mirabelle had sauntered out from the chair in the kitchen.

"Well, who are you?" Seth asked.

Caprice hadn't yet filled Seth in on Alanna Goodwin's death, and taking in Mirabelle. The story was too complicated to go into an e-mail. Wasn't it? Was that the real reason she hadn't told him about any of it? Or was it because she sent an e-mail into cyberspace and didn't know exactly how much attention Seth gave to it? His replies were usually short and chipper, but not crammed with details. Maybe she hadn't wanted to overload *him* with too many details.

"It's a long story," she said.

He took her hand. "You can tell me all about it over dinner. We can really catch up."

"Do we need a reservation?"

"I already made one, hoping you'd be free."

"You took a chance, driving to Kismet. What if I hadn't been here?"

"I would have waited. Even an hour with you would have been worth it."

She stood on tiptoe and kissed him. "Why don't you go get your duffel while I change."

"Sure," he said. "I can use your downstairs bathroom. But before I get that duffel . . ."

He looked concerned now and Caprice wondered what was wrong. "What is it?"

"I noticed your car is parked in the driveway. Are you waiting for a tow or something?"

"No, why?"

"Because I'm pretty sure you have two flat tires—the back ones."

"You're kidding." She went to the door and looked out.

"Take an umbrella if you go out there. It's really coming down."

"I was going to take a shower anyway, so I can get all dressed up," she teased. "I'm going to take a look."

"I'm already damp and I can dry off in a hurry. Come on, if you want to check them."

They ran outside and Caprice ducked around her car, examining the tires. Yes, the two back ones were indeed flat, and she had a feeling she hadn't run over any nails. Could Len have done this? Someone else?

"I might as well have it towed," she muttered. "Don't get any wetter than you have to. Get your duffel."

She ran inside to use her cell phone, and soon Seth was inside, too.

Her AAA membership came in handy. Seth assured her she could get dressed for dinner and he'd wait for the tow truck.

An hour later, her Camaro was being dragged from the driveway and Caprice was still running through the possibilities of who could have damaged her tires. She was having the car towed to Don Rodriguez's garage and body shop. He'd become an acquaintance during her last murder investigation. When he took care of her car tomorrow, he'd tell her exactly what had happened to those tires. She had his cell number and called him before she showered. He promised her he knew exactly what kind of tires to put on that Camaro and he'd give her a report the next day.

Seth had already taken Lady outside by the time Caprice dressed. He also changed his clothing and looked amazingly handsome in the white shirt and tie. As they drove to the B and B, which was in the country, she filled him in on what had happened with Alanna Goodwin and Ace. When she was finished, they'd arrived in the parking lot by the bed-and-breakfast, and the rain had almost stopped.

"Why didn't you tell me about any of this in our e-mails?" he asked after turning off the ignition.

"Because it was complicated, and one event just seemed to snowball into the next."

"That happens when you investigate a murder," he said soberly.

"I suppose so."

He said, "Stay put and I'll come around and get you. It's still drizzling a bit. We'll take the umbrella inside just in case it pours again."

Caprice didn't argue. She wondered if Seth had wished she'd shared the murder investigation with him. But it wasn't as if he had time to really study it with her. It wasn't as if he had time to solve the puzzle with her.

Seth hung his arm around Caprice's shoulders as they took the flagstone path around to the front entrance of the B and B. They were greeted by owner and manager Holly Swope, who was dressed all in purple. Caprice only had a passing acquaintance with Holly from Chamber of Commerce dinners and breakfast meetings. Nikki knew her better. Before the B and B had opened the restaurant, Nikki had catered events there.

Holly was about five-two, with close-cropped black hair and beautiful blue eyes. Older than Caprice, she was also single and devoted all of her time and attention to the bed-and-breakfast. The Purple Iris had gotten its name from the stained-glass windows of irises—one in the foyer, and the other on the landing that led to the rooms upstairs. Of course, the rooms were all done in iris motifs and the flower beds outside were filled with irises of every shape and color. In the spring, the beds were magnificent and some of the irises were even reblooming.

Holly and Caprice exchanged greetings, and Caprice introduced Seth. Holly checked her list. "Dr. Randolph, you called this morning and asked for our best table. I'm happy to say it was free." She picked up two leather-bound menus from the desk. "Follow me and I'll show you to it."

Caprice hadn't been in the restaurant since it opened. She smiled at the lilac-colored drapes, yellow-and-purple pin-striped wallpaper, framed iris prints, and metal sculptures. The tables were covered with white linens, and the glassware and silverware sparkled under white enamel and crystal chandeliers.

"This is charming," she said to Holly as Seth seated her and Holly handed them both menus.

"It was a huge investment for me," Holly admitted. "But the restaurant has really enhanced the bed-and-breakfast. We're drawing clients from Washington and Baltimore, as well as Harrisburg. Who knows? With the

Chamber of Commerce's efforts to draw more business to Kismet, we might become a tourist town."

"I haven't been to a Chamber meeting for a while," Caprice said.

"You should come," Holly encouraged her. "Changes are afoot. We have a tourism committee now. I'm thinking of hosting the next breakfast meeting right here. Watch for the date in your e-mail."

Once Holly had left, Caprice was about to open her menu, when Seth covered her hand with his. "I'm worried about your tires being damaged. Do you think you should call the cops?"

She sighed. "If I tell Detective Carstead, then he's going to ask whose feathers I might have ruffled."

"Maybe you should tell him *exactly* whose feathers you ruffled. It sounds as if this Len character could be dangerous, especially if he did steal Ace's guitars."

"If Don confirms that someone slashed my tires, I'll call him."

Seth squeezed her hand. "I don't want anything to happen to you."

"I don't want anything to happen to me, either. I'll be careful. I'll tell Detective Carstead anything I find out that's important."

She was about to open her menu again, but Seth tapped the bracelet he'd given her, which she'd worn tonight. "I'm glad to see you're wearing this."

"I usually do," she said honestly. "It reminds me of Valentine's Day, our dance, our talk until three." Actually, they'd kissed more than talked.

"I have something to ask you," Seth said. "It's one of the reasons I wanted to see you."

Caprice suddenly felt breathless. "You couldn't ask in an e-mail or over the phone?"

He shook his head. "I've kept track of your house

stagings, and when they're scheduled. You don't have one next weekend, right?"

No, she didn't. For a very good reason. Her birthday was on Sunday and she usually spent it with her family or had dinner with friends. "Right," she answered. "No staging. Why do you ask?"

"I'd like you to drive to Virginia with me to meet my parents. I can pick you up Friday evening and we'll be back by Sunday afternoon. What do you say?"

There was only one thing she *could* say. She grinned at him. "Yes."

Caprice's evening with Seth seemed like a dream the following day as she arrived at Isaac Hobbs's antique shop with Lady . . . and a loaf of chocolate-coffee bread. Their dinner at the Purple Iris had lasted two hours! Afterward, they'd gone back to the house and discussed plans for the weekend. When he'd left, though, she'd felt . . . unsettled. Her relationship with Seth seemed like a relationship when she was with him. But when she wasn't, she wondered exactly what they shared except for conversation and kisses. Maybe spending a weekend with him would settle her feelings for him.

She entered Isaac's shop, letting the beauty of the past awe her. Isaac collected antiques as if they were more valuable than the prices he put on them. When she walked into Older and Better today, he was finishing up with a customer.

Caprice nodded to the older woman, who was carrying a carton with a milk glass lamp, as she passed her and exited the shop.

As soon as Caprice and Lady approached the cash

desk, Isaac gave her a wry smile. "You're on the hunt, aren't you? And not for anything I have in my shop."

"Just how do you know that?"

"I know you."

Part of Isaac's profession was noting details about any item he looked at—whether it was old, new, valuable, or not, and whether he was capable of reselling it.

"This is for you," she said, offering him the chocolate-coffee loaf.

He grinned. "New recipe?"

"Sure is. You're a great taste tester."

Isaac tucked the loaf under the counter. "I'll save this for dinner tonight."

As he sat in one of the chairs, Isaac noticed the bracelet she was wearing and pointed to it. "Very cute. Is that new?"

"Valentine's Day. Seth gave it to me."

"Oh, ho! You've gone beyond flowers. Just what does that mean?"

She felt herself blushing. This was Isaac. She could be honest with him. "I'm going to be meeting his family this coming weekend."

"Then things are getting serious."

"I don't know about that," she admitted. "He has so little time for us. When his fellowship ends, he could be off to another part of the country."

"Or he could come back here."

Instead of sniffing around the antique furniture as she sometimes did, Lady went around the desk to Isaac. She was after the treats he kept there for her.

As Isaac gave the canine a treat, Caprice thought about Seth and his future. He wasn't necessarily filled with ambition, but his work was all-important to him. If he decided trauma surgery was what he preferred, he'd want to be practicing in the best trauma center in the country. She knew that.

"Didn't you tell me Seth's dad is a GP?" Isaac asked.

"Yes. I'm nervous about meeting his parents."

"What do you have to be nervous about?"

"Maybe they won't like me, what I do. Maybe they'll think it's frivolous. Maybe they don't have a soft spot for animals. Maybe—"

"Do not 'maybe' yourself to death, Caprice. All you have to do is be yourself and you'll be fine."

That sounded exactly like the advice Nana would give her.

"Are you staying overnight?" Isaac asked.

"Yes. I guess I'll have to be the perfect houseguest."

"Or, just show them how much you care about Seth."

Again, that was advice her mom or Nana would give her.

"You should start an advice column or a blog."

Isaac laughed. "Anyone who reaches my age should have some life experience to share. The problem is, nobody listens. Now, why did you really come today?"

"I need a few crystal vases, but I also need information."

"Aha, just as I thought. What kind of information?"

"What's the best way to sell a valuable guitar?"

Isaac gestured to the coffeepot. "I just made a fresh one."

"Sounds good," she said, settling deeper into the captain's chair and getting comfortable on its red plaid cushion. Lady was already sitting by Isaac's foot.

After Isaac had given Lady another treat and poured two mugs of coffee, adding milk and sugar for Caprice, he sat across from her. "Are you talking a valuable guitar from a legitimate seller?"

"No, I'm talking about a stolen guitar."

"There are fences for that type of thing. That's what white-collar crime is all about. But for the highest offer, some type of auction would be best. Of course, we're not talking about an auction on eBay. It would have to be private and probably online. What kind of valuable guitar?"

She took her phone from her pocket and checked the notepad. "A 1936 Martin D-45 and a 1958 Gibson Les Paul Standard."

Isaac took a tablet from the counter and wrote down what she'd said. "Let me check around and I'll get back to you. I know a couple of people who can tell if anything like that's on the market."

"You're such an asset when I'm snooping."

"And you're such a reliable customer. I can always count on selling you something."

This time, she laughed. "Do you still have that antique garnet-and-pearl ring that I liked so much?"

"Yes, I do. It's sitting in a corner of my safe just waiting for you to buy it."

"I don't need it," she said with a sigh. "Maybe you should just put it back in your showcase."

"There's no hurry."

Maybe Isaac wasn't in a hurry to sell the ring, but she was in a hurry to solve this murder. She had the feeling that if she didn't, someone else could get hurt.

An hour later, Caprice considered one more errand before she met Juan and their client at the glass house. She wanted to visit her uncle Dom. Maybe she should stay out of it. Maybe she should let Nana and her parents and her uncle Dom settle everything themselves. But if she could see so clearly what was happening with Nana, maybe the others were too close to it to see it, too. She knew her mom and dad would be at work, and she was hoping she could catch her uncle in the privacy of their home. If he wasn't there, she'd visit Nana.

Caprice mounted the steps to her childhood home, past the brown rope pillars, to the side door entrance. She knocked because sometimes the bell at this entrance didn't work. It had always been that way, one of many quirks about the house. Her dad had tried to fix it, but the doorbell seemed to have a mind of its own. Besides, usually she walked right in. But today, she wanted to alert her uncle she was there. The dynamics of a household changed when a houseguest was present.

Her uncle opened the door, looking tired and about ten years older than his age—until he saw her and Lady. Then his whole countenance brightened and his eyes even sparkled a bit.

"Hi, there." He stooped down to pet Lady, and she butted her head into his hand and rubbed against his ankle and shin.

"She really likes you," Caprice said.

"I really like her. I like all animals a whole lot. Once I get a place of my own again, I might get a dog or a cat or both." He stood and motioned her inside. "You didn't have to knock just because I'm here."

"I thought it was the polite thing to do."

He grimaced. "You certainly weren't disturbing me. I was just going over want ads and checking online job sites. One of the things Ronnie didn't manage to take in the divorce was my laptop computer, thank goodness."

In the large foyer, which led to the living room and dining room and the upstairs, Caprice unleashed Lady and asked her uncle, "Can we talk?"

"Sure. Come on in." He led her into the living room, where he took a seat in an old wooden rocker with an upholstered seat and back, which her mom had had redone in a pretty blue-and-tan stripe that matched the décor. Caprice curled up in the arm of the sofa as she had so many times before. Lady hopped up on the sofa beside her, and she petted her, knowing her mom wouldn't mind her on the couch. Pets were family, too.

"I'd like to talk to you about Nana," Caprice said.

At that topic of conversation, her uncle frowned. "She won't rest, but thank goodness she has that kitten you gave her. When Valentine curls up on her lap, at least she sits still for a while and watches her favorite program on TV."

"I'm not her doctor, and I'm certainly not a medical professional, but I think part of the problem, part of her condition, could be the stress and tension in the house between the two of you."

Her uncle looked thoughtful. "You think my coming back is what caused this."

"No, not your being here. I think she's glad you're here, that you came to your family for help. But I think the past has to be resolved between the two of you. Can you make amends with Nana so the tension in the house fades? Have you ever thought about apologizing for cutting her out of your life?"

The expression on her uncle's face was a mixture of annoyance, anger, and regret. "Maybe you shouldn't poke your good intentions into this, Caprice."

She knew sometimes she could be too blunt, but some occasions called for bluntness. She looked her uncle straight in the eye. "You cut Nana out of your life for twelve years. She's still hurting over that. She's still hurting over you. She's been in my life, *all* of my life. I care about her, Uncle Dom, and I care about you, too. Maybe you'd both feel better if you both gave a little."

He was silent a long time; then he finally said, "I fell in love with the wrong woman."

"It happens," Caprice responded softly. "But that doesn't mean one mistake has to become three or four or five."

"I should have married someone my mother would approve of."

"I don't think Nana wanted you to marry someone for *her,* but someone who would be the best for *you.*"

He gave a mirthless laugh. "Ronnie wasn't the best for me."

"Can you tell Nana that?"

When Caprice saw how hard that conversation would be for him, she suggested, "Can you just think about what I've said?"

He gave a resigned sigh, and then he patted her hand. "I'll think about it."

What more could she ask for?

Chapter Fourteen

It was finally spring.

At least that's what the weather felt like in the morning when Caprice took Lady for a walk.

The birds were chirping and the trees budded with green—elms and maples and poplars, too. She thought her street was one of the prettiest in Kismet, but, of course, she was prejudiced.

As Caprice and Lady neared home after their walk, she spotted Dulcina carrying bags of groceries from her car to her front door.

After crossing the street, Caprice called to Dulcina so she wouldn't startle her by coming up behind her.

Her neighbor opened her front door and then turned to greet her. "Good morning. Isn't it a beautiful one? This kind of day reminds me winter doesn't last forever. Just give me a minute to take these grocery bags to the kitchen, and then I'll give Lady the attention she deserves. Maybe one of those treats she likes so much, too. I picked up the peanut butter and bacon ones at Perky Paws."

Caprice laughed. "She'll want to live with you if you buy her those."

Once in Dulcina's house, Caprice unleashed Lady and they followed her neighbor to the kitchen. Sun streamed in from the adjacent glass-enclosed room as well as from the window over the sink. Dulcina wore a smile as she went to a canister she kept on the counter, detached the lid, and took out a cookie treat. It looked as good as any cookie Caprice could make.

Lady stood on her hind legs, her paws in the air.

"You don't have to beg," Dulcina said. "Here you go."

Lady took the treat in her mouth, then hunkered down on the floor with it, positioning it between her paws. She took a dainty bite, then looked up at Caprice.

"I guess you're going to make it last."

Lady gave a little bark as if to say, *You bet I am.*

"Coffee?" Dulcina asked.

"Sure. You know I can't pass up a cup of your coffee."

"Then you should get one of these machines," Dulcina added.

"I don't know. I did see one that uses a carafe or you can do the individual pods. It's tempting."

"When you have a man living with you, you'll want to be able to make a pot."

"Who says I'm going to have a man living with me?"

"You told me about the flowers Dr. Randolph sent and the bracelet he gave you. He cares."

"He asked me to go to Virginia with him this weekend to meet his family. Talk about nervous. I really don't know much about them. His father's a doctor and his mother's a nurse in his dad's office. And that's about all I know."

"Can't you give him the third degree in a few e-mails?"

"He won't have time to answer."

"That time thing is a real issue with you, isn't it?"

"I have this philosophy," Caprice explained. "It comes from something my dad once told me. My guess is he got it from Nana, because it sounds like similar advice she's given me. Anyway, he says no matter how busy you are, no matter what you make time for, you make time for what matters most to you. And that's true for me. Getting Mirabelle settled in my house is as important to me as the new client who has a house staging."

"So you take care of Mirabelle first," Dulcina guessed.

"I do. She's been removed from a life she knew and now she's in new surroundings with other animals. She doesn't know if she likes Sophia, let alone Lady, so Mirabelle is getting my attention. And as far as work, it's getting done."

Dulcina said, "I agree we make time for what we consider most important. You're nervous about the weekend. I'm nervous about tonight." She motioned to the groceries. "I'm going to be cooking for Rod and his daughters. He's finally going to introduce me to them. I'm so excited about it. I want to spend time with them."

Time seemed to be one commodity Seth didn't have. Would he ever?

"Talking about what's important to you—" Dulcina put a coffee pod in the machine, then inserted a mug under it. "While you're sipping coffee, you can tell me all about this Mirabelle."

"She's the sweetest cat," Caprice said with a sigh.

"Are you keeping her?"

"I'm not sure. If she and Sophia become friends, I might."

"Cats aren't much different from humans. Harmony will take time. They'll figure out their relationship eventually. Besides, that poor animal probably needs a lot of loving after having Alanna Goodwin for an owner."

"You know something about Alanna's life?"

"More about her personality than her life."

Everyone in Kismet knew Alanna by sight. She made sure of that with her photo in the newspaper all the time.

"Before Christmas, I went to the Blue Moon Grille for dinner with a friend. Alanna and a younger man were having dinner there and they looked very chummy. After dinner arrived, Alanna had a fit and said her chicken was too done. She sent it back. The man simply looked embarrassed."

"But you don't know who the man was? Can you describe him?"

"Oh, sure. He was good-looking, taller than Alanna, at least five years younger. He was solicitous of her. I could tell by the way he leaned toward her and touched her hand."

Caprice wondered if that man could have been Archer Ford.

As she sipped coffee with Dulcina and thought about Archer, she suspected there were secrets to be dug out, and she might as well be the one to do the digging.

Caprice and Dulcina were chatting when Caprice's cell phone played.

Dulcina said, "I don't mind if you take it. I'll make us another cup of coffee."

Caprice knew she really should get going, but sometimes she sensed Dulcina was lonely. Another fifteen minutes of conversation wouldn't put her day too far behind.

After she saw Isaac's face on the phone screen, she answered. "Hi, Isaac. Did you find out anything?"

"I found out what the guitars are worth," he responded quickly. "Even beat my estimation. The Martin is worth three hundred twenty thousand to four hundred thousand dollars, and the Les Paul ranges from three hundred thousand to three hundred seventy-five thousand dollars."

"Wow," Caprice said.

"Double wow. That could fund my retirement."

"Did you discover anything about auctions for guitars?"

"I fished around online and accessed sites of some of the private auctioneers who travel down a gray road."

"What does that mean?"

"That means their customers don't care particularly where the merchandise comes from. They just want to own it. One of the auctioneers has a Martin listed for the beginning of May."

Caprice considered whether she should send this information Detective Carstead's way. After his attitude the last time she spoke with him, she was tempted not to.

"Thank you, Isaac. The information could come in handy. I guess I can't get into these sites to look around."

"No, not unless you use a hacker. I have creds as an antique dealer. That's why they let me in. They think I might see something a client wants. I'll keep trolling the sites and maybe something else will pop up. If Ace's band member stole those guitars, he might have his own fence. From his connections in L.A. or anywhere, he could know someone who wants those guitars."

"And he'd be that much richer."

"He would. If he's been a two-bit keyboard player up until now, that money could change his life."

"A trip to South America and retirement at a little village where he doesn't have to pay taxes," Caprice surmised.

"Sometimes I think that's not a bad idea."

"Isaac, you'd never do that."

"Are you saying I'm too stodgy to find another life?"

"No. I'm saying you like connections. You wouldn't want to leave old friends . . . or your shop."

She heard him give a resigned sigh.

"I guess my days of dreaming of becoming a beach bum are gone."

"You could still go to the beach."

He laughed. "Ever the optimist. I'll give you a call if I find out anything else."

"Thank you," she said again, and ended the call.

Could Len run away with over five hundred thousand dollars? It was a definite possibility.

Most of the afternoon, as Caprice worked in her home office, she was debating whether or not to call Detective Carstead about the guitar information, and then she received a call from Don Rodriguez, confirming her tires had been slashed. Still, the slashed tires could have been a kid's prank.

But what if it hadn't been a kid's prank?

What if someone didn't want her asking any more questions? What if someone thought she knew too much already?

Just what did she know?

Not nearly enough.

After the afternoon at her computer, she decided exercise, meaning a swim at Shape Up, could do her a lot of good. Often while she swam, she sorted her thoughts. Often while she swam, a new idea popped up that she could act on.

However, as she stopped at Perky Paws to pick up dog and cat food on her way to the gym, as she drove through downtown Kismet and approached the police station, guilt weighed her down. She had told Detective Carstead she'd keep him informed, so that's what she'd do.

She'd stop in. If he wasn't there, she'd put what she knew in her back pocket and leave him a voice mail.

When she approached the desk, she could tell the officer there recognized her. His name tag read, OFFICER JOHN PLATT, and she'd noticed him at several of the crime scenes she'd had the misfortune to witness.

"Is Detective Carstead in?" she asked.

"Do you have an appointment?" he responded.

"No, but I do have some information he might want."

The officer picked up the phone and pressed the button. A few seconds later, he said, "Miss De Luca's here. She says she has information for you. What would you like me to do?"

He hung up the phone moments later. "He'll be right out."

Detective Carstead was frowning when he met her at the desk. "You could have left me a message."

"I could have, but I was driving by."

He motioned her to follow him. "Come on back. You know the way."

Yes, she did.

After they were seated in his office, he looked her up and down, from her striped blouse, with its Peter Pan collar, to her high-waisted, grass green slacks, which matched one of the stripes in the blouse. She just felt a fifties-style outfit suited her today.

She wasn't too sure the detective thought so, because he frowned again. "So, what do you have for me?"

"My tires were slashed."

His eyes widened a little at that. "When was this?"

"Sunday. A friend came over and he told me my tires looked odd. When we examined them, we saw the back two were flat. Today Don Rodriguez confirmed they'd been slashed."

"Why didn't you call me then?"

"Because we were on our way to dinner and I didn't know for sure."

Detective Carstead looked like he was about to erupt.

"Don't go ballistic on me. It was pouring down rain. There was nothing you could do. I didn't want to go through the hassle of filing a police report. I still don't. I'm just telling you what happened."

He eyed her suspiciously. "And what had you been doing on Sunday before this happened?"

She'd been afraid he'd ask that. She gave a little shrug. "I visited Len Lowery, Ace Richland's keyboard player."

"And?" Detective Carstead prompted.

"And . . . he wasn't friendly. And I practically accused him of stealing the guitars."

Carstead started shaking his head. "I told you, if you got in the way of this investigation, you could end up in jail."

"I'm not in the way. Ace is probably still your prime suspect, right?"

"No comment."

"You want me to spill everything, but you don't want to tell me anything. All right, I'll spill some more. Both guitars are valuable and together could be worth over five hundred thousand dollars. There are online auctions with dealers who don't walk the straight and narrow. One of them has a Martin for sale at the beginning of May."

"And you know this how?" Carstead's tone told her not to mess around with him.

"I know this because I asked Isaac Hobbs to investigate a little. He gets around on the auction sites. They let him in because he's an antique dealer."

"I never thought of Hobbs," Carstead admitted. "I

have an officer searching auction sites, but I need to find the underground ones."

"I don't know if Isaac would help you."

"But he'd help *you*?"

"We're friends."

"I'm beginning to think you have too many friends in Kismet, friends who could give you the wrong information."

Caprice stood. "Kismet is a small-enough town that there aren't many degrees of separation. One person knows someone who knows someone else. I came to tell you what I know. Now I've done that. Good afternoon, Detective Carstead."

She'd made it to the door when Carstead warned, "You could get hurt."

"I'll be careful. I won't intentionally put myself in danger."

"Your intentions have nothing to do with it. A murderer doesn't care about your intentions, good or bad." He sighed. "I've learned to respect the information you collect. If you find out anything else, let me know . . . im-me-di-ate-ly." He drew out the last word so she got his message.

"Got it," she said with a nod, and left his office. She heard him mumble something about contrary females, but she kept walking. She'd done her duty and she'd keep doing her duty.

But now she needed that swim.

Caprice's swim at Shape Up was therapeutic. She tried to blank her mind while she swam laps and experienced the push of the water against her limbs, the beat of her heart, the fulfilling experience of working her muscles. Swimming was usually like that for her. That's why it was the only exercise she actually enjoyed.

The one thing she didn't like about it was the scent of chlorine. Everything smelled like it when she was finished. Some days, especially in warm weather, she waited to shower when she got home. But today, she just wanted the chemical off her skin and out of her hair.

She couldn't keep all of her thoughts at bay while she dried her hair with one of the facility's dryers and brushed through it. The shower area of the women's locker room was separate from the lockers. She was the only one using it right now. She could hear women's voices in the other section, but she didn't pay much attention.

She did pay attention to the thoughts that came and went, but she could no longer push away. Mostly, they were about her visit to Seth's family and what it was going to be like. She was usually a roll-with-the-punches kind of girl. This time, she wasn't.

Why was that? Because too much was riding on the experience? She was looking forward to the weekend with Seth with too much anticipation? Or maybe it was just her sixth sense telling her something she didn't want to hear?

After she dressed, she pulled Seth's bracelet from her purse. She studied it for a few moments, looking at each little charm. The kitten, the flower, and the peace sign, plus the colorful beads, always made her smile. Now it jingled as she slipped it on her wrist and fastened it. She picked up her duffel bag and left the locker room.

She automatically glanced around the exercise area. She often saw some of her clients here . . . or friends. Even her brother had taken out a membership, but he usually worked out in the late evening or early morning.

To her surprise, over in a corner near the floor mats, she spotted Twyla. Not hesitating, she headed her way. Twyla was using one of the exercise balls to stretch her back. She was stretched over the red ball, her hands on the floor on one side, her feet on the floor on the other.

Caprice set her duffel on the floor, not wanting to interrupt.

Twyla opened her eyes and saw her—upside down, grant you, but apparently she recognized her.

"Hi, Caprice."

Caprice didn't know how Twyla could talk upside down. She knew she probably wouldn't be able to do it. But then she'd never tried the exercise ball.

Twyla rolled off the ball and sat in a cross-legged position on the mat, looking up. "This place is great."

"You decided to join?" Caprice asked, wondering if Twyla had made the decision to stay in Kismet.

"I took out a temporary membership. I can pay week by week. It fits for now. It will be a big decision whether I want to move here or not. I'm just not sure. Actually, I'd like to go over the pros and cons with you, if you wouldn't mind—sell Alanna's house or keep it. By the way, how's Mirabelle doing?"

"She's settling in, not hiding nearly as much. She and Lady get along fine, and Mirabelle and Sophia are sleeping in the same room together now. That's definite progress. When would you like me to stop by to talk about the house?"

"How about tomorrow afternoon? Would that suit you? I'm going to spend some time here now, and I have an appointment with Alanna's lawyer later."

"Tomorrow afternoon would suit just fine." Caprice picked up her duffel bag. "Have a good workout."

Twyla squatted onto the exercise ball again. "I will. See you tomorrow."

The following afternoon, Nikki took Caprice to the body shop to pick up her Camaro. Afterward, Caprice drove to White Pillars, armed with a list of pros and cons. She'd brought along facts about Kismet and the surrounding area, and the advantages of living in south central Pennsylvania. She was a neutral party here. She'd made her fee on the staging, so whether Twyla sold or didn't sell White Pillars didn't really matter to her. She was glad she had this meeting today. When she was sitting at her computer, designing, or in between phone calls, she thought too much about Seth and the upcoming weekend.

She parked in the driveway and hurried up to the front door of the mansion. To her surprise, the huge white door was hanging open. Yes, Twyla was expecting her, but that seemed a little unusual.

She called inside. "Twyla?"

There was no answer. She could try to call her from her cell, but that was silly. There was no reason she couldn't step inside that luscious foyer and yell.

But when she stepped inside the foyer, the tall vase usually on the center table was pushed to one side. And when she peered into the living room . . .

There was Twyla, lying on the floor; a crock of some kind had shattered into several pieces, which were scattered nearby.

Oh no, Alanna's sister couldn't be dead, could she?

Caprice raced to her. As she sank down on her knees beside Twyla, the woman moaned. Thank goodness.

Caprice slid her hand along Twyla's cheek. "Twyla?"

Caprice could see an abrasion on the side of Twyla's

head, which was bleeding. *If that crock had had a rough edge . . .*

Twyla's eyes fluttered open and it took her a moment to focus. When she saw Caprice, she tried to sit up.

"Stay put," Caprice warned her. "I should call the paramedics."

"I don't want to go to the hospital."

"They could treat you right here."

Twyla had already come to a sitting position and was shaking her head. That caused her to close her eyes and wince.

She pointed to the nearby antique pie safe, its doors hanging wide open. "There was a man in a ski mask and gloves stealing something from there."

Just what had been worth stealing in Alanna Goodwin's antique pie safe?

Chapter Fifteen

"You were unconscious, Twyla. That's not something to ignore," Caprice reminded her as she took the handkerchief Nana had advised her to always carry and pressed it against Twyla's wound.

Twyla held it, while with a tissue Caprice wiped away the blood that had trickled down the side of Alanna's sister's face. "I do think we should call the police," Twyla said in a thready voice.

They both looked toward the pie safe.

"Do you have any idea of what was in there?" Caprice asked.

Twyla shook her head carefully this time. "No. But the man was removing papers when I spotted him."

"How could you tell the burglar was a man?"

"It was his build and height."

"What kind of papers did he take?"

"I don't know," Twyla responded. "They were folded up. There's so much to sort through in this house that I haven't even gotten to the living room."

Caprice desperately wanted to go look in the pie safe, but she knew she shouldn't touch anything. Or even move around. Evidence could be found anywhere.

"I'll call Detective Carstead," she agreed. "But I know he'll dispatch the paramedics, too. You need them."

This time, Twyla closed her eyes and murmured, "Go ahead. I have a headache that probably won't quit any time soon."

Caprice called Carstead's cell number. To her relief, he answered. She knew how Carstead worked and she didn't gloss over anything. She told him, "I found Twyla Horton unconscious on the floor in the living room at White Pillars. A man in a ski mask knocked her out when she found him pulling papers from a pie safe. We're still in the living room, sitting on the floor where I found her, and we won't move if you or the para-medics can get here in a decent amount of time."

"I'll be there with a patrol car in five minutes," he assured her. "The medics will be right behind me."

Caprice figured it would be more like ten minutes, but the detective must have used a siren and lights be-cause it wasn't much past five minutes when he strode in the front door. At the same time, she heard the am-bulance bleeping a sound as it pulled up in front of the property.

Caprice had helped Twyla prop herself against the sofa, but she looked pale and shaky. From what Caprice had seen, Twyla's wound looked jagged and deep and might need stitches.

After Carstead took in the scene at a glance, he crossed to Twyla and asked, "What happened?"

"I was upstairs," Twyla responded. "Stupidly, I didn't have the alarm turned on. I had just come in and was changing clothes for my meeting with Caprice."

"Why were you two having a meeting?" Carstead asked.

Caprice answered this time. "Twyla has to decide whether or not she's going to sell the house. That's what we were going to talk about. But when I arrived, the front door was open and I found Twyla in here, on the floor."

Carstead studied the floor as if he was looking for footprints or some evidence of the man's arrival and departure.

He studied the pie safe. "From what I understand, you had an open house here before Mrs. Goodwin was murdered. About how many people attended?"

"Easily fifty," Caprice answered.

"And we had a reception here after the funeral," Twyla told him.

"Another fifty?" he inquired with his brow creasing.

Twyla and Caprice both nodded.

"Did you have a cleaning service come in afterward?"

Still holding the handkerchief to her wound, Twyla shook her head. "No. I just didn't want to be . . . bothered. Alanna's regular cleaning service was going to start again next week. I had to sign a new contract with them in my name."

Suddenly the clatter of a gurney broke their conversation. Two paramedics rushed to Twyla and began their examination, first taking vital signs, then asking her questions and checking her wound.

As they worked, Detective Carstead scanned the whole room again and his focus targeted the foyer.

"I only saw one thing amiss when I came in," Caprice told him. "The vase that usually sits on that table out there was pushed off center."

"As if someone running past it elbowed or bumped it?" Carstead asked.

"That would be my guess," Caprice agreed.

"We'll check it for prints. But if the intruder wore gloves, I doubt if we'll find anything useful."

He walked toward the pie safe, took a pair of latex gloves from his pocket, and slipped them on. After a moment of examining the open door, he peered into the shelved interior, spending a good long time examining the inside.

Taking a penlight from his pocket, he shone it into the shelves then, obviously finding something notable, Carstead took out his mobile unit, pressed a button, and said, "Thompkins, bring in an evidence bag. Any sign of anybody out there?"

As he listened, Caprice saw him frown.

"A motorcycle, maybe?" he asked. "Good catch. The evidence techs will be here as soon as they can. Let Monroe guard the scene. You bring in the bag."

Less than a minute later, a patrol officer had come in with a brown paper evidence bag and tag. Carstead extracted a small tool kit from his jacket pocket and pulled out what looked like forceps.

As Caprice watched, he used them to draw out whatever was in the back of the pie safe.

After he pulled out a small scrap of paper, he studied it. "Whatever papers were in there must have caught on the rough back edge of the shelf." He held a good-sized corner in the forceps. "My mother made me take piano lessons when I was a kid. I even had a crack at writing music. That's what this looks like."

"Can I take a closer look?" Caprice asked.

"Why should I let you do that?" Carstead asked.

She had a very good reason. "Because Ace often handwrites songs in his early stages of composing. I've seen the notebook he keeps."

Carstead thought it over. "All right. But don't touch it. Don't breathe on it."

Of course, she knew better not to touch it or breathe on it. She simply stared at the notes and the handwritten words under the music staff. The scrawl looked very much like the handwriting she'd seen in Ace's notebook. Had someone stolen his music, as well as his guitars? Had it been Len? And since it was in Alanna's house, had Alanna known about it? Maybe instigated the theft?

Caprice certainly didn't want to say that out loud near Twyla. Nevertheless, her gaze met Carstead's and she guessed he knew what she was thinking.

She gave a nod that she was finished looking, and he dropped the piece of sheet music into the evidence bag.

Once again, Carstead peered into the pie safe, but apparently found nothing else of importance. After he handed the bag to Officer Thompkins and the patrolman left, Carstead crossed to Twyla, who was now lying on the gurney.

"You'll probably be at the hospital for hours. That should give us enough time to process the scene." He took a card from his pocket and handed it to her. "When you're through in the ER, call me to make sure the forensics unit is finished here."

Twyla took the card, but looked a bit lost. "My purse is in the kitchen."

"I'll get it," Caprice offered. "And I'll go with you to the hospital. You'll need a ride when you're finished."

"I don't want to impose . . . ," Twyla began.

But Caprice brushed her concern away. "You're not imposing. I brought my laptop along. I can work while I wait." And she'd call her uncle to see if he could puppysit, since Detective Carstead was possibly right and Twyla wouldn't be coming home for a few hours.

This day had definitely turned out differently than she'd expected! Differently than Twyla had expected, too. Her whole ordeal in Kismet had been traumatic. Caprice could certainly understand if she didn't want to keep this house and the bad memories associated with it.

The ER physician decided to admit Twyla and keep an eye on her overnight. He ordered a CT scan and other tests. Twyla insisted Caprice not wait around and promised to call her later with an update. Caprice assured her she would pick her up the following day and return her to White Pillars.

On the way home, Caprice gave Ace a call and they decided to meet at his house to talk in person. When she asked if she could bring Lady, Ace responded, "You don't even have to ask."

After thanking her uncle for petsitting and giving him a loaf of pepperoni-cheddar bread to take along, Caprice drove her van out of town along the long expanse of mostly deserted road. Just what did Detective Carstead think about the sheet music?

No way to know what was in the detective's head.

Mrs. Wannamaker let Caprice and Lady inside at Ace's house. She said, "Mr. Richland's in his den. He was pretty upset when that detective left. Maybe you can calm him down."

She didn't know about calming him down, but maybe together they could figure out exactly what was going on.

As Caprice followed the housekeeper to Ace's den, Lady trotted along beside her. When they reached the room where Ace spent much of his time while he was here, she spotted him pacing.

She said, "You're going to wear out the shine on those beautiful hardwood floors."

He stopped and turned.

"I didn't think I'd have to announce her," Mrs. Wannamaker said.

"No, Caprice announces herself."

Lady ran toward Ace. With a wry expression of resignation mixed with pleasure, Ace crouched down to give the dog a good rubdown. Lady wriggled and rolled over, but then she sat back on her haunches and stared up at Ace. After a moment, she licked his face.

Caprice's heart always warmed at how intuitive animals could be. Just by the vibrations in the room, Lady knew Ace was upset, and she was trying to comfort him. Caprice silently sent the message, *Good dog, Lady. You're such a good dog.*

Ace looked as if Lady's kindness might have choked him up a bit. When he stood, he cleared his throat. "Have a seat."

"Shall I bring coffee?" Mrs. Wannamaker asked.

"Good and dark," Ace said. Then he glanced at Caprice. "Double cream and sugar in hers. Maybe you can bring a couple of Brindle's treats for Lady, too."

The housekeeper exited the room without a word, knowing exactly what to do.

Caprice sat in the comfy, butter-soft leather club chair across from Ace. "So Detective Carstead was here?"

"Oh yes. What in the blazes happened? He asked me a lot of questions and gave me the minimum amount of information. Something about Twyla Horton having been assaulted at White Pillars and someone had stolen sheet music. Turns out it was *my* sheet music."

"He showed you a torn piece?" Caprice asked.

"Yes, he did. I checked my binder. Six songs were missing. I was still working on them."

"How many people know about that binder?"

Ace thought about that. "My band members know, my agent, any production people I bring in. Mrs. Wannamaker knows about it . . . and Marsha and Trista."

"Did Alanna know about it?"

Ace was silent for a few moments. Lady curled up at his feet and leaned her head over his shoe. There was that comfort again.

Ace finally answered, "Yes, she knew about it."

"Where do you keep the binder? In here?" This was his major headquarters when working from home other than his production area in the basement.

"No, I don't keep it in here."

She knew from the tone of Ace's voice what was coming. "Where?" she prompted.

"I keep it in a dresser drawer in my bedroom."

"And how many people know that?"

He closed his eyes for a moment. "My housekeeper . . . and Alanna knew. She also knew I haven't written or worked on new songs lately. I've been too busy polishing what I'm going to perform on tour."

"Ace, I'm sorry."

"Because you don't think my housekeeper stole them?" he inquired with some irritation as he ran his hand over his face. "Of course, she didn't. Alanna was in cahoots with Len in a stupid plot that I don't understand. Why would she steal my sheet music?"

"Maybe to give it to Len in exchange for sabotaging your tour?"

"She had enough money to give him."

"My guess is that she was going to give him money, too, but he might have demanded more. Like the chance to make it big with music *you* wrote. If Alanna wanted you to quit your tour and stay home with her, she'd adhere to Len's demands to accomplish that."

"Did she think I wouldn't miss the music?"

"Maybe she thought you wouldn't return to the binder for a while. Maybe she thought because you were so busy, and would be even busier planning a wedding and moving her in, you wouldn't notice. On

the other hand, maybe she was going to make copies
and put them back and just didn't have time to do that."

"So if Len stole them and eventually sold the songs
or had them produced, did he think I wouldn't notice?
I would have sued someone!"

"Not if Len changed them just enough. It could have
come down to your word against his. He could even
claim he coauthored them."

Ace kept shaking his head as if he couldn't believe
any of it. "This is like some crazy nightmare. If Len
stole that music, he obviously knew Alanna had it and
where she kept it."

"I don't know the answer to that one. It's possible
Alanna told him where she kept them, like a carrot on
a stick. Then when he accomplished what she wanted,
she'd hand them over."

"Maybe I can believe this of Len Lowery. After all,
I really didn't know him well. I only did a surface back-
ground check. But Alanna?" Ace looked devastated.
"Carstead didn't tell me where the music was hidden.
I suppose you aren't supposed to tell me, either?"

"Probably not."

He nodded. "He did tell me one thing, though.
There's a BOLO out on Len Lowery and his vehicle. It
shouldn't be too long before they bring him in for questioning. If he murdered Alanna—"

Ace looked as if he'd strangle the man with his bare
hands. Caprice just hoped the police got hold of Len
before Ace ever could.

The following day as Lady bounded into Nana's
small suite, Caprice saw her dog stop short as if she had
put on the brakes. Then she realized why.

Nana laughed. "She's still not sure of Valentine

being here. It's like Lady is always surprised to find a pip-squeak of a gray tabby."

The three-month-old kitten had been a big surprise one cold night when Caprice had found her in her backyard . . . or rather Lady had. The kitten had only been six weeks old then. When Caprice had told Nana about her, Nana had decided she might like a pet. And she did. Valentine entertained her, got her to smile a lot more often, and kept her company all day and night. The kitten was a cuddler, and that was just what Nana had needed.

Seeing Valentine, Lady sat and stretched out her front paws. The kitten ran up to her, did a little sideways dance in front of her, then bumped her nose against Lady's. Lady didn't react much, just sniffed Valentine whenever she got within sniffing distance. Valentine then ran to the cat condo Nana had purchased for her, that sat at the window. She perched up on the top shelf.

Lady chased after her and sat beneath the condo, gazing up.

"They'll entertain each other," Nana said. "Would you like a cup of tea and biscotti?"

"You know I would," Caprice assured Nana, following her to the kitchen. "So, how are you feeling?"

"Is that why you stopped by? So you can hover over me like everybody else?"

"No hovering. I'm just hoping you're feeling better."

As Nana put filtered water into the teakettle and settled the kettle on the stove to heat, she didn't speak. But then she turned and eyed Caprice studiously. "A little birdie told me you visited Dom."

"What little birdie was that?" Caprice wondered who the tattletale could be. No one else had been home when she'd visited her uncle.

"Our neighbor next door. She's my age, lives alone,

and we check on each other. She knows your car and van, of course. She said you stopped by."

"I just wanted to catch up with him," Caprice said vaguely.

"Well, catching up must have worked, because Dom and I had a talk—a very long talk."

Actually, Caprice didn't want to pry. If Nana wanted to tell her what they talked about, she would.

She found the can of biscotti Nana kept on the counter. It was a pretty decorative canister with tulips painted on the lid. She took a few biscotti out and placed them on a plate. Then she set the plate on the small table for two.

Seeing the water was ready for the tea, Nana poured it into a white porcelain teapot decorated with roses.

While the tea steeped, Nana sat across from her. Finally she confided, "Dom apologized for not staying in touch, for being foolish because of love."

Nana was silent again, but then pushed the plate of biscotti across to Caprice. "Eat," she directed.

Caprice took a cookie and bit into the soft biscuit with the lemon icing. Nana's biscotti weren't like the twice-baked ones most people thought of as biscotti. These had a soft texture and melted in her mouth.

Nana said, "I suppose I can understand how he felt. Love makes everyone do foolish things."

"You included?" Caprice asked.

Nana shrugged. "I would have followed your grandfather anywhere. I would have stood by him even if the barbershop hadn't been successful. I would have done anything for him."

"And you did." Caprice remembered how Nana had made a loving home, how as a couple her grandparents had been strong and loving, affectionate and unified—a wonderful example of marriage.

"So you're feeling better about Uncle Dominic?"

"I've forgiven him. Holding on to hurt wasn't hurting anybody but me. I could see that, but I didn't know what to do about it. Our talk settled things." She reached over and took Caprice's hand. "So thank you for your visit, whatever you said."

Caprice felt a bit embarrassed. She didn't want thanks. "Time to pour the tea. What kind do we have today?"

"Bilberry. I know you didn't come here just to drink tea. What's on your mind?"

"Alanna Goodwin's murder is on my mind. I found Twyla Horton unconscious yesterday afternoon." The whole story spilled out as the contents of her mind and heart were wont to do whenever she talked to Nana. "Twyla's tests were okay and she's supposed to be discharged later. But what happened is puzzling. If Len murdered Alanna, why didn't he steal the sheet music then?"

"This case seems more complicated than any you've attempted to solve—stolen guitars, stolen sheet music, and an attempt to sabotage Ace's tour. It all seems to point to this keyboard player, doesn't it?"

"It seems to. But then there's Alanna's former lover, Barton's illegitimate son, Archer Ford. If Alanna was having an affair with him after Barton died, why did she suddenly drop him and start dating Ace?"

"Because Ace had more of what she wanted?" Nana asked.

Caprice wasn't exactly sure what that might be.

"Then there's Ace, who I suppose is still a suspect," Nana said. "Maybe Alanna was going to go back to Archer and Ace found out, and in a passionate rage killed her. After all, you said he has a short temper sometimes."

"Oh, Nana. I can't believe that of Ace. I just can't. I won't. He might have a short fuse now and then, but he has a good, kind heart. He could never hurt anyone."

"You said he broke Len Lowery's nose."

Caprice sighed. "He did, but he was provoked."

Nana arched a brow just as Caprice's cell phone played. Nana said, "Go ahead and answer it. I'll check on Lady and Valentine."

After Caprice fished her phone from her purse, she was astonished to see Seth's face. Her heart began to beat a worry rhythm.

"Hi, Seth. This is a surprise."

"I just have a few minutes," he said. "I'm sorry, but I have to cancel our plans for the weekend. I have a critical patient and I can't leave. I promise I'll make it up to you, and we'll visit my parents."

"I understand," Caprice said automatically, but as she said the words, she felt tears gathering in her eyes.

"I've got to go," Seth told her. "I'll be in touch soon."

A tear rolled down her cheek.

Nana took her by the shoulders. "What's wrong?"

Caprice dropped her phone onto the table. "Seth can't make it this weekend. He has a critical patient."

Nana gave her a huge hug. She asked, "Does he know your birthday is on Sunday?"

Caprice sniffled. "No. I didn't tell him yet."

Nana leaned back and said, "This is the life of a doctor, *tesorina mia*. Are you ready for that?"

Chapter Sixteen

The more Caprice thought about her wrecked weekend with Seth and his one-minute call—well, maybe two minutes—the more upset she got. She didn't know if she was upset with Seth, the situation, or herself for expecting too much. Nana had told her once that she shouldn't have expectations, but how could she not? How could a woman dream without expectations?

She couldn't fault Seth for wanting his career, for following his dream, for making his path in a profession he loved. But was there room for a woman beside him? More important, was there *time* for a woman beside him? Yes, this experience at Johns Hopkins was demanding in every way possible. But wouldn't his on-going career be demanding, too? Especially if he chose one in trauma medicine. Where would he end up? New York? Boston? Possibly Chicago, Portland, or L.A.?

His career was one thing. Their relationship was another. Was she as important to him as he could be to her? Flowers and gifts were wonderful. Seth was good at those. But time and commitment were even more important.

After Caprice took Lady home, they went on a walk.

A fine mist began to fall as she answered her cell phone when it played again. This time, the caller was Twyla. "Do you need me to pick you up?"

"No," Twyla said, sounding fatigued. "I'm back at White Pillars. I took a cab back. I didn't want to impose more."

Caprice wouldn't have minded. "How do you feel?"

"Tired. But all my tests checked out okay. When this headache lets up, I'll give you a call and we can have lunch or dinner."

"That sounds good."

Caprice pocketed her phone to protect it from the rain as she and Lady hurried back to the house. Sitting at her desk at a computer this afternoon wouldn't be helpful to her mind-set or her work. She'd think about her thirty-third birthday . . . and Seth.

After she settled Lady with her ball that dispensed treats, secure in the kitchen with the pet gates in place, she gave Mirabelle and Sophia petting attention and then went to her purse. After she pulled out the photo of a little girl that she'd found at Alanna's, she studied it. She Googled the dance studio on her phone and checked the hours. As she suspected, after-school slots for classes would be busy ones. It was time to elicit answers about Alanna and her past. Yes, Len was an obvious suspect, but she had a feeling there were a few suspects who weren't so obvious.

The dance studio was located in a strip shopping center in West York. The front of the studio was plate glass. Photographs of what Caprice supposed were dance recitals decorated that window. Professional shots of two girls, three girls, and up to fifteen girls were the subjects in each photograph. All wore different types of costumes from ballet to hip-hop to jazz.

As Caprice opened the door to step inside, she found

herself in a brightly colored reception area. The chairs were a bright royal blue and the side tables were pink. Pale yellow walls surrounded her. Several women sat in the waiting area perusing magazines. One held an electronic reader, and another was scrolling down her smartphone. The beats of music came from inside a studio and Caprice noted a line of women, probably mothers, watching a dance class through a Plexiglas partition.

The receptionist at the desk looked up at Caprice and smiled. "Can I help you?"

Suddenly a flood of little girls came pouring out of the doorway of the closest studio. Caprice wasn't exactly sure how to go about this, but she did know she wanted to talk to one of the teachers. These facilities usually had a head instructor and an assistant.

She extended her hand. "I'm Caprice De Luca. I have a concern about one of your students, and I wondered if I could talk to the instructor?"

The receptionist looked stumped for a moment as if she wasn't sure what to do.

Caprice handed her a business card.

The receptionist said, "Class just let out. Rhonda has about fifteen minutes, where she can catch her breath and down a bottle of water. Come on. I'll take you to her."

Mothers and girls had flowed from the studio and chatter emanated from the reception area. Caprice followed the receptionist into the now-empty studio and waited while the woman introduced her. "Rhonda, this is Caprice De Luca. She says she has a concern about one of the students." The assistant handed Caprice's business card to Rhonda.

The brunette, dressed in a leotard and leggings, with wavy hair arranged in a topknot, looked wary. "I can't talk to you about the students unless your name is on their card as a parent or an emergency contact."

The assistant glanced awkwardly from Caprice to Rhonda and then said, "I have to go back to the desk."

Caprice understood the rules at an establishment like this. They were set in place for the safety of the students. So she had to go about this in a way that didn't threaten anyone.

"May I show you a photo?" Caprice asked.

"No harm in that, I suppose," Rhonda agreed, but she crossed her arms over her chest. Caprice saw it for the defensive gesture that it was.

Before Caprice showed her the photo, she explained, "I'm looking into a murder, and I need information. Background often helps the police find new leads. I won't ask for anything you consider confidential."

Now Rhonda looked as if she relaxed a bit.

Pulling the photo from her macramé bag, Caprice handed it to the dance instructor. Although the teacher tried to keep her expression neutral, Caprice saw recognition in her eyes.

"I understand if you can't give me a name. But can you tell me if she's a student of yours? The name of your studio is stamped on the back."

"Then you've already guessed that she is."

"But I don't know if she's a student now or was in the past."

"This is a murder investigation and you're with the police?" Rhonda asked, still wary, still protecting her students.

"I'm not with the police," Caprice admitted honestly. "I have a friend who I believe is being wrongly suspected and questioned, so I'm trying to get to the bottom of the murder."

"You realize I can't tell you any specifics."

"I understand that."

After studying the photo and glancing toward the reception area, Rhonda relented. "I can tell you that this photo is a recent one. I can also tell you that this little girl and her mom will be coming in for the next class. You might recognize her among the students. If you do, that's not on me."

"I understand," Caprice said. "I *am* legit. You won't be sorry."

"Whose murder are we talking about?" Rhonda wanted to know.

"Alanna Goodwin in Kismet."

Rhonda's eyes widened. "And you know Ace Richland?" She guessed that was the suspect Caprice was talking about. "What happens in Kismet reaches York, too," she added. "I heard that community concert was pretty much a fiasco. Someone asked if Ace Richland killed her. Gossip about that travels fast. Do you really know him?"

"I do. As you can see from my card, I'm a home stager. I staged the house he bought. We've become friends since then."

"Is he as wild as they say?"

"He's not wild anymore, not in the sense you mean. Just as you won't talk about your students, I won't talk about my friends."

Rhonda looked less cautious and gave a little nod. "If you sit in the reception area, the students will soon start filing in."

"And I've taken up your break time."

"If I down a bottle of water, I'll be good to go until the next break. I love what I do."

Caprice smiled because she understood that. When she was staging a house, she could go all day without eating . . . without cooking . . . without stopping for a big breath. When you loved what you did, you became engrossed in it.

After Caprice thanked Rhonda again, she crossed to the reception area and took a seat. Most of them were empty now. Consulting her phone, she checked messages.

Two and then four and then two more little girls ran into the empty studio, some of the moms following. More children and parents flowed through the door. It wasn't long before Caprice spotted the child she was looking for. The girl was carrying a duffel bag, and Caprice could see the tag on it. She took out her phone and zoomed in, snapping a quick shot. The girl's name was Sherry Duncan.

After a brief exchange between mother and daughter, the mom gave Sherry a hug and a kiss on the forehead. Then Sherry went running off to join the others in the dance studio.

Before the woman took a seat, Caprice approached her. "Are you Sherry's mom?"

The woman looked concerned. "Yes, I am. Are you a new instructor? Is there a change in the schedule?"

"No, I'm not an instructor. Could we go over here to the corner and talk for a few minutes?"

The woman gave her a cautious look. There were other moms seated in the reception area now, but she seemed to make a decision and they crossed to a vending machine.

Caprice took out the photo again. "Are you Ms. Duncan?"

The mom's face was stoic. "Why do you want to know?"

"This is your daughter, correct?" Caprice asked, showing her the photo.

Finally the little girl's mom admitted, "It's Sherry's performance photo. How did you get it?"

"It was in Alanna Goodwin's desk."

Ms. Duncan paled considerably, her face almost going white. She asked, "Are you with the police?"

Caprice wished she could lie, but it just wasn't in her nature. "No, I'm not. But I'm helping a friend who cared about Alanna and is being questioned in connection with the murder. Can you tell me your connection to Alanna Goodwin?"

"No, I can't," the woman said adamantly.

"You can't, or you won't?"

"I can't *and* I won't."

Caprice took out another business card and handed it to Ms. Duncan. "The detective in charge of the murder investigation doesn't know about this photo yet. He doesn't know your connection to Alanna Goodwin. Maybe the photo means something and maybe it doesn't. But if I don't hear from you by Monday, I'm going to give this photo and your name to the homicide detective investigating the case."

A panicked look entered Ms. Duncan's eyes. "You have no right to interfere."

"Maybe, maybe not. But Alanna's murderer needs to be brought to justice. The only way we can do that is if we have all the facts."

She waited, hoping the woman would fill her in on how she knew Alanna. But she didn't.

However, she did slip Caprice's card into her purse. "We're done here." Then she hurried to the ladies' room, which was down the hall across from the studio.

Caprice would give the woman the weekend. But then she would do what she said she was going to do. She'd pass the photo to Detective Carstead.

Since the dance studio was located in West York, Caprice decided to stop at one of her nana's favorite shops. It was one of those gift stores that sold hand-made craft items, trinkets, and a little bit of home décor. Caprice shopped there, too, looking for incidentals for stagings. She was happy to find some of Nana's favorite sachets created with rose petals. Her mom's birthday was coming up in May and she spotted an embroidered table runner that she knew she'd like. It was easy to spend an hour examining all the nooks and crannies, the mugs and key chains, necklaces and scarves.

But Caprice had another stop to make as well—an Italian deli nearby, which sold mortadella, prosciutto, salami, and other favorites that seemed more flavorful than the ones she bought at the grocery store. She was almost tempted to buy the wedding cookies in the glass case—macaroons rolled in pine nuts, fragile almond crescents, leaf-shaped chocolate wafers. But she resis-ted. She bought a frozen container of whipped topping from their refrigerator case, and now she stuffed that, with the meats surrounding it, into a cooler that she kept in her trunk. After zipping it up, she was ready to head back home to her animals and the possibility of solving Alanna's murder, once Sherry Duncan's mother called her. If she was any judge of character, she was pretty sure Sherry's mother would.

Because this was a high traffic time, Caprice decided to take back roads to Kismet instead of staying on Route 30. The landscape was coming alive with spring. In this area of York county, she also passed many farms that were slowly giving way to urban sprawl, but hadn't yet.

Still thinking about her canceled weekend with Seth and her confused feelings about the whole matter, she stared straight in front of her, her gaze on the ribbon of road. It wound up and down and around curves. She barely noticed the trees budding with green leaves, the red barns, the horses dotting the landscape now and then.

Her gaze suddenly spotted a pretty chestnut filly, with a black mane, running along the roadside fence.

She wasn't sure when she noticed the sound of something behind her. Maybe it was when the chestnut loped out of view. Maybe it was when she glanced at the dashboard to see what speed she was going. Maybe it was some sixth sense, or, most likely, the sound the vehicle behind her made. That *vroom* didn't project from her Camaro.

As the *vroom* became louder, Caprice's gaze shifted to her rearview mirror. Her heart seemed to leap to her throat. The rusty brown mud-splashed pickup truck approached fast. At first, Caprice thought it was going to pass her. A speed demon eager to get home from work?

But then, the speed-demon truck surged forward and hit the back of her Camaro!

She knew everything there was to know about her car's handling. The whiplash effect didn't affect the car as much as her sense of balance and her confidence in what she should do next. Speed up? Pull over? Duck down?

The truck rammed her again. Before she could come up with a plan of action, it dropped back and sped forward. This time, it didn't ram her in the rear bumper. It slid up beside her left side; then before she knew it, it had plunged into her left fender.

The steering wheel slipped through her fingers in spite of her efforts to direct the car where she wanted to go. Her Camaro lurched into a muddy ditch on the right side of the road. As Caprice struggled to recover from the shock, she heard the pickup's gunned engine as it sped away, disappearing over the rise of a hill.

Caprice's left shoulder had hit the door. She felt woozy, whether from an overwhelming sense of disbelief or the accident itself, she didn't know.

Taking several deep breaths, she took stock of her situation. Unhooking her lap belt, she moved her arms first and winced. Her left shoulder was definitely bruised. She moved her hand and fingers. All of that was in working order. She turned her head from left to right. No problem there. She leaned forward a little, then moved each leg. There was always an adrenaline rush after an accident, and the people involved didn't always realize how badly they were injured. But she really did think she was okay.

Her car might be another matter. The idea that her car was badly damaged almost brought tears to her eyes. She loved this car.

She managed to pry her door open. The car leaned to the right and it was a huge step to reach the ground.

When she did, she sank into mud over her instep. These shoes might not survive the accident, either.

After a look at how the Camaro was leaning and a glance around at all the mud, she knew her vehicle would have to be towed. Pulling her cell phone from the pocket of her bell-bottoms, she touched contacts, then the number for the auto service. A dispatcher informed her someone would be there between forty-five minutes and an hour.

Still standing in mud, worrying whether or not her car could be repaired, analyzing who could have done this to her, she felt frustrated and out of sorts, weary and teary. Before she thought better of it, she speed-dialed Grant.

Ten minutes later, Caprice sat in her car, thinking that was the safest place to be, when she spotted Grant's vehicle coming from the opposite direction. He must have broken all the speed limits. The shoulder on the other side of the road wasn't as muddy, and he managed to pull off. Exiting his car, he rushed over to hers.

She pushed open her door again, fighting against gravity. But she didn't have to exert too great an effort because Grant was there, standing in the mud, opening it the whole way.

His eyes were an intense gray. "Are you sure you're all right? We can still call the paramedics."

He looked all macho and worried and completely unconcerned that his navy suit slacks were soon going to have mud edged around the hem that might not be so easy to get off.

"I'm okay," she assured him.

He held out his hands to her. "Let me help you out. You can sit in my car until the auto service and police arrive."

"I didn't call the police."

"I'm calling them now." He dialed 9-1-1 and gave them the appropriate information.

They were out of Kismet jurisdiction, but whoever responded would file a report. She would contact Detective Carstead later to fill him in . . . if he didn't get to her first.

After Grant was finished, he said, "It isn't safe to stay in your car. Let's go to mine."

No, sitting here wasn't safe. Apparently, driving on this back road hadn't been safe. Watching a horse gallop as she cruised by him hadn't been safe. She took

Grant's hands and slid forward on the seat, but the bucket was an impediment to her sliding out easily. She couldn't help but wince when she moved her shoulder forward.

Grant muttered something unintelligible; then he leaned forward, wrapped his arms around her, and, more or less, carried her free from the car. Once she was on solid ground that wasn't oozing water and dirt, he took her hand and guided her to his SUV.

At the passenger door, she murmured, "I've got mud all over my shoes and pants, and your car's going to be a mess."

"I am not worried about the car," he said in a firm, strained tone.

After she slid inside, and he took another look at her from head to toe—probably to make sure she wasn't going to faint on him or something worse—he shut the door. The words "white knight" kept running through Caprice's head and she wondered if she hadn't been shaken up more than she thought.

An hour and a half later, Caprice was settled on her sofa, an ice bag on her shoulder, Lady at her feet, Mirabelle to one side of her, Sophia peering down from her cat tree. Oh yes . . . and Grant was bringing her a cup of hot peach tea.

"Are you sure you don't want something to eat?" he asked. "Your hands are still shaking."

After a sip of tea, she put the cup and saucer on the coffee table right next to her silent butler. What had been her affirmation this morning? *Breathe and enjoy your day.*

It had been some day.

"Talk to me some more about what you were doing in York," Grant said as he sat beside her.

She'd given him a very brief explanation when she'd phoned him. Just that she'd been visiting a dance studio. She'd been too tired and upset to talk on the way home and Grant had respected that.

Now she went into more detail. "When I was staging Alanna's house, I saw Alanna studying a photograph of a little girl, which she quickly hid in her desk drawer."

"Hid?"

"That's the way it seemed to me. She didn't want me to see it. I didn't think a lot about it then, but after the funeral reception, I asked Twyla if we could see if it was still there, and it was. The little girl was dressed in a recital costume and the name of the dance studio was on the back. Twyla let me take it with me. So today I went to the dance studio. At first, the instructor was reluctant to tell me anything, but then she realized I was searching for a murderer."

"Do you hear yourself?" Grant asked. "Do you know how chilling that statement is?"

After what had just happened to her, she realized exactly how chilling it was.

"I was simply searching out clues. The little girl and her mom came to the next dance session, and I approached the mom."

Grant groaned. "You never should have done that. You should have given the picture to Carstead."

"Maybe, but what good was the photo without information to go with it?"

Grant's jaw was a chiseled, stubborn line; and his expression, more than anything, told her that he didn't approve of any of this. Yet, he let her go on without saying he didn't approve . . . without saying, *I told you so.*

"I was reasonable about this, Grant, really I was. I told Sherry Duncan's mother she had until Monday. If I didn't hear from her before then, I would give the photo to the detective in charge, and she'd have to answer his questions instead of mine."

Grant's jaw became a little less stonelike, and the look in his eyes softened. "That made sense. But what if *she* was the one who tried to run you off the road? About fifty yards up that road, there was a line of decades-old maples. Do you realize if you'd been run off the road there and crashed into one of those trees, you'd be dead?"

His voice wasn't filled with disapproval now. It was filled with so much concern that Caprice's throat tightened and tears threatened once again.

He must have seen her eyes glisten because he wrapped his arm around her and pulled her tight against him. "You make me crazy sometimes," he murmured, looking deeply into her eyes.

She searched his face. Exactly what did that mean? She made him crazy? Crazy with—?

In the next moment, she found out. For Grant, "crazy" meant he wanted her, he needed her, and he cared about her. As the ice bag slipped from her shoulder, his lips on hers told her all that. The kiss was passionate and masterful and absolutely everything a first kiss should be.

A first kiss.
Grant.

When he leaned away, their eyes locked and neither of them seemed able to speak.

He cleared his throat and spoke first. "That kiss was a long time in coming."

"Do you regret it?" she asked, thinking he might. After all, everything up until now with Grant had been tense, sometimes awkward, but always filled with a bond they didn't want to admit they shared.

"I don't regret it. How about you? You're involved with Seth Randolph."

She let out a sigh and shook her head. "Can I talk to you honestly about this?"

"You mean—do I want to hear I'm in second place?"

"Nothing like that. I'm beginning to think that Seth and I . . . maybe I was infatuated with the idea that a handsome doctor would want to date me. Maybe I was infatuated with the idea of connecting again with a man who thought I was special."

Grant frowned. "Maybe *I* think you're special."

"Yes, but you didn't want to admit it. You didn't want to admit anything, not even honest-to-goodness friendship. On Valentine's Day, I was so disappointed you didn't ask me to dance. I was so disappointed you left. I was so disappointed that we couldn't talk about . . . us."

"I wasn't ready," Grant admitted.

"I know, and I didn't want to push you. I also really thought Seth and I had something that might last."

Grant cocked his head and studied her. "So, what makes you think differently now?"

"I was supposed to meet his family this weekend."

Grant's eyebrows shot up and his mouth tightened.

"But he called yesterday and canceled. He had a critical patient and he had to stay. And I understand that. I feel terrible thinking that we don't have a relationship because of his career. But he's never here.

Even when he's here, I get the feeling he's not. He doesn't know what's going to happen after Baltimore, and he'll go where the best job is. He'll go where his career leads him."

"And you?"

"I don't want to go anywhere. I want to stay here with my family."

Grant opened his mouth to say something, but then he closed it again.

"What?" she prodded. "I want you to be honest with me and tell me what you're thinking."

"I'm thinking that if you really love this guy, you'd follow him anywhere. Yes, family is important to you. But so are love and a relationship and having a family of your own." Then he shook his head. "But I'm the wrong one to talk to about this, because I'm totally prejudiced. Now that *that kiss* happened, I'd like it to happen again."

She'd like that, too.

Grant gently touched her face and pushed her hair behind her ear. He ran his thumb over her chin and afterward placed his hand on her shoulder. "How does this feel?"

"Like I need ice on it again."

"I'll get the other cold pack in your freezer. What kind of takeout do you want?"

"I don't do takeout. I cook."

"Not tonight."

She sighed. "Morelli's has steak sandwiches to die for, and they deliver. The number's on my refrigerator."

"So you don't do takeout?" he asked with a smile.

"Once in a very blue moon."

"I'll check the color of the moon tonight. And while

I'm calling to order, you need to call Carstead and ask him if he received the police report."

That was a call she didn't want to make because she suspected his reaction would be even more vociferous than Grant's. She'd much rather just sit here and think about Grant's kiss. She'd much rather just sit here and consider the future.

Since that was so confusing, however, she took out her phone and she made the call.

Chapter Seventeen

When Caprice's mom phoned her early Saturday and asked her to come to Sunday dinner, Caprice was grateful she'd be spending her birthday with her family. She just hoped they wouldn't want to talk about her canceled weekend with Seth . . . or her feelings about it. So many mixed feelings about beginnings and endings, family and commitment. Nana and Grandpa De Luca had always been there for each other. Her parents' devotion to each other had never wavered. If her mom called her dad for help, he was there. If her dad needed her mom's strength, she gave it. Marriage was about giving 100 percent to a relationship. It was about putting your partner first.

To be honest, most of her thoughts had returned to Grant and his kiss and the conversation they'd had. That had occupied her waking moments.

Turning her attention to work, she planned for the open house fast approaching on Tuesday. While she did, the murder suspects ran through her head. Would she hear from Sherry Duncan's mother? Because if she didn't, she'd be calling Detective Carstead again. It was the right thing to do. When she'd called him last evening, the desk officer had informed her the detective was unavailable until Monday. Working on the case? A personal matter? None of her business. She'd simply left a message, asking him to call her as soon as he could.

Caprice had managed to convince Grant she'd be perfectly safe on her own until Carstead knew the situation. But Grant had insisted Juan pick her up today and bring her home from her work staging the glass house. She'd acquiesced.

Studying the glass walls, moving her shoulder a little to work out the stiffness, she decided the house, after a few hours of work, was stunning. The amount of sunlight flowing through the windows gave the interior an otherworldly feel as light bounced off the glass tables, as well as the crystal vases. Russet and green upholstered love seats, along with sofas and drapes, brought the exterior colors inside as the real estate agent shot photos and videotape. Caprice hoped for lots of sunlight on Tuesday to make the staging dramatic for the open house.

After early Mass on Sunday, Caprice walked through her neighborhood with Lady, making it a Zen experience. She breathed in deeply, took notice of every color and bud, listened to birdsong. Today was *her* day that she was going to enjoy in the ways she liked best— walking her dog, gardening, and spending time with family. What better way to spend her birthday.

Mirabelle, Sophia, and Lady thanked her for an extra round of treats with meows, purrs, and, in Lady's case, a little yip. Sophia and Mirabelle seemed to have drawn a truce. But Mirabelle still ran from Sophia, now and then, when Sophia gave her that big golden-eyed stare. Animals could communicate in telepathic ways so much easier than humans could.

Caprice gave thought to what she wanted to wear that evening and pulled out several outfits for Mirabelle and Lady's approval. Sprawled comfortably on Caprice's bed, Mirabelle slept through her first two choices. Lady cocked her head at each one, but she gave a flap of her ears that appeared to indicate she wasn't impressed.

Caprice finally pulled out a bohemian-style maxiskirt with ecru lace around the flowing handkerchief-style hem. The top was the same material as the skirt, with three-quarter bell sleeves trimmed with the same ecru lace as the hem.

At this choice, Mirabelle raised her head, yawned, then purred in approval. Lady stood, came to sniff at the hem, and then sat at Caprice's feet, looking up at her with an expression that suggested, *This one works*. From atop the chest of drawers, Sophia lounged, raised a white paw to her orange ear, and nodded.

"Okay, then," Caprice told them. "All I need to complete it is that cute marcasite kitty necklace I found at the flea market."

After she attached the necklace, she caught sight of Seth's bracelet stretched out on her dresser. Tonight she'd leave it at home. She wasn't angry with Seth because of the canceled weekend. Anger didn't enter into it at all. She was disappointed they hadn't talked further about it. She was upset he hadn't called again. Most of all, she was confused by what had happened with Grant and what it meant going forward.

Dinner with her family tonight was just what she needed to ground her.

She soon discovered that grounding might have to come from somewhere else.

Her van and her uncle Dom's car were the only vehicles parked in front of the family home. That wasn't unusual, since there was a detached garage around the back where her parents parked. Lady seemed abundantly eager as she and Caprice exited the van, climbed the steps to the yard, and then those to the porch. At the door, Lady did something she rarely did. She scratched at it.

Caprice laid her hand gently on Lady's head. "Whoa, girl. Eh-eh. Not something we do," she said in a firm voice.

Lady just looked up at her and whined.

So, what was that about? A new behavior she'd have to work on discouraging?

When Caprice opened the door and stepped inside the foyer, she was surprised at all the quiet. Her mom, her dad, Nana, and her uncle did not come out to greet her. Had something terrible happened that she didn't know about? Certainly, someone would have called her.

Lady, however, didn't wait for questions to be answered. She ran ahead into the dining room; and to Caprice's amazement, two dogs came to meet her—Dylan and Patches.

Before she knew it, she was moving forward and then everyone was shouting, "Surprise!"

With her mouth agape, she scanned the crowd gathered and found not only her family, including Vince and Roz, Nikki, Bella, Joe and the kids, but Grant and—marvel of marvels—Seth.

"Happy birthday," she heard again from her left, and there was Isaac Hobbs, and beside him was Dulcina. It was quite a gathering, and the table was laden with so much food she thought it might spill off.

"What did you do?" she asked her mother in a stern tone.

"It was Nana's idea," her mom responded with a shrug and a broad smile.

When she rushed forward to hug them both, tears sprang to her eyes. Her thirty-third birthday was going to be an occasion she wouldn't soon forget. In a corner beside the buffet, which was loaded with beverages, Caprice caught a glimpse of a stack of presents. As the dogs ran into the living room to play, Caprice began a round of hugs for her other guests.

Isaac looked a bit embarrassed when she kissed him on the cheek. Then he muttered, "I couldn't miss my best customer's birthday."

She laughed.

Dulcina said, "Your family knows how to make a girl feel at home. When your mom called, I knew I had to be here. Everyone's been so welcoming."

"That's my family," Caprice agreed. "Quirky but welcoming. I'm so glad you could come."

After hugging the rest of her family, Grant came next. He was looking at her as if he wanted to kiss her again. He was smiling, but there was something else lurking in those gray eyes. She wondered if she'd find out tonight what it was.

"I'm glad you could be here," she whispered into his neck as he hugged her.

He leaned away, but kept his arms around her. "I'm glad I could be here, too." His voice was a bit husky and she wondered what else was going on in his mind. But this definitely wasn't the time or place to ask.

When she hugged Roz, Roz told her, "Your mom said Dylan was welcome to come."

"He and Patches and Lady can have their own party," Caprice assured her friend.

The last guest she was ready to welcome was Seth. He looked apologetic as he said, "Hi. I was surprised when your mom e-mailed me. I didn't know it was your birthday. I can't stay long, but I didn't want to miss your party. I thought it would be better to talk face-to-face than over the phone. Do you think we could snatch a few minutes later?"

How much later? How long could he stay? Would "can't stay long" mean he'd be here an hour . . . two hours?

"Sure," she assured him. "We can talk later. Just let me get my bearings and see what Mom has planned."

When she moved away from Seth to speak with her mom, she realized she and Seth hadn't even hugged.

Her mom clapped her hands to catch everybody's attention. She announced, "First we're all going to enjoy some of this delicious food. Nikki and Bella and Nana and I don't want any leftovers. We set up folding chairs in the living room and the library. Pile up your plates and find a place to land. Then Caprice can open her presents and we'll have birthday cake. It's not an ordinary cake. Nana made one of her famous rum cakes, with a vanilla-cream center."

"I hope it's big enough for all Caprice's candles," Vince joked.

"Plenty of room for the candles," Nana assured him. "And Dom will make certain we don't light anything on fire."

When Nana gazed at her son, Caprice could see that her grandmother really had forgiven him. Maybe the tension would leave the family now.

However, as Caprice took a seat in the living room

with a full plate, and found Seth on one side of her and Grant on the other, she could feel plenty of tension. In the past, when Seth was around, Grant had just taken a backseat . . . or left.

Tonight, however, he was doing neither.

Because of all the guests, Isaac's colorful anecdotes about his customers, a discussion of whether a school day should be longer than it was, her father's input on new houses that were being constructed, and Bella and Nikki discussing a few new recipes, her conversation with Grant and Seth was kept to a minimum. She tried to give them equal time—talking to Grant about the renovations Kismet was planning to make for the dog park, and conversing with Seth about the traffic from Baltimore and if his patient was recovering. The man was. It seemed Seth had helped save another life. Caprice so admired his dedication, but . . .

She about felt torn in two, sitting between Grant and Seth. After everyone had finished with their plates, and her father had gathered all of the paper into a large trash bag, Uncle Dom theatrically set a folding table in front of Caprice.

"Your Nana's rum cake needs a sturdy place to sit."

"Now if we can convince the dogs not to run into the table . . . ," Caprice said with a laugh.

Bella heard her. "Or Megan or Timmy!" She pointed to them as they sat with their electronic games on the other side of the room. They'd obviously had their orders to behave.

"After cake, if they're bored, they can play with the dogs on the sun porch. They won't be able to hurt anything in there."

Bella just rolled her eyes. "We know how that goes."

Joe chimed in. "I'll watch them so they don't get too

rowdy." He was holding baby Benedict and rocking him back and forth. "I can't believe Benny is still sleeping. I wish I could sleep that good."

Caprice and Nikki and Vince were Benny's godparents. She hadn't spent as much time lately with him as she'd like. "Can I hold him for a little while? Until the cake comes in, anyway?"

Joe helped transfer the baby to her arms. He was three months old now and looked like a cherub as he slept. Caprice knew he could squall with the best of them, but holding him like this tugged on a corner of her heart. She wanted her own family. She wanted children. She glanced from Grant to Seth, and her heart began giving her answers. Nana had told her when Caprice figured out what she wanted, she should jump without a net. She might just have to do that tonight.

Nana's cake was absolutely scrumptious, even though Caprice was out of breath from blowing out thirty-three candles. And after the cake—who didn't like receiving presents? She was delighted by Isaac's present, a creamer shaped like a cat, reminiscent of the 1950s. Dulcina knew how much she liked flowers and had gifted her with four colorful place mats decorated with hydrangea sprays for her table.

And on it went. Roz gave her a vintage purse. Nana presented her with a beautiful turquoise sweater that had tiny pearl buttons. By the time she reached Grant's present, she didn't know what to expect. It was a gift box, about a foot square, wrapped in fuchsia paper, topped with a yellow bow. He knew she liked those sixties colors.

When she lifted the lid from the box and brushed the tissue aside, she gasped. It was a *Lady and the Tramp* statue. The two dogs were seated at a table covered with a checkered cloth sharing a spaghetti dinner. Grant knew *Lady and the Tramp* was her favorite Disney animated film. Was there a subtle message behind the gift? She and Grant were different in so many ways. Yet, when it came to gazing into each other's eyes over a spaghetti dinner . . . maybe differences were what made life spicy.

After opening her uncle's gift, a book about gardening, she gave him a hug. Apparently, he'd been listening when she talked about what flowers she planted in her yard.

Next she turned to Seth's gift. He handed her an envelope. Inside she found a birthday card, as well as a generous gift card to her favorite online bookseller.

More presents, another piece of cake, and a second cup of coffee. The group was engrossed in animated conversation as Patches, Lady, and Dylan slept together near the fireplace hearth.

Seth stood and extended a hand to her. She had promised to give him a few minutes alone so they could talk. But as she stood, Grant touched her elbow. "Are you leaving?"

She looked around at all the guests who had come to celebrate with her. "No, I'm not leaving."

He nodded. "Good, because I want to talk to you about having dinner later in the week."

He obviously wanted to spend more time with her. She wanted to spend more time with him.

"I won't be too long," she said, giving him a smile. She knew Seth would be leaving . . . as he'd left before.

Since everyone else was gathered in the living room, she and Seth meandered into the foyer and through the dining room into the kitchen, passing through the cooking area. They stood near the kitchen table in the eat-in area.

This had been the room that Caprice probably had the fondest memories of. It was painted pale yellow above the white wainscoting. Gingham curtains graced the windows. She remembered helping her mom make pie dough at this table, squabbling with her sisters and brother, doing homework under her dad's guidance while her mom graded papers. They'd played board games here—Candy Land to Scrabble— and card games—Crazy Eights to poker. The gray Formica-topped table had been smeared with finger paints, as well as tomato sauce. The ladder-back chairs had been caned and recaned, one by one, by an old friend of her dad's. This room always brought back a deluge of memories, which she welcomed.

Now, standing here with Seth, she didn't know what was coming next.

He looked serious. "I know canceling plans for the weekend was a big disappointment."

"Yes, it was." *More than a disappointment, really. A reality check.*

"I don't want either of us to be disappointed again like that, but my career is a fluid life choice, and I'm going where the flow takes me. So I have a question for you. When my fellowship is ended, would you go with me, wherever I take a job?"

That question shocked her. Exactly what was he asking her? "Go with you as—be in the same city with you? Live with you?" This was the time to ask the hard questions.

"I haven't thought way ahead," he admitted. "But we could live together."

Live together, she mentally repeated. Those words

didn't bring to mind a lifelong commitment, vows, a wedding veil, and babies. "Living together" was an interim thing, a placebo when you didn't know what you wanted. Caprice wanted more than living together with a man—even a man as handsome and sexy as Seth Randolph. She wanted more than having plans dashed, appointments canceled, and celebrations denied. Maybe the whole problem was, she'd been infatuated with Seth. Today she'd realized that she loved Grant. Her heart was telling her what she needed to do and where her future lay. Her future was here in Kismet with her family and friends . . . and Grant. She couldn't live on a romantic notion and maybes.

As if Seth could see the decision in her eyes, he frowned. "You don't want to leave your family and . . . what you have here."

"Seth, I'm sorry. I've loved the time we've spent together."

"But I can't make a commitment to anything but my career, and you need more than that." He sighed. "I understand that, Caprice, really I do. I wish only the best for you."

"And I wish only the best for you."

Seth wrapped his arms around her in a huge hug. Then he gave her a gentle good-bye kiss on the forehead. A door led outside from the kitchen to the porch.

"I didn't bring a coat," he said. "I can leave from here."

He gave her one of those smiles that had convinced her to date him, a smile that could reassure patients and give them hope.

As he went out the door, Caprice felt as if she'd been through a storm, and she stood there for a very long time.

She'd made the right decision. She wanted to explore what she and Grant could have.

While she was catching her breath from a variety of emotions, her cell phone played. She automatically plucked it from her pocket. When she read the caller ID displayed on the screen, her heart thumped. She answered, not knowing what to expect. "Hello?"

"Miss De Luca?"

"Yes."

"This is Diane Duncan. I think we should meet."

Chapter Eighteen

The party was winding down when Grant placed his hand on Caprice's shoulder. "Can we talk?"

Dulcina and Isaac had left and her family was milling about. Her stomach did a flip-flop as she gestured toward the library. "Let's go in here."

Once in the library, Grant stuffed his hands into the pockets of his black jeans. "I was surprised to see Seth here."

"So was I." Her heart beat faster as she tried to read Grant's face and what was coming.

"He left abruptly."

"Yes, he did. He had to get back . . . to his patients. To his career." She plunged in, eager to tell Grant all of it. "He asked me if, after his fellowship ended, I'd follow him to wherever he practiced."

Grant's brows drew together, his gray eyes stormy. "What did you say?"

Taking a deep breath, she jumped without a net. "I told him I couldn't leave Kismet . . . that my family was here . . . and my future." The world stopped spinning as she waited for Grant's response.

"Am I in that future?"

"If you want to be."

All of a sudden, Bella came sweeping into the library. "Mom wants to know if Grant would like a piece of rum cake to take along." Glancing from one of them to the other, she asked, "Did I interrupt something?"

Caprice blew out a breath. Sometimes her sister could be so tactless.

But Grant just smiled at Bella. "I'd appreciate a piece of rum cake."

Bella winked at Caprice and tossed over her shoulder, "I'll tell Mom."

Caprice muttered, "We won't get time alone here."

"We'll have time alone . . . soon," Grant promised. "You enjoy the rest of the evening with your family. Not everyone can have this much caring around them."

Just then Megan and Timmy ran into the living room with the dogs and settled near the library's doorway.

With another sigh, Caprice said, "I suppose not."

Grant ran his finger down her cheek.

Caprice wanted to close her eyes and simply think about her future with Grant. But she did have something to tell him. "Diane Duncan called me. I'm meeting her early tomorrow morning."

"Alone?" Grant asked with concern.

"I'll see if Nikki can go with me."

"Carstead didn't call you yet?"

Caprice shook her head.

"After your meeting, go straight to the police station and talk to Detective Jones if you have to."

Realizing Grant was right about this, she assured him, "I will."

"And if Nikki can't go with you tomorrow, call me. I'll rearrange appointments."

"Thank you."

He looked as if he wanted to kiss her again. But with Megan and Timmy sitting right outside of the room . . .

Caprice's dad called to her, "We're going to play charades. As the birthday girl, you can go first."

Anything personal between her and Grant would have to wait.

But a future with Grant was worth waiting for.

Caprice had set up the meeting with Diane Duncan at a park in York. Nikki waited in her car . . . and watched as Caprice approached the bench where Diane sat.

The woman didn't look at Caprice when Caprice took the bench beside her, but rather stared straight ahead.

"I bring my daughter here a lot," she said.

"Tell me about your daughter," Caprice prompted, leading into the conversation.

"Before I do that, I have to know what you're going to do with this information."

"That depends. If it directly impacts the murder investigation, I'll have to tell Detective Carstead . . . or you will."

Diane's face practically crumpled, and Caprice felt sorry for her. "I suppose secrets can't stay secrets forever," Diane said.

"Secrets between adults are difficult enough, but when they involve a child, somehow they have even more impact."

After biting her lip in an obvious emotional dilemma, Diane revealed, "I can't tell you about my daughter without talking to you about Alanna."

"Alanna's secrets are possibly the reason she was

killed," Caprice responded softly, remaining calm although she might soon have the answers she needed to solve this murder.

Diane seemed to absorb what she'd said. "Do you know about Archer Ford and Barton Goodwin?"

"I know that Archer is supposedly his illegitimate son."

Diane nodded, winding her fingers together in her lap. "After Archer came forward to make contact with his father, he and Alanna formed a friendship. Barton Goodwin wasn't always kind, and I think a woman always has need for kindness. So her friendship with Archer became more than friendship. They had an affair and Alanna got pregnant."

Caprice had already pieced some of this together on her own . . . or at least suspected it. It was good to have it confirmed. "How do you know this?"

"She told me her story when we met, so I'd understand her situation and what she had to do."

"Did she tell Barton?"

"She did. I don't know if she told him out of spite, out of resentment, or if she wanted him to be jealous. But she did tell him. She never expected he'd give her an ultimatum—either a divorce or an abortion."

"He was a hard man," Caprice murmured.

"Alanna was a strong woman. Most of all, she was a negotiator. In spite of her affair, she believed her husband really loved her. She told him she could never abort the baby, but she didn't want a divorce, either. She promised him she'd give up the baby for adoption and never look back."

"Never look back? Never know what happened to her child? I don't understand how a mother can promise that."

"She wasn't thinking in terms of being a mother

then, just a woman who wanted to hold her marriage together. That seemed to be her main purpose."

"She didn't tell Archer about her pregnancy?"

"No. Under Barton's instructions, his lawyer, Jeremy Travers, arranged for a private adoption. Alanna went to an undisclosed getaway and had the baby. She told me she set the wheels in motion for gossipmongers to spread the word she was in Europe, but she really went to a clinic in New England. Barton's lawyer set up a trust fund for the baby and the transaction was supposed to be over with once the child was born."

"How did Alanna or the lawyer find you?"

"I had once worked with Jeremy Travers as a paralegal. We remained friends even when he left the firm. He was sort of like a mentor to me. I couldn't have children because of a severe case of endometriosis and he knew that. He also knew a boyfriend had left me because of it. I wanted a child and I talked to him about possibly finding an unwed mother who wanted to give up her baby. When Alanna needed a mother for her child, he called me about the situation. After Sherry was born, Alanna wasn't supposed to have any contact with me or her."

"But Alanna didn't stick to her end of the bargain," Caprice guessed.

"What mother could?" Diane asked, sounding as if she understood perfectly. She took out her phone, tapped the gallery app, and showed Caprice a photo. "That's the first picture I took of Sherry a week after she was born. What mom would walk away and not want to know exactly what kind of life she had?"

Caprice studied the photo of the baby.

Diane was silent a few moments. "I think regrets got the best of Alanna. When Sherry was a year old, Alanna called me. She said she didn't want to interfere in my life, but she needed to know how her daughter was. So every now and then, I'd send her a photo. That was the new agreement between the two of us. I'd keep her informed and e-mail her photos, but she wouldn't have contact with Sherry."

"What changed?" Caprice was sure something had.

"I mailed her Sherry's recital photo, the one you had with you at the dance studio."

"It's a beautiful photo. You have a lovely daughter."

Diane smiled. "It has less to do with me and everything to do with Sherry. She's a sweetheart, and all I want to do is protect her from life's bumps and from emotional trauma. But I didn't know how I was going to do that anymore. Last month, Alanna called me and tried to convince me to let her reveal the truth to Ace Richland before she married him."

"Were you going to let her do it?"

"I was so torn. I eventually was going to tell Sherry who her birth mother was. But after Alanna called me, I was scared. She had a lot of money. If she married Ace Richland, she'd have even more than that. She could pull strings. She could possibly get Sherry back. I didn't know what to do. I didn't know whom to confide in. I was still trying to decide, and then I heard she was murdered."

What a powerful motive for murder for Diane. Of course, she was going to have to tell Detective Carstead about this. Of course, Diane would have to talk to him herself.

She had one more question for Diane Duncan. "Did you try to run me off the road on Friday?"

Diane's shock looked genuine. "Of course, I didn't."

Could Caprice believe her?

* * *

After Caprice's meeting with Diane, she found messages from Detective Carstead and Twyla on her phone. The detective had been out of town at his sister's wedding. He'd be at the station all morning. Twyla had made the decision to return to Mississippi. She thought it best to pull out the rental furniture and empty the house. Caprice would return her call when she had time to discuss it all.

Nikki's foot was heavy on her accelerator as she drove Caprice to the police station. Her meeting with the detective went as expected. He disapproved of her pursuing the investigation. He went stony-jawed about the police report of her accident. Still, he listened and jotted down Diane's number.

After her visit to Carstead, Caprice insisted Nikki take her home. She'd care for her furry family, then drive herself where she needed to go in her van. She didn't need a chauffeur. She'd be careful.

She just hoped Don Rodriguez could restore her Camaro to its beautiful condition before the accident. He'd assured her he could.

Breaking into Caprice's thoughts, Nikki said, "Promise to call me every couple of hours so I know you're okay."

"I will," Caprice promised. Certainly, a visit to see Barton's lawyer couldn't be considered dangerous.

At three o'clock on the dot, Caprice sat outside the office of the general counsel of Goodwin Enterprises. She hadn't exactly told him what this was about when she'd called asking for a meeting. She'd simply said she was looking into Alanna's background for the murder investigation and she needed to talk with him. He hadn't asked about her credentials.

A tall, thin, long-necked man—her vision of Ichabod Crane—opened the door and nodded to his secretary.

"Miss De Luca?" he asked.

Jeremy Travers's wire-rimmed glasses were high on his narrow nose. He might look like a gangly character from literature, but she spotted quick intelligence and an alertness in his hazel eyes, which she'd expect in a lawyer.

He beckoned her inside with one thin arm.

Although he gave her a cursory once-over, he didn't linger on anything about her appearance, her tie-dyed shirt or her pleated skirt and saddle shoes. That meant he was all business. Good. She could be as well.

He motioned to the leather chair in front of his desk. "It's good to meet you, Miss De Luca. Alanna told me you were staging her house. You have a reputation in this part of the country for doing a bang-up job of that."

A bit of flattery to get them started. She couldn't do the same for him because she didn't know him, or his position in Alanna's life. So she asked, "Were you Alanna's confidant?"

He studied her for a few moments before rounding the desk and lowering himself into the high-backed, cushy-looking, wheeled office chair. "Are you asking out of curiosity or because you're hoping to solve a murder before the police do? I've read the articles on you."

"This isn't a competition, Mr. Travers. If I discover anything of importance, I'll be calling Detective Carstead, the lead detective on the case."

"Oh, I know him. He's already interviewed me regarding Alanna's position on the board."

"I'm not here about Alanna's position on the board."

Ichabod's, or rather Jeremy's, eyebrows arched. "If I was a confidant, I would claim lawyer-client privilege."

"Alanna's dead, Mr. Travers."

He seemed to go a shade paler. "Believe me, I know that."

She should just get to the point. "I know about the adoption. I know you were Barton's lawyer and handled it. I learned the whole story from Diane Duncan."

He seemed appalled at that. "How did you find out? How did you ever find Diane?"

Caprice basically explained about the photo she'd seen in Alanna's hands and tracking down the dance studio, as well as the child and her mother.

"You should be a detective," he muttered. "Or maybe a PI."

"I don't want to be either. Ace Richland is my friend, and he wants to know what happened to Alanna. He needs to know, and I would like to clear his name. So, will you answer a few questions for me?"

"I suppose there's no harm in hearing what they are," he agreed reluctantly.

"You arranged the adoption, correct?"

"How do I know you really *did* talk to Diane?"

"Because she showed me this." Caprice took out her phone, found a photo in the gallery, and presented it to Jeremy Travers. It was the baby picture of Sherry that, on Caprice's request, Diane had texted to her.

He sat back in his chair and then steepled his fingers in his lap. "What do you want to know?"

"I know all about the adoption, how there wasn't supposed to be any contact between Alanna and Diane. I want to know Alanna's state of mind after her baby's birth."

The attorney seemed surprised by that. "She was angry. She was angry at me, angry at Barton, angry at the world, and, most of all, angry at herself."

"And that anger changed her," Caprice guessed, remembering what Muriel had told her.

"It certainly did. When Barton first married her, she was the proverbial steel magnolia, but not unbendingly hard. During her first years of marriage, she found out Barton wasn't the man she expected him to be. He certainly wasn't any armored knight on a pedestal, though he did armor himself. She found out about all of his flaws, his armor, and how his ruthless nature could sometimes take over. When I arranged that adoption, she thought she'd lost total control of her life."

"Were you privy to how the affair with Archer came about?"

"As I said, she'd become disillusioned with Barton and their marriage. When Barton was so adamant about not recognizing Archer as his son, not taking a DNA test, not letting any of it come to light, Alanna saw yet another side of him. She liked Archer. He was younger than she was, but closer to her age than Barton. They connected. They really connected."

"So, why didn't she just run off with Archer and divorce Barton? Why agree to his terms in giving up the baby?"

"That's where you need to understand the real Alanna and how insecure she could be. Barton confided in me about her from the moment he'd met her. I wasn't sure marriage between them was a good idea because of their diverse backgrounds . . . as well as their age difference. But he fell head over heels. He loved her until the day he died."

"But his love wasn't enough?"

"Archer was kind, younger, energetic, affectionate even. I found all that out when Alanna was ranting about the adoption. I think she really loved Archer, but she agreed to Barton's terms because she needed the security of his wealth. She'd had nothing growing up, and she was determined never to return to that kind of living. So she traded her child for security, and she hated herself for it."

Caprice could easily see how that self-hatred would happen. She had to find out something else. "Did she confide in you about her relationship with Ace?"

"She did."

"Because she wanted to tell him about her daughter."

"Yes. I believe she had true feelings for him." Then he added, "But not for his lifestyle. Barton had traveled too much and she didn't want to go down that same road in another relationship."

"Did you know about Alanna's deal with Len Lowery to sabotage Ace's road trip?"

Mr. Travers looked blank. "No, I didn't know about that, yet it doesn't surprise me. She had confided she was going to do something to have the life she wanted with Ace."

"Thank you for being forthcoming with me."

"I want to see Alanna's murderer brought to justice. It's true, I was Barton's lawyer. But after he died, Alanna had to depend on me in many ways. She didn't want to take over the reins of running the business, and I had to make sure it ran smoothly."

"What happens to the business now?"

"It will be sold to the highest bidder."

"And then it will become part of Alanna's estate?"

"Actually, no, it won't. Barton had arranged for a separate type of trust for the business. Once it's sold, the proceeds will be divided among all the shareholders—those individuals who helped him get started, who backed his patents, who made Goodwin Enterprises a success."

"Did the shareholders know this?"

"No, they did not. They do now, since Alanna's will was read. But if you're looking for motive, there was none there."

"Are you a shareholder?" Caprice asked.

He looked uncomfortable for a moment. "Yes, I am."

"Then you had motive."

"You could see it that way," he said. "But Detective Carstead knows all about that and he hasn't pulled me in for further interrogation, so I don't think I'm a suspect. Besides, I had a solid alibi for the day Alanna was murdered."

Good, Caprice thought. She didn't need another suspect to add to her list.

After she left her meeting with Travers, she exited the building, climbed into her van, and thought about everything she'd learned. Alanna wasn't as cold as she'd seemed. Her motivation had come from insecurity rather than malice. If she loved Archer Ford and dumped him, *he* had motive for murder. She needed to find out more about him, but she probably shouldn't do that alone. Maybe Grant would like to go along.

She would have to put another trip to York aside while she attended the open house tomorrow. A weekday open house was unusual but not unheard of, especially when the showing was by invitation only. The luxury broker representing the house had told her she had at least thirty people on her list who were coming, and there were the other real estate agents from York, Baltimore, and even D.C. who had claimed they had interested clients. Yes, tomorrow would be a busy day. And tonight?

Tonight she was going to call Ace and tell him what she'd learned about Alanna. He might feel better knowing that Alanna had true feelings for him, feelings deep enough that she wanted to tell him about her daughter.

And then she'd call Grant to see if he wanted to do a little sleuthing with her . . . and maybe to see if their relationship could grow into a permanent commitment.

The magnificent house with its walls of glass was all modern architecture. That's why Caprice had gone with a minimalist theme. It sat atop a hill, stone and wood enhancing the glass and steel. In some ways, its angles stood out against the rhythm of the rolling grass, the swaths of trees, the bubbling creek below, and the hills in the distance.

But this house wasn't supposed to fit into its landscape. It was supposed to make an architectural statement. That's what Caprice had tried to do, too, using the sunlight that sometimes glared and sometimes sifted into each and every room. She'd decorated one bedroom in hunter green. The bed frame was that color, along with the headboard, the nightstands, and the round rug that lay in front of the bed. That green brought the outside forest in, and you could almost smell the scent of pine from looking at it. The foyer and living room further highlighted the glass by being wood wrapped, bestowing warmth in spite of the house's angles and edges. A gas fireplace was encased in stone and faced the sectional black sofa, where anyone could stare into the flames.

Glass gave off a miraculous amount of light and Nikki was playing with that. The light and darkness and minimalist theme was reflected in her food. One of her hors d'oeuvres—deviled eggs with a caviar top, couched on a romaine leaf—was an example of that.

Other offerings included shrimp-topped parsley sauce, pecan-encrusted Brussels sprouts on a bed of couscous, and a plate of beef stew surrounding a scoop of white rice. Fresh, beautifully red strawberries nestled on meringue. Nikki had combined color with natural ingredients to present an unusual buffet.

When Caprice approached Nikki, her sister was arranging tangerine slices around a sprig of green grapes.

"Everything looks fabulous, as always," Caprice complimented her.

"I'll accept that compliment today because I'm feeling fabulous . . . like I've got my mojo back."

"You always have mojo," Caprice teased.

"Drew Pierson took it away for a while."

"I saw your social media pages. You're having lots of contact with members of the community and great interaction. Your campaign to pull in new clients is in full swing."

"It is. Two of the guests from our last open house signed on with me for catering jobs last week and gave my information to friends."

Caprice's cell phone played. When she slipped it from her pocket and checked the screen, she saw Ace's picture.

"It's Ace," she told Nikki. "I'd better take this."

Nikki just nodded and returned to arranging tangerine slices.

"Hi, Ace. What's up?"

"I didn't break anybody's nose again, if that's what you're thinking."

"It never entered my mind," she lied.

He laughed. "What a friend you are. I just wanted to tell you I sent Marsha and Trista over to your open house. Is that okay?"

"For this open house we have a restricted list, but I'll put Marsha and Trista on it. Is there a reason they want to see this place?"

"Marsha was intrigued when I told her about the glass. And the thing is . . ."

Caprice just waited.

"The thing is," Ace repeated, "Marsha's thinking about moving here with Trista. I want her to have a place she really likes, somewhere where Trista can have her friends over. The house does have a media room, doesn't it?"

"On the lower level. The glass is equipped with darkening shades, just like the first two stories."

If she was surprised Marsha was thinking about moving to Kismet, she didn't let it show. But she couldn't contain her curiosity. "Did you and Marsha come to some agreement about Trista?"

"I went to Virginia to visit them last weekend and we had a long talk. You know I want to spend more time with Trista. Less traveling back and forth would make that easier. It's not as if Marsha has a job or anything. In fact, she's thinking about going back to school. We have colleges within about an hour from Kismet—Gettysburg, Millersville in Lancaster . . . even McDaniel in Westminster. There are Penn State annex campuses. We're close to Harrisburg for cultural events, and York has plenty of shopping centers. I think Marsha could be happy here."

Maybe after Ace recovered from Alanna's death, or at least the grieving eased, he and Marsha could find their way back to each other.

However, before that could happen, Alanna's murderer had to be found. Caprice remembered her phone call to Grant, his easy acceptance of her invitation for him

to accompany her to talk to Archer Ford's neighbors.
Neighbors often held the lowdown on comings and
goings . . . as well as personality traits. And having
Grant along?

That would be a bonus.

Chapter Nineteen

As Grant drew up in front of a brick bungalow, with black shutters and unassuming landscaping with box-woods, Caprice felt like wringing her hands. They'd made small talk the whole way down—about their dogs, about her family, about Grant taking Patches along to work and what the dog might need there to keep him happy. She wanted to talk about the two of *them*.

On the other hand, that could be a long, face-to-face discussion and they had investigating on their minds now. Didn't they?

After they'd climbed out of Grant's SUV, and studied Archer's property, Caprice was less sure about what she was going to do here.

"How do you know he won't come home unexpectedly?" Grant asked.

"It's not like I'm going to break and enter. I called the hotel and he's working until ten."

Grant's brows arched and she noted the lines around his eyes that hadn't come from laughter.

"They gave you that information?" he asked.

"I told the person who answered I had business I

wanted to discuss with him and asked how long he'd be there."

"I think you're getting too good at this," Grant muttered as he took a few steps closer to the porch. He nodded to the back lawn. "I think you might be in luck. His neighbor is pruning her roses."

The properties on this block in West York were fairly close together, maybe only twenty to twenty-five feet separating the houses. The home to the east side of Archer's was a little bungalow, with white siding and blue shutters. It was an L-shape, with a garage sitting forward in the front. Caprice caught sight of the neighbor now, her straw gardening hat obvious against the forsythia hedge that bloomed along the back of her yard. A row of freshly pruned roses was a boundary between her property and Archer's.

Caprice was ready with a list of questions. "Let's see what she has to say."

Grant caught her arm. When he did, his fingers were warm on her bare skin under her lime green bell sleeve. As she looked up at him, her breath caught.

"Do you know what you're going to say?" he wanted to know.

"If all else fails, I'm going to say he's dating my sister and I want to know more about him."

Grant shook his head. "As I said, you're getting too good at this."

As they walked toward the older woman, Caprice studied Grant in his wine-striped Henley shirt and black jeans. Her eyes could linger on him all day. Instead of indulging that whim, she turned her focus onto Archer's neighbor. She could see now that the woman was older, maybe in her sixties. She wore bright blue glasses and a pink-and-yellow-flowered, long-sleeved blouse over a white T-shirt and pale blue dungarees.

Even her sneakers were decorated with flowers. It was obvious she was a gardener, which gave Caprice a starting point.

Approaching the woman, she smiled. "Hi. Your forsythia is fabulous. They're so airy and pretty when they're free form."

The woman looked a little wary as her focus turned to tall, broad-shouldered Grant. "Did you ring my doorbell?"

"No, we didn't," Caprice answered. "We came to see Archer, but he's not here."

"Oh, my, no. Not on a Wednesday. He always works late. He works most weekends, too. It's a shame, really, but he doesn't seem to mind. I'm glad to see he does have friends. His work schedule doesn't leave him much time for socializing."

"I know what you mean. Evening work doesn't help, either."

"That's for sure," the neighbor agreed. "He used to switch hours with somebody so he'd have a few evenings off. It's lucky for me, though, that he's here many mornings."

"How so?" Grant asked.

"He helps me with things I can't do anymore—like changing light bulbs or the batteries in my smoke alarms. He even trims my bushes for me sometimes."

"So you like living next door to Archer?" Caprice asked.

"He's a kind young man. I just wish I were thirty years younger so I could snatch him up."

Caprice laughed. "I'm surprised he's still single."

"He was dating someone for a while," the chatty neighbor told them. "I saw him come home with a snazzy suit. I recognized the name of the men's shop. He told me the woman he was dating expected men to dress as well as she did. I never saw her. He always went out, never brought her home."

"Maybe he thought his house wasn't grand enough," Caprice guessed.

"I don't know about that. He has a nice little place, smaller than mine, but it's well kept. When I cook, I often take him a casserole or a cake. I kid him his place is never messed up, and he always says that's because he's not there very much. A cleaning service comes in every two weeks."

Caprice and Grant exchanged a look, because obviously this woman saw everything that went on next door.

"You said he was dating someone," Grant prompted. "When we're around him, I haven't heard him talk about anybody lately."

"That's just like a man, not talking about personal details. I think he broke up with her around Christmas. He seemed pretty down to me over the holidays. After all, I know *down*. When my kids don't get home for Christmas, it's lonely. But he didn't want to talk about it, and he worked on Christmas Day. My daughter was here and we baked a ham, so I took some of that over to him the following day. He just didn't have the Christmas spirit. He even took down the lights he'd hung around the door before New Year's Day."

Caprice could see into the yard on the other side of Archer's house, too. There was a swing set and one of those jungle gyms with a sliding-board attachment.

Archer's neighbor caught Caprice looking that way and she smiled. "You should see Archer with Donald's kids. They climb all over him like he's a favorite uncle."

"I hope they're not too big," Caprice said.

"Four and six, an adorably active age when they have to be doing something constantly. Little Barney—

he's the six-year-old—had a birthday party last month. Archer planned a scavenger hunt for them. It was a big hit. He had to leave the party early to go to work, but he helped supervise the activities while he was there. But you probably know all of that."

"We only met Archer recently," Caprice explained, "so we have a lot of history to catch up on." Before Archer's neighbor decided she wanted to know their names, Caprice gave her another smile. "I don't want to take up any more of your time. When I see Archer, I'll tell him he's lucky to have a neighbor like you, who even feeds him!"

The older woman flushed with the compliment. Before she regained her composure, Caprice and Grant excused themselves and returned to Grant's SUV.

Once in the vehicle, Grant didn't switch on the ignition, rather he angled toward her. "Archer Ford sounds like a decent guy."

"Yes, he does," Caprice said thoughtfully. "Maybe he should know he has a daughter."

"Maybe, or maybe not. He's still a suspect, and any revelations should wait until the murder investigation is over."

"Will it *be* over?"

"Someone's going to solve this puzzle, Caprice. I don't know if it will be you or Carstead or Jones. But I do know none of you give up easily."

"I want to clear Ace."

He took her hand. "I know you do. That's how I know you won't give up." His thumb rested on the top of her hand and she got lost in the feel of it for a moment. Then Grant asked, "Will you answer a question for me?"

"If I can."

"Can you tell me the honest-to-goodness reason you broke off your relationship with Seth?"

Above all, Caprice knew honesty was important with Grant. "I broke it off with Seth because I can't date two men. I just want to date one man. *You.*"

Grant's only comment to that was a kiss Caprice wouldn't soon forget.

Caprice was still floating on air from Grant's kiss and the possibilities of the future when she arrived at Twyla's the next day. She needed to remove her additions to Alanna's belongings as well as oversee the rental company withdrawing their furniture. The sky was gray with dark clouds and a brewing storm. Hopefully, they could load the truck and her van before rain poured down.

After an hour, there were already hollow sounds in the house. Juan was going through the upstairs with his clipboard to make sure everything on Caprice's list was back in her van. The rental-company employees had already left.

Thunder grumbled as Caprice stared at the taupe love seat she kept in her own storage shed. She and Alanna had fought over removing two settees and replacing them with this love seat. But she'd won that battle.

When Twyla entered the living room, Caprice asked, "What are you going to do with the rest of the furniture?"

"An antique dealer from Baltimore is coming tomorrow with a U-Haul. He insisted he could get me better prices than anyone locally."

Caprice knew that was probably true. Isaac was

good at what he did, but his market didn't extend as far as the shops in Baltimore's might.

"Are you going to stay here until the house is empty?"

Twyla nodded. "I thought I would. I'm keeping one of the guest bedroom furniture suites and moving that to Biloxi. So I'll have my own little haven until the rest is gone and I leave."

Caprice pulled a cushion from the love seat and propped it on the floor.

"If the vacant house doesn't sell in a few months, maybe I'll contract with you again to stage it more simply," Twyla added as she looked over everything that was still there.

"All you have to do is call," Caprice assured her.

After Caprice moved the second cushion on the love seat and propped it against the first, something shiny in the seam of the piece of furniture caught her eye. She bent to pick it up. It was a silver bangle bracelet, with a disc charm hanging from it with the letter *T*.

Caprice held it up. "Look what I found."

Twyla came closer to examine it. "Oh, my goodness. That's mine. I lost it the last time I was here. Thanks for finding it for me." She took it from Caprice.

Returning her attention to the love seat, Caprice said, "I'm going to take the cushions out to my van."

Ten minutes later, Juan had loaded the frame of the love seat into the van also, and Caprice was ready to go. It was a good thing, too, because another April storm was imminent.

Rain began to splat against her windshield. Although she should be headed to her storage shed, she was suddenly compelled to drive into town for a stop at the local pharmacy and a talk with Phyllis Trenton, a friend of her mother's. Phyllis worked the day shift and she wasn't averse to gossiping. With her gift of remembering even the slightest details, she might be able to help Caprice solve a murder.

Fortunately, when Caprice arrived at the pharmacy, no one else was in the store. The pharmacist stood behind the raised dais and the glass counter, and Phyllis was stocking shelves. Caprice crossed to her and asked, "Phyllis, can I talk to you for a minute?"

The small, birdlike woman popped up from a crouched position. "Sure you can, Caprice. I'm almost finished here. What do you need? An umbrella?" There were a few folding ones in a display at the front of the store.

Thunder rumbled outside as Caprice lowered her voice. "I need some information."

Phyllis's blue eyes lit up. "What kind of information?"

"I know what a great memory you have."

A smile twitched Phyllis's lips. "Indeed, I do have a good memory."

"Did you know Alanna Goodwin?"

"I knew who she was. After all, everyone in Kismet stops in here at one time or another."

That's what Caprice was counting on. "Did she ever come in with her sister?"

"You mean Twyla? That's such an unusual name that I remember it. Alanna never bought cosmetics here. She liked the expensive stuff. But Twyla often stopped in when she was in town. She needed over-the-counter allergy medication because of Alanna's cat. She was so different from her sister. She didn't treat me like gum on her shoe the way Alanna did."

Allergy medication. Exactly what Caprice had been betting on. When being around cats and dogs was a sometimes occurrence, over-the-counter medication would do.

"Now this is the important question," Caprice warned before she asked it.

Phyllis tilted her head a little and leaned closer.

"Do you remember the last time Twyla stopped in here for allergy medication?" This guessing game might not pay off. Maybe Twyla came to Kismet prepared. But just maybe on a quick trip here . . .

Phyllis thought about it and then her face brightened. "I remember exactly. It was March thirtieth. I remember because that's my daughter Barb's birthday. I wanted to get home sooner rather than later, and Miss Horton was the last customer who came in."

Five minutes later, Caprice rushed through fat, plopping raindrops to her van, cell phone in hand as she dialed Detective Carstead. Twyla had told her she'd lost the bracelet Caprice had found in the love seat the last time she was in Kismet, but she had also stated the last time she was in Kismet was over the holidays. That love seat where Caprice found the bracelet wasn't in Alanna's house over the holidays. Caprice had moved it in when she'd staged the house.

Reaching Detective Carstead's voice mail, she left the message that Twyla had been in Kismet on March thirtieth. He could take the investigation from there. Had she flown to Kismet? Driven to Kismet? That was for Detective Carstead to find out.

A shiver ran down Caprice's back. Twyla Horton could be the murderer. Or maybe she had a good reason—other than murder—for not wanting anyone to know she'd been in town. That wasn't for Caprice to figure out. She'd let the police handle it. She wanted to just go home and wait until she heard from Detective Carstead. She wanted to be with her animals, lock her doors, and hope that everything would be okay. And soon.

When Caprice entered her driveway, she pressed the remote for the garage door and drove into the garage.

Snatching up her purse, she opened the door that led to her small back porch and heard Lady barking.

That was odd. Lady didn't usually bark even when she heard her coming. Not those kinds of barks anyhow. She gave little yips of joy. Maybe the storm had spooked her. Maybe the thunder had stressed her out.

When Caprice unlocked the door and entered the kitchen, Lady pranced all around her, keeping up the barking. Had something happened with one of the cats, making Lady frantic to escape into the rest of the house?

Caprice dropped her purse on the counter, patted Lady, ruffled her ears, and said, "Calm down, girl, it's okay." When she hurried to the pet gate that led into the dining room and released the catch, Mirabelle and Sophia sat on the dining-room table. They meowed at her.

"Are you two spooked by the storm, too?" she asked.

Mirabelle and Sophia didn't answer, but Twyla Horton did. She stood in the dining room by the hutch, with a gun in her hand.

"The storm didn't seem to bother them, but my gun does. I picked your lock, if you're wondering. You really need a more up-to-date system."

Caprice's breath stopped for a moment and she warned herself to stay calm.

Twyla said, "I've had training and I'm a good marksman, so don't try anything funny."

Twyla's voice was a little different than usual—more nasal—and Caprice noticed she was already stuffy from being in the same area with the animals.

"Put your dog in her crate," Alanna's sister ordered. "I would have done it, but I didn't know if she'd bite me, and I didn't want you to be suspicious when you walked in."

No way did Caprice want to crate Lady, but Twyla's accent wasn't so sweet now, her words, not as drawn out. Had all that sweet Southern charm been an act?

"I'm going to give her a treat so she goes in more easily," Caprice told Twyla.

"Fine, just hurry up," Twyla ordered. "Who did you call and tell about me? When you found that bracelet, I knew you'd figure it out—if not right away, then in a short amount of time. You're a smart girl."

Straightening her shoulders, Caprice said, "I called Detective Carstead." Then she realized that might not have been the smartest thing to say.

"Then we're going to make this short. Get that dog in her crate. I wish you could do something with these two."

If Twyla even thought about hurting Sophia or Mirabelle, she'd find out what a pet lover's rage could do. But rage wouldn't help Caprice right now. She had to keep her sense. She had to figure out what to do next. She had to remember everything she'd learned in her self-defense course.

Sophia meowed again, hopped to the floor, and jumped up onto her cat tree in the living room. But Mirabelle stayed on the dining-room table, her eyes on Twyla.

Since Lady readily obeyed Caprice's orders, she went into her crate. With her hands shaking, Caprice praised her and gave her a treat from the pouch on the counter, but not with the usual enthusiasm.

Caprice didn't know if she was going to die today or not. But she was going to do her best to get out of this mess. She had too much to live for. Not only her family and her pets . . . but Grant, too. Thinking about all of them gave her strength . . . and objectivity.

Twyla was too cagey to give her much time when

Detective Carstead knew who the murderer was. Still . . .
Caprice took a stab at stalling. "Why did you kill
Alanna? You were *sisters*."

"Why did I kill her? Because she told me she'd included Archer in her will. All my life, I wanted to
depend on Alanna. But she was always too concerned
about herself and where *she* was headed. She never
even thought about me."

"Why did you come to Kismet last month?"

"To talk about her wedding. Would you believe she
didn't even offer to pay for my airfare? So I drove. I
was only supposed to stay two nights. She wanted to
show me bridesmaid gowns and talk about designer
shoes. She was going to pay for them. I told her I
couldn't be in her rock star wedding if she didn't."

"So, why did you strangle her?"

"Because she was *so* condescending. Because I
asked her to get me a good-paying job at Barton's fancy
company and she wouldn't. Because that night she told
me I didn't have enough drive or ambition to ever be in
her league. I just got so angry because I felt so less than
she was. Just because I screwed up a few times when I
was a kid, she thought she was so much better than me.
She went to the sideboard to pick up dress swatches. I
picked up the tieback and wrapped it around her pretty
neck."

Twyla worked out at the gym. She had strength in
those arms. Caprice could see the muscles now.

"Enough of that," Twyla said. She pointed her gun
directly at Caprice's chest. "Get down on your knees,"
she ordered.

Thinking again of her family, a possible future with
Grant, Caprice took a very deep breath and told herself
she was *not* going to pass out. Then she fell to her knees
and saw Twyla take plastic ties from her jeans pocket.

Caprice knew those ties were going to secure her hands.

"Raise your hands above your head," Twyla directed harshly.

As Caprice did that, Twyla sneezed.

Strategies from the refresher self-defense course gelled in Caprice's mind. Instinct took over with them. Using her elbow, she rammed it into the side of Twyla's knee.

Alanna's sister cried out and went down hard. The gun flew, sliding near Lady's crate. Caprice grabbed it, then jumped on to Twyla, sitting on her, holding the gun to the woman's head.

Removing her phone from her pocket, she shakily dialed 9-1-1.

Epilogue

Lady trotted beside Caprice. Patches walked beside Grant. The two of them strolled down the path into the York playground. The swings and sliding board were empty as Caprice stopped with Grant beside a tall sycamore.

"Do you think they'll show up?" Grant asked.

"I think they will," Caprice assured him.

The past month had been a roller-coaster ride. Caprice had gone from nearly getting killed to dating Grant. They'd attended a carnival, enjoyed a day at Hersheypark, had dinner at a new fifties diner, and spent time together, giving their pups exercise.

"How's Ace doing?" Grant asked.

"Much better now that Len has been apprehended and is being charged with larceny for stealing the guitars and sheet music, as well as assault and battery for attacking Twyla. They couldn't pin slashing my tires on him without proof. Ace is still shaking his head over the fact that Twyla murdered Alanna . . . that Alanna stole his music . . . that Len planned to promote it as his. It's mind-boggling for anyone. He trusted Len and Alanna and they both betrayed him. He thought Twyla was a sweet Southern woman. Little did anyone except Detective Carstead know that Twyla had a juvie record. I never would have believed she'd spent a stint in a juvenile detention center for breaking and entering and theft, if Detective Carstead hadn't told you."

"You thought she was sweet, just as Ace did," Grant pointed out.

"True." Caprice glanced toward the swings again, wondering how she'd been so wrong. Twyla had admitted nothing to the police, though.

As if he'd read her thoughts, Grant went on to assure her: "The DA's office has a pile of evidence against Twyla, from the security video at a gas station near York on March thirtieth to the tieback she kept in her closet in Biloxi as a souvenir. And Alanna's gardener said he'd testify that she borrowed his truck the day she followed you. Telling him she'd scraped a fence and giving him cash to have it fixed didn't keep him quiet once he'd learned she'd been charged with her sister's murder. I'm not sure she intended to run you off the road . . . at first. She just wanted to know what you were up to. But when she saw the chance to maybe eliminate you . . ."

Those words gave Caprice the shivers. Along with the murder charge, the DA had added reckless endangerment and aggravated assault with a motor vehicle to the list.

Twyla Horton had been arraigned and was awaiting trial, and Caprice was ready to testify, along with Alanna's gardener.

"The motive was *partly* money," Caprice said, still analyzing everything that had happened. "Twyla was tired of living the way she was in Mississippi. And she

wanted Alanna's estate. But mostly, she'd been jealous
of Alanna for a long time—since they were kids. Alanna
always seemed to get what she wanted. At least that's
the way it looked to Twyla. She never knew about her
sister's heartache in giving up a child."

"And speaking of children," Grant murmured.

Diane Duncan saw them and waved. She'd come in
from the other side of the playground, and she was
holding her daughter's hand. She looked a bit pale.

After Diane introduced her daughter to Caprice and
Grant, Sherry looked up at them. "Can I play with your
dogs?"

"Sure," Grant said. He took a ball from his pocket.
"I always carry this because Patches likes to fetch."
He pointed to the grassy area, where kids sometimes
played softball. "Why don't you go over there with
them, okay?"

Sherry grinned at them and ran toward the grassy
area, the dogs scampering beside her.

"I'm nervous," Diane admitted.

"I understand that," Caprice said as Archer walked
in the same entrance she and Grant had.

The next couple of minutes were awkward as Caprice introduced Archer to Diane. He nodded to the
swings. "Why don't we go over there and talk?"

Diane gave him a shaky smile and nodded.

As Diane and Archer sat on the swings to have one
of the most important conversations of their lives,
Grant wrapped his arm around Caprice. "What do you
think they'll decide?"

"If they have Sherry's best interest at heart, I think
they'll figure out a way to share her. Archer knows he
can't just jump into their lives. But I think Diane will
make room for Sherry having a dad."

As Sherry's laughter rang out, as Diane and Archer leaned toward each other, intent in conversation, Grant's arm tightened around Caprice. "I know you didn't put yourself in harm's way on purpose this time, but I worry about you solving murders."

"There might never be another murder to solve."

After giving her a look that told Caprice he'd like to kiss her when they were in a more private place, Grant muttered, "I can only hope."

Original Recipes

Caprice's Chicken Cacciatore

Preheat oven to 350°
1-hour prep time
Approximately 1½ hours baking time

- 1 pound Italian sausage cut into 1-inch pieces
  (sweet or hot—your choice!)
- 1 tablespoon vegetable oil
- 1 cup chopped onion (about 1 medium onion)
- 1 cup chopped sweet bell pepper (about 1 large
  pepper)
- 1 cup chopped celery
- 3 cans fire roasted tomatoes (14.5 oz cans)
- 1 tablespoon sugar
- ¼ teaspoon pepper
- 1 teaspoon smoked paprika
- 1½ teaspoons salt
- Add ¼ teaspoon crushed red pepper (if using
  mild sausage)

Brown the sausage pieces in vegetable oil for about
10 minutes on medium, stirring to brown on all sides.

(Do not burn. You want the oil with sausage drippings to coat the onion, pepper, and celery.) Add onion, pepper, and celery and sauté for about 3 minutes. To this mixture, add the 3 cans of fire-roasted tomatoes and the spices. Simmer on low while browning the thighs.

    8 chicken thighs (3½ pounds)
    1½ cups flour
    3 teaspoons salt
    ½ teaspoon pepper
    2 tablespoons oregano
    4 tablespoons butter

Put flour, salt, pepper, and oregano in a Ziploc bag and shake to mix. Melt butter in 11-inch to 12-inch deep-sided skillet. Drop thighs into the bag with flour mixture, 2 at a time, and shake until they are coated. Then brown the thighs in the skillet on medium high until all sides are golden brown. Place the browned thighs in a lasagna pan. Pour sausage mixture over the thighs. Bake uncovered at 350° about 1½ hours until thighs are tender and falling off the bone. Use meat thermometer to assure proper doneness.

This dish can be served over pasta of your choice (I cook a pound) or complemented by side dishes such as mashed potatoes.

Serves 4 to 6.

Fran's Yummy Baked Cinnamon Apples

Preheat oven to 350°

    6 cups sliced apples (I use Granny Smith!)
    3 tablespoons brown sugar
    1 teaspoon cinnamon
    1 tablespoon flour
    2 tablespoons butter
    ¼ cup chopped walnuts
    ¼ cup water

Slice apples and measure into a large bowl. Pour ¼ cup water into 2-quart casserole. I use one with a lid. Mix brown sugar, cinnamon, and flour in a small dish, then pour over the sliced apples and coat them. Blend in walnuts. Pour all into the casserole. Slice the butter into thin pats on top. Cover the casserole.

Bake at 350° about 45 to 50 minutes until apples are tender and can be pierced easily with a fork. Stir the apples before serving to coat more evenly in the cinnamon syrup.

Makes 4 to 6 servings, depending on how much your guests like apples!

Caprice's Chocolate-Coffee Loaf

Preheat oven to 350°

2½ cups flour
1½ cups sugar
1½ teaspoons baking powder
1 teaspoon baking soda
½ cup cocoa
¾ teaspoon salt
½ cup oil
2 eggs
½ cup strong coffee (cold)
½ cup sour milk (To make sour milk, add
    ½ tablespoon apple cider vinegar to whole
    milk)
1 teaspoon vanilla
1 cup chocolate chips

Grease and flour two 8¼-inch x 4½-inch pans. Mix together all ingredients in mixer. Pour into greased pans and bake for 40 to 42 minutes until tester comes out clean.

After 10 minutes, slip a knife along sides to make sure bread isn't sticking. Remove from pans and cool. Top with powdered sugar or whipped cream for serving.

Please turn the page for an exciting sneak peek of
Karen Rose Smith's
next Caprice De Luca Home Staging mystery

SILENCE OF THE LAMPS

coming in May 2016!

Chapter One

Caprice De Luca caught sight of the guest who stepped over the threshold. She braced for trouble.

Spinning on her kitten-heels, her long brown hair flowing over her shoulder, she rushed to the living room of the four-thousand square foot, stone and stucco house. She'd staged it with the theme of French Country Flair. Bringing the rustic country flavor from the outside in, she'd used the colors of lavender and green, rust and yellow, mixing them for inviting warmth. Carved curved legs on the furniture, upholstered in toile with its pastoral scene, mixed with the gray distressed wood side tables.

Prospective buyers who entered should have been screened by real estate agents. So how had Drew Pierson ended up standing in the foyer of today's open house?

The chef was her sister Nikki's arch enemy. Ever since he'd opened Portable Edibles, a catering company that competed with Nikki's Catered Capers, the two of them had been in a battle to make their businesses succeed.

Just why was he here?

Caprice hurried to the dining room with its almost wall-length, whitewashed-wood glass-doored hutch, passed the table with its pale blue tablecloth and white gently scalloped stoneware dinnerware, and headed for the smells emanating from the grand kitchen. She hardly noticed the still-life paintings of flowers that she'd arranged on the walls.

The floor of the kitchen mimicked rustic brick, reflecting the colors in the floor-to-ceiling fireplace. Blue and rust plaid cushions graced the bay-windowed breakfast nook as well as the plate glass window over the sink. Two-toned cupboards, white on top, dark cherry on the bottom, along with the copper pots hanging over the granite island, made the space inviting for cooking or family-centered activities.

Nikki and her servers had almost finished readying the chafing dishes and serving platters in the state-of-the-art kitchen. The combination of Nikki's culinary skills and Caprice's staging talent would pull in prospective buyers. More often than not, they sold houses quickly because of their efforts, and the real estate agent on board made a hefty profit. The luxury broker today was Denise Langford, and Caprice wondered if Drew Pierson knew her and that's how he'd added his name to her list.

While one server poured vin d'orange into crystal glasses, another took a cheese soufflé from the double oven. Nikki's assistant was stirring soupe au pistou, a thick vegetable soup with vermicelli while a platter of pan bagnat hors d'oeuvres, which were basically tuna, tomato, green pepper, olive, and sliced hard boiled egg sandwiches stood beside her.

Since Caprice had gone over the menu carefully with Nikki, she knew other chafing dishes held blanquette de veau—veal in white sauce with carrots, leeks, onions, and cloves as well as poulet basquaise which was pan-fried chicken dipped in pepper sauce. Nikki herself was stirring the boeuf bourguignon. The braised beef cooked in red wine with carrots and potatoes and garnished with bacon smelled wonderful.

Nikki was so intent on stirring the dish in front of her that she didn't see Caprice approach. Caprice was about to warn her that Drew Pierson had arrived when he appeared beside Caprice, looking over the offerings of food for the prospective house buyers.

"I thought I'd stop by and see what my competition was offering today," he said smoothly.

At the sound of Drew's voice, Nikki's head snapped up, her eyes widened, and she frowned.

"You're thinking of buying a French country bungalow?" Caprice asked, giving her sister time to compose herself.

"I told Denise Langford I wouldn't mind having a look at this place."

This "place" was definitely out of Drew's budget since he was a fledgling business owner. Portable Edibles couldn't be making *that* much money yet.

Drew ignored Caprice and stared down at the boeuf bourguignon, sniffed it, then smiled at Nikki. "Anyone can make boeuf bourguignon, but I see you added bacon. Nice touch."

"Don't think I'm going to serve you any of my food," Nikki responded, her tone kept in tight restraint. "If it were up to me, I'd have you removed from the property."

Drew clicked his tongue against his teeth. "Your envy is showing. I guess you heard I'll be catering the fundraising high brow dinner at the Country Squire Golf and Recreation Club. My bid came in lower than yours."

Caprice had to wonder about that conclusion. Nikki's

bids were more than competitive. It was quite possible that someone on the selection committee for the dinner had favored Drew. She could read her sister well, and she saw that Nikki was thinking the same thing.

"Just because you won that job doesn't mean your food will win the taste test," Nikki offered. "I have a growing client base. Do you? I have repeat customers. Do you?"

"Your social media following is pitiful," he responded with bitterness, and Caprice wondered where that bitterness was coming from. What had Nikki ever done to Drew? They'd actually worked well together when she'd first hired him to assist her in a few catering jobs. It was after she'd turned him down as a partner that their relationship had fallen apart.

"I believe in growing my business one happy customer at a time," Nikki returned. "My followings will grow. The way ten thousand followers suddenly flowed into your Twitter stream, I suspect you bought them. How loyal do you think they're going to be?"

Everyone in the vicinity was listening and watching now, and Caprice knew the sparring match between Nikki and Drew would only escalate.

Caprice leaned a little closer to him. "We'll serve you if you want so you can sample Nikki's food to see exactly how delicious it is. But I don't think you want a scene here any more than she does. That could be bad for business, and business is what you're all about, isn't it?"

She didn't know what had made her throw that question in. But when she saw the look on Drew's face, she understood this wasn't just about business. There was something personal underlying his rancor for Nikki. Still, she must have gotten through to him.